ALEX MCKENNA & THE GERANIUM DEATHS

ALSO BY VICKI-ANN BUSH

Alex McKenna & The Geranium Deaths

Alex McKenna & The Academy of Souls

Alex McKenna & A Winter's Night

Alex McKenna Death is Not the Beginning

Liminal Space

The Darkest Light

UNTHREADED

Ophelia

The Garden of Two

Saving A Life

The Queen of IT

Winslow Willow the Woodland Fairy

Short Stories

The Joshua Tree

ALEX MCKENNA & THE GERANIUM DEATHS

VICKI-ANN BUSH

Published in the United States by Creative James Media.

www.creativejamesmedia.com

978-1-956183-77-1 (hardback)

First U.S. Edition 2023

ALEX MCKENNA

LaBoccetta/Russo Family Tree

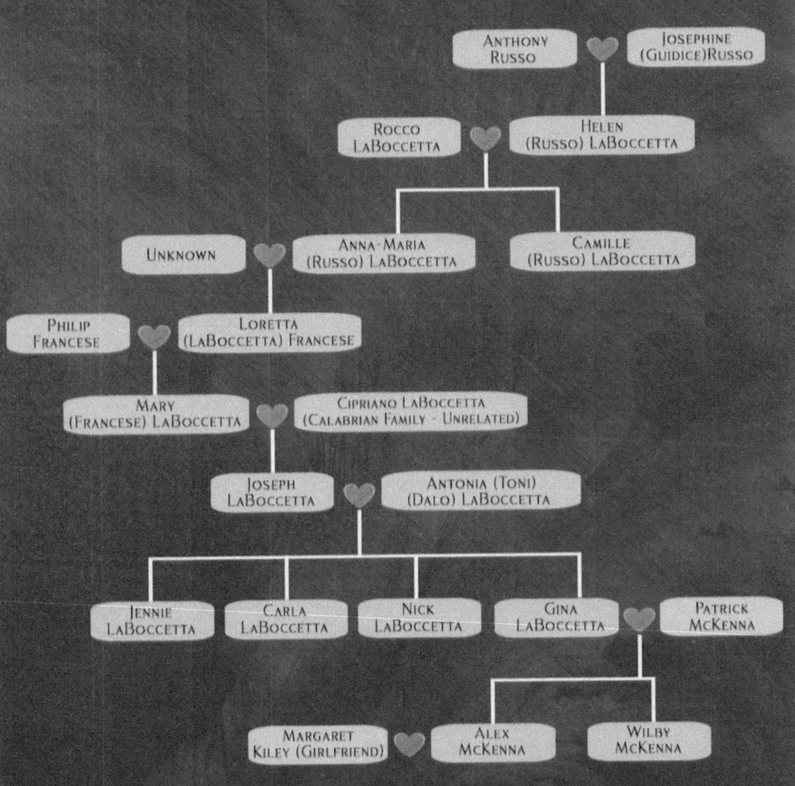

To Dean

Without you there is no Alex. You are my light on the darkest day and my strength at my weakest moment. I love your laughter, wit, and clever way you manage to hold Papa and me in the palm of your hand. When you were born the world changed for the better. I love you forever.

THE KNOW

Alex held Margaret, his firm hand pressing her head to his shoulder. His breath brushed across her ear. "Don't look, no matter what you hear. That's how it gets you."

All the other victims had turned to ice. Alex couldn't understand why, but the rules didn't apply to him. None of the deceased were family, so maybe that was his armor. His family history protected him somehow.

They were huddled behind the furnace in the basement while they attempted to construct an escape plan. Although in a frenzy, Alex knew the level of heat from the unit should be enough to throw the beast temporarily off their trail. The foul spirit followed the warmth from the living, which made hiding from its ghostly grips difficult. The tighter he held Margaret, the more he worried about Wilby. His little brother had bolted in the other direction.

Alex was careful not to touch the hot metal tank as he peered around it. He made the mistake a few years back of carelessly brushing against it while moving some boxes. The scar on his right arm left a permanent reminder. Alex crinkled his nose—the damp walls and seventy-year-old pipes needed more than a little fresh air.

It was dark in every corner except for a sliver of light emanating from the single ground-level window. He hated the basement, and especially the furnace room. It was the part of the below-ground space that wasn't finished, and he felt like he stepped into a portal to hell every time he was there. He could sense the darkened soul still lurking in the shadows but couldn't home in on it. Only the goosebumps standing to attention on his arms confirmed his suspicions. He eased back behind the tank. His plan worked for the moment, but it also limited their options. Now he needed a solid way to find Wilby and escape.

"I think I know how we can get out of the house." Alex spoke softly. "But you're gonna have to trust me."

She nodded, her eyes widened with fear. Neither were normally the type to rattle easily, this one had them both off-balance.

"I know you're really scared right now. So am I. But I also know you can do this. I'm going to lead the creature toward the attic."

"Alex. No." Margaret grabbed his T-shirt and gripped tightly. He softly smiled.

"It will follow me. Then you get the hell out of here and find Wilby. Try my mom's room first; he used to hide under her bed when he was little. It made him feel safe."

"Luckily, that thing stayed on our heels. I know the darkness is down here with us. My bumps are strong. After I get its attention, I'll run for the stairs. You give it a minute or two before following. Get Wilby, and then head back down here and out that window." Alex pointed to the ground window. It was big enough for Wilby and Margaret to fit through. "See the large wrench on the bench? Use it to break the glass. My mom has rags over there, too. Line the ledge so you guys don't get cut."

"Why don't we just break one of the windows in the den? They're larger."

"No. It would be harder to break through one of the double panes, and it would attract a lot more attention. This way you'll barely be heard."

Margaret shook her head. "I can't leave you." A tear streamed down her cheek.

"I need you to do this for Wilby." Alex hesitated. He yearned to kiss her but settled for a pal hug. "Text me when both of you are out."

"How are you going to get the hell out of the house?"

"Don't worry, I got a plan." There was no plan, but he had to tell her something so she would agree. Margaret's fierce when it comes to protecting the ones she loves.

He pulled away and eased out into the open. A chill ran up his spine—it was close. Alex squinted, trying to distinguish the difference in the shadows. He took a step forward; a blast of cold air startled him, raising the hair on his arms and roiling the butterflies in his stomach. He was headed straight toward the evil spirit.

A low, gravelly hum tainted his ears. Could Margaret hear it? He shook his head. No, he was not about to call out and give up her location. He shifted his eyes toward the right, his heart pounding. The beast lunged forward and reached out with a translucent, icy hand. Alex ducked and swerved. Spinning around, he ran straight for the door, and crossed the threshold before it could stop him. He scrambled up the stairs and made the mistake of turning back. It was a costly move. He tripped, and his body hit the floorboards, scraping his knees. He could feel stinging cuts but chose to ignore it.

A frozen grip seized his leg and a layer of ice spread across the denim like a fungus. Furiously, Alex kicked free and scrambled back to his feet, running for the staircase to the second level. The entrance to the attic was in the hallway. Once he got the spirit there, he could buy Margaret the time she needed.

He reached the top of the staircase, rounded the corner, and reached for the knob. There was no need. The door flew open, slamming it into the wall. Chips of plaster exploded and nicked Alex near his left eye. He didn't stop. Taking the steep steps two at a time, he ran to the center of the room. He heard the door slam and knew his plan had worked.

He was alone with the dark soul and nowhere to go.

Days Earlier

OCTOBER WAS by far the most vibrant month in Floral Park. Alex preferred the crisp, cold air over the heat of the summer, and would patiently wait each September for it to escort out the ninety-degree temperatures to make way for the aromatic Autumn nights and warm covers piled on the bed.

He'd worked over the summer at the community pool, saving nearly everything he'd earned. Now, with winter and the holidays coming, he was hoping to get a job after school; the means to his goal of buying a car. If he could save up three grand, his mom would match it. Only eighteen hundred and forty-eight bucks to go.

Jumping in the shower, he barely had time for the water to get hot. The alarm beeped, but the flashing numbers indicated another power outage during the night. He only realized how late it was after he checked his phone for messages from Margaret. He briskly dried off and stepped into the confines of his second skin, pulling it up inch by inch. It seemed to help when he wiggled and twisted a little. He slowly wriggled it past his hips and waist, then yanked it up to his chest. He adjusted it, straightening and smoothing, before slipping on his T-shirt, jeans, and a hoodie, and he was out the door.

He had missed the bus, so he pulled out his current mode of transportation. At sixteen, it wasn't the coolest to show up at school riding a bike, but it was a lot quicker than walking. Alex didn't spend much time worrying what others thought. Live and let live was his motto.

Alex pedaled past Mrs. Carricchio's house—the elderly woman was raking leaves from her front lawn. Her only son had been killed in the Vietnam War, and she'd lost her husband to a heart attack two years ago. Sometimes he and Margaret brought her pasta, a care package from his mom.

Alex waved, but she didn't see him.

Pulling up to the bike rack, he saw Margaret pacing in front of the school, her brows furrowed. He latched the front frame securely to the rack, adjusted his backpack, and hustled over.

"Hey. Why are you waiting out here? You're missing first period." He grabbed her arm and pulled her through the academic cave.

"I was getting worried. I texted you like three times."

"I'm sorry. The power went off and I overslept. Did you lose power at your house, too?"

Margaret's eyes narrowed. "Lose power? No. Alex, you could have at least texted me back. With all the weird crap that's been going on around here, that wasn't fair."

Alex sighed to himself. She was his person. The one that he could confide anything to and know his words would be safe. They took care of each other.

"Speaking of weird, did you hear what happen last night outside the church?" Alex grabbed a science book out of his backpack. "I'd better get this out now. I'm already late, and Mr. Klein is going to be pissed enough."

"You are so frustrating sometimes. What happened at the church?" Margaret crossed her arms.

"They found Craig Earley dead on the back path to the rectory. His body was frozen."

"What the hell? Frozen? Did they say how?"

"No. They don't know yet. It was all over the late-night news. I can't believe you didn't hear anything."

"I went to bed around ten o'clock. I was exhausted from studying for that pointless calculus test today. I swear, I will never understand why we have to take some of these bullshit classes. I want to go to art school, not become some damn engineer." Margaret's disdain faded into concern. "Your eyes look sunken in. How late did you stay up last night?"

"About one o'clock. My head was killing me. I've had so many headaches lately. So has my mom. It's a pain in the ass." Alex dropped his chin toward his chest.

"How you doing now?" Margret reached for him, but quickly pulled back.

"Better. They only seem to come at night. Poor Mr. Earley. His family . . . I know his son Oliver."

"I know. He was a really nice man. He and my dad would golf together."

They agreed to meet on the football field at lunch. He watched her rush down the opposite end of the hallway. He had that feeling again—the one that told him things were about to get stranger. At times, he hated the *spidey sense*—the superhero terminology that Margaret used to describe his abilities.

The morning lulled on with little excitement. Mr. Klein went easy on him for being late, and Alex was sure it was because of the news about Mr. Earley. His strange death was just the latest oddity that had been plaguing the town for the last two weeks. The bodies were starting to pile up, and in every case, the victim's head was frozen solid.

Alex wasn't sure what was responsible for this latest string of occurrences, but he did know he needed to call his great grandmother, or Gram as he always referred to her. She was the go-to for weirdness in the family, and he knew his mom wasn't going to do it. She tried to ignore all the strangeness that surrounded their family, hoping it would protect them. The problem was, you couldn't deny it. It was always there, and it wasn't denying you, so you learned how to work with it. Gram had been teaching him, showing him how to cope with his gifts and how to use them.

He watched the hands of the large clock hanging above Mr. Klein's desk. Three more classes until lunch. Ugh.

Thankfully, he was seated by the window in his next two classes, which was a welcome distraction. The puzzle pieces of the murders floated around in his mind, frustrating him. *Multiple deaths by the hand of what?* He had never seen a case like this, and it frightened him.

After the lunch bell rang, he headed to the field. He got there early, so he whipped out his phone and Googled *how long does it take to freeze to death.* Alex turned his head just as Margaret rounded the corner of the bleachers. She jumped up to the second level and sat beside him. He quickly turned his phone screen off, giving her his full attention.

A natural beauty, her chestnut hair flowed in a curtain down her back, falling freely unless they were on a case. Then, it was pulled back in a loose ponytail for some serious research. Her eyes melted him every time. Light brown with flecks of gold, he could lose his soul in those eyes. *Best friends forever.* He repeated the phrase in his mind.

"What are you doing?" Margaret lightly punched his shoulder.

Alex squirmed. "I was checking how long it would take to freeze to death. You'd think one of them might have gotten away."

"The whole thing is disturbing. It's like there's a serial Mr. Freeze in Floral Park."

"How was your morning?" Alex put his phone back in his pocket.

"Long and boring. I swear, I can't wait until we graduate. College has to be better than this."

Alex furrowed his brow. "I don't know, but at least it will be our choice to go. I hate the confines of being told it's required."

"I know, me too. What's our next move?"

"I'm calling my gram later. She might be able to give us some insight."

"Sounds good. How's Wilby doing with training? You haven't mentioned it lately."

Wilby—real name William—was Alex's younger brother and the newest member of the family to start his ghostly training.

"He's training fine. I'm worried he doesn't have the *know*. I remember going to preschool and seeing things others didn't. Wilby hasn't experienced that yet. He knows strange things happen, but it's because he's told, not that he senses them. I'm hoping he's just a late starter. I know others in the family that didn't have their abilities show up until they were eight or nine. So, I keep waiting. Not that it's easy having this thing, but at least I'd know he'd have a better chance of dealing with something if he could see it. And since it seems to circle my family wherever we are, he'd be better equipped."

"Do you ever think that maybe it's easier for Wilby *not* to see things? I mean, if he doesn't see it, he doesn't deal with it."

"No. I know what you mean, but it's all around him anyway. As long as he's near me, Mom, or almost anyone on that side of the family, he's susceptible. I think my dad would have learned to deal with it, but my mom turning a blind eye made it harder. Things would happen, and she didn't want to talk about it. He was left with one foot in the strange and the other in everyday life. I think, for a lot of years, it frustrated him."

"You think that's why he left?"

"I don't know. Maybe. He seems better now that they're apart. Divorce turned him into a real father of the year. New wife, new kids, new outlook."

Margaret smirked. She clasped Alex's arm and weaved it with hers, and laid her head on his shoulder, allowing her hair to fall across his chest.

"I'm glad we're best friends, Alex McKenna."

A whiff of mint tickled his nostrils, and he turned his cheek toward her silky locks. "Uh-huh, me too."

FROZEN HEADS

The house was empty when Alex arrived home. A note on the fridge left dinner undecided. His mom was out with friends, and Wilby was spending the night at their dad's house. His brother adjusted a lot easier to the divorce and their dad's new family. He had remarried a woman who had a kid of her own—Shea—named after the New York Mets. His dad's new family were devoted fans. Shea was twelve, and Wilby adored him. When Sariya, their little sister, came along, the little family was complete.

Alex felt like an outsider. Maybe it was because he suspected his abilities made his new stepmother nervous; he hoped not. That would mean she might act differently toward Wilby once he got the *know.*

It was quiet with no one home, and he liked that. He had time to think and do some uninterrupted research. There was homework, but it took a backseat to the more pressing issue— murder. Over the years, he had managed to figure out the balance. Even when things were out of hand in the spirit world, he found a way to make up for what he missed in the living one. Not to say it wasn't difficult.

A second search through Google produced several failed attempts at learning any new information until he came across a small paragraph. The only thing that could remotely explain the frozen bodies was Flash Freezing. The victims would have had to come into contact with liquid nitrogen at a deadly -320.8°F, which could have been feasible for Mr. Earley if he were frozen and then dumped. Or, Grace Johnson. However, none of that explains Mrs. Brewster. How would the murderer just freeze her head while it was still attached to her body? No. This was definitely not an earthly serial killer. He figured it was time for that call to his gram. He wanted to speak to her before his mom got home so he could avoid any unwanted explanations.

His great grandma, Mary LaBoccetta, lived in Stony Brook —a quaint community further out on Long Island, about an hour's drive away. Alex preferred it out on the Island and would have rather lived with her this past year. It would have been easier for him with his ability growing stronger. His mom's lack of participation just added to the anxiety. He dialed her number on his phone, and she picked up after one ring.

"Hello, my little Bonzetta."

Alex chuckled. His great grandma was first generation American. Her parents had come to the U.S. from Naples, Italy in 1928. Literally translated, "Bonzetta" means "breast of veal that has a pocket cut out for stuffing." But she just meant it as a term of endearment. "Hi, Gram. Wait, how did you know it was me? Oh, never mind. Stupid question."

"I've been waiting all day for your call. I could feel something was not right."

"Gram, have you been watching the news? There's a load of strange crap going on here."

"No, I've been busy with my bridge club. We're planning the annual Christmas event with the Senior Center. Lots of sign-ups for this year. It's so sad how so many of the elderly are alone. You said strange. Not the usual encounter?"

"Uh, this is anything but usual. This is weird even by our family's standards."

Alex gave her a brief account of the murders, finishing with his concerns for Wilby.

"Tesoro, have you seen anything new lately?" She cleared her throat.

Alex hesitated. "Nothing yet. It's more like a queasiness in the pit of my stomach. This one is really bad. I can feel it. I mean, yes, the deaths tell even the normal person that whatever is doing this is evil, but Gram, it's so much more. I just know it."

"When did you say this started?"

"About two weeks ago. I think the first death was on the seventh. That was followed by the second body found on the thirteenth. And now, Mr. Earley."

Alex heard rustling and knew she must be fiddling with the calendar she kept by the kitchen phone.

"That's another six days."

"Huh. I didn't see that pattern. Do you think there's something to it?"

"Maybe. If you keep adding six days to each death and the murders continue, it leads us to Halloween."

"Oh, Gram, you're brilliant!"

"Well, only if it means something. Let me do some reading, and I'll get back to you. In the meantime, keep Wilby close. If you're feeling something, heed the warning."

"I will. Thanks, Gram. I'm gonna do some digging here, too. If you're right, we only have six more days to prevent another murder."

Alex hung up and plopped on the couch. Staring at the ceiling, he repeated the words to himself. *It's time.* A twinge of guilt heated his belly. He hadn't been completely honest with his grandmother. He wasn't sure what it was he was seeing in the house; the new occurrences started right before the first death. Still, it could just be a coincidence. It would be easier not to get her worried. She might drive down, and that would just start conflict with his mom. He made a pact with himself: no worrying until there was something to worry about. A loud growl followed by gurgling in his stomach poked at his senses, and he went into the kitchen to make something for dinner.

In Italian mom fashion, there were always cold cuts for sandwiches in the fridge. He pulled out some Genoa salami and Provolone cheese—his favorite combination. There were two loaves of crusty bread from the Italian deli on the counter, which was another staple of the McKenna household. Reaching for a knife to slice the bread, Alex hesitated.

I guess it's not really the McKenna household anymore, he thought to himself. Sure, he and Wilby still had his dad's last name, but his mom didn't. After the divorce, she changed it back to her maiden name of LaBoccetta. Loosely translated, it means "little mouth," which was a phrase that tickled his humor. The Italian side of the family was not known for its quiet demeanor. He grabbed a handful of chips and put them on the plate next to his sandwich. A culinary delight.

He took his dinner up to his room; the search for answers paired well with food.

He started typing in "Halloween" when a buzz from his cell interrupted him. He glanced over. It was a call from Margaret. He quickly chewed the bite of sandwich he had just attacked, washed it down with some Dr. Pepper, and tapped her picture on his phone.

"Hey, you call your gram yet?" Margaret sounded tired.

"Yeah. She's gonna do some checking. In fact, that's what I was just about to do. Gram figured out that the deaths were each six days apart. Don't know if that means anything, but if you keep adding six days, they lead you right to Halloween."

"So what, six more days and there will be another dead body?" Margaret's voice squeaked.

"That's what we're thinking. But this is all just guessing at this point. You okay?"

"A little weirded out. Your *spidey sense* has led me to believe in some strange crap, but those people, the ghosts . . . They're already gone. These are people we know that are dying. And now you're saying there might be more, and we have no way of knowing who. Which means we can't even warn them—or help ourselves, for that matter. Not that I can't take care of myself, but what if the connection goes back to you and your family? What if it's something that knows you know, or wants you gone so you can't prevent what's happening? Alex . . ."

"Slow down. We know nothing yet, and you've gone from zero to a hundred in half a second. Just like every other case, we'll research and get answers. Then we'll help. Or, in this case, stop it. I'm not gonna lie, this thing is bad. But I don't think you needed me to figure that one out. I will get this and end it. Do you believe me?"

"Yeah. I do. I didn't mean to overreact. When it comes to you being in danger, it sets me off. I got some homework to do, but I'll see if I can pull up anything useful, too. Maybe *my* abilities as a super sleuth, fact-gathering, kick ass Wonder Woman can find something you're missing."

"Really? Wonder Woman?" Alex laughed. "I'll meet you by the bleachers."

Margaret didn't need him to be the brave one. She was strong on her own. But he was responsible for getting her into the strangeness that was his world. In the past, he thought it might be better for her if he stepped back. Danger was his to carry, not hers. One time, he went so far as to suggest she back off from working cases. They didn't talk for a week. It was then he realized he couldn't be without her.

He pecked in *Halloween* again, but this time, sleep took precedence to research. He decided to get up early and do some checking before school. If his gram was right, they didn't have a lot of time.

FLORAL PARK, New York 1928

MR. AND MRS. BISHOP stood in front of the three-bedroom, one-bathroom structure that was nearly finished, and the original move in date would be sooner than anticipated. The four of them had been living in a cramped apartment in Brooklyn for over three years, and now they would finally have their dream house. Standing there now, it was all worth it. Jim could finally stop working two jobs.

"Honey, isn't it perfect?" Carol nestled her head on Jim's shoulder.

"Yes, it is. And it's all ours. Well, ours and the bank's." He laughed.

"I think the kids are going to be overwhelmed with all this space. I was thinking, would it be very costly to finish the basement? It would be a great playroom for them." Carol rubbed her hand over Jim's heart. That always got to him.

He grabbed her hand and kissed it. "No, I don't think it would be costly at all. I'm sure my brother would help me. We can do the main area and leave the furnace room alone. No need to waste money prettying up a bunch of pipes."

"Thank you." Carol stood on her toes and kissed his cheek. She was about to move to his lips, but they were interrupted by the foreman on their property, Jake Warner.

"Mr. Bishop, we have a small problem. Nothing that can't be fixed, but it needs your attention. I'm actually thankful you were both out here today. It could have delayed us but getting your decision on the spot will keep everything on track."

"What is it, Jake?" Jim lit a cigar.

Carol frowned as she waved away the billows of smoke from her face.

The foreman took out a blueprint and rolled it onto the hood of his black Ford truck. "The original plan had the option of a second half bathroom down in the laundry room. Just a toilet and sink. I know you both opted to save a few bucks and not have that installed. However, my guys neglected to refer to this before adding the connection in the laundry room, and they put in the sink. Now, that's my crew's mistake, so I'll absorb that cost. But if you would like the toilet, the plumbing is there. We can put one in for real cheap. I'll give it to you for cost plus ten percent. That might come in handy with two kids."

Carol tried to temper her excitement after Jim winked at her. For years, they had used only one bathroom; two would be heaven. Jim put his arm on the foreman's shoulder. The two men walked away to speak.

"Carol, I'll be back in a few minutes. Why don't you see where you are going to plant that garden you keep telling me about?"

Carol knew this was her husband's way of saying this talk was for the men. He was a take charge kind of man. While walking the perimeter of the property, she imagined the plethora of foliage and luscious green grass she had always envisioned. One of her dreams was to plant a row of rose bushes lining the yard, giving privacy from the street and the sidewalk. She could enjoy a ribbon of pastels and her favorite, white. A thriving garden would need plenty of sunlight, so she decided, after much turning of her head from one side of the yard to the other, that the perfect spot would be the northeast patch of dirt. She could involve the kids, and they could work on it together. Maybe even a small area for a vegetable garden.

It wasn't long before Jim came strolling into the back yard. He was smiling, which excited her. They must be getting that toilet.

"So, Mr. Bishop, have you worked your magic and gotten us a reprieve from long waits to use the bathroom?" She grinned.

"Not only are we getting the extra facility, but at five percent above cost instead of ten."

Carol threw her arms around him and planted a robust kiss on his lips. "I knew it!"

"Oh? How did you know that we would have that second toilet?" Jim said sheepishly.

"Because you always take care of us, and I know Jake was offering a great deal. You just got him to sweeten it." She squeezed him tight and showed him her plans for the location of the garden. Carol began to shiver, and briskly rubbed her arms to warm them. Jim grabbed her hand and led her back to the car.

"I'm going to say our goodbyes to Jake and the crew. You get in and stay warm, and I'll be back in a few minutes." Jim opened the car door and escorted her into the front seat. Carol's gaze followed her husband as he went into the house. *Everything was going to be perfect.*

GRAM

lex had set the alarm for five o'clock, an hour earlier than usual. This would give him a small jump on some research. He decided to start with the history of the neighborhood.

Floral Park was a fairly quiet town, so any news was big news—which was why he was surprised when he spotted a small paragraph about a devastating house fire in 1932. The inferno had ignited in the bitter cold month of January, the ice and snow fatefully slowing the response time of the fire department. The blaze raged through the south part of the house while the family lay sleeping. A father and his young son were able to get out, but rescuers were unable to reach his wife and daughter, who perished in the flames.

Alex jumped when an abrupt knock on the door startled him. "Come in." He swiveled his chair to face the doorway. "What's up, Ma?"

"I wanted to talk to you. You know I'm pretty lenient and give you space, but I got a call from the school yesterday. They said you missed math class a couple of times last week. Is there something going on? Are your shots making you sick? Because the doctor said any side-effects and he . . ."

"No, everything's fine. I'm not getting sick or anything. I missed math class because I had a really bad headache again. Not from my meds; it's like a sinus thing. You said you were getting them, too."

"I have been, and I think if they persist, we're both going to the doctor. No more missing class without telling me. Got it?" His mom glared.

"Yes, I got it. I'll tell you next time. I promise."

"I've got a conference call this morning, so I'll be home for a few hours. In case anyone feels the need to come home sick." She narrowed her eyes. "Also, your dad's driving Wilby straight to school this morning. So if you were counting on him to swing by and pick you up, it's not happening."

"It doesn't matter; I was planning on taking the bus."

"Okay, watch the time and don't be late. I won't be able to stop the call to take you. Have a great day, Bella Mia."

Alex turned back to the computer screen. It had gone dark, and he could see his reflection. Leaning in, he rubbed his hand over his jawline and chin. Smooth as a baby's butt. He frowned and went back to his search.

Scouring the internet for more information, he stumbled on the actual article from the front page of the Floral Park Community Review paper. Now this made more sense. A house fire would have been on the tip of everyone's tongue in town. As he read the details, Alex stiffened. It was the first of a series of horrors that plagued the small community that year. There was a string of unusual and deadly occurrences beginning with the fateful one in January and rampaging over the next several months until their abrupt ending on October thirty-first. Chills raced up the middle of his back as he looked away from the screen. He must have read it wrong. He had to have. He took a breath and looked at it again. The address of the fire that spawned the beginning of horror for the once quiet neighborhood was fifty-five Geranium Ave . . . his house.

Alex stood up and, pushing the chair back, stepped away from the computer as if the very act would somehow erase the words he had read. Impossible. His house had begun the terror for the people in town that year. It was the root cause for the avalanche that would follow. This was confusing. He hadn't felt anything evil or negative. Why wasn't his know picking up on this? His ability to see the dead, feel the paranormal energy around him, never failed. It had to mean something. Alex didn't believe in coincidence; he had witnessed too many things. There was always a reason—always.

He glanced at his phone. It was 6:15, and he needed to run. He grabbed his jacket off the doorknob, threw his backpack on his shoulder, and raced to catch the bus. He made it just as the yellow metal carriage was about to pull away. Good thing Gloria liked him. She had been the driver for the high school for about twenty years. Kids would come and go, and she could remember every one of their names. She started watching out for Alex shortly after he started the ninth grade. That was an exceptionally hard year for him. The physical changes started to get more prevalent, and the occasional ignorant comments by some of the other kids really started to get to him. Gloria would distract him with stories about all the odd things she'd seen in her years of driving. Alex welcomed the reprieve from dealing with the inevitable closed minds, and when he started seeing the doctor and getting on track, things settled down. Mostly.

"Morning, Gloria. Thanks for waiting for me."

"Okay, Alex, get your late self behind the line and in a seat. Honestly, you're gonna be late for your own funeral."

Alex grinned and sat in the empty seat right behind her.

"Any news?" Alex knew if there was something new to be heard about things going on in town, Gloria was the go-to.

"You mean anything new since the gruesome death of Mr. Earley yesterday? Nope. That would be enough for now. Don't you agree?" She peered at him through the rear-view mirror. Gloria was one of the few people in town who knew about Alex's *spidey sense.*

"Agreed." Alex slouched down in his seat, put his ear buds in, and switched on some Arctic Monkeys. It helped him think. He watched the houses whisking by and couldn't help thinking, who would be next?

He turned his head to glance at the empty seat across from his. Well, empty to everyone else. He nodded to the young girl dressed in a cheerleader's uniform, and she smiled back. He shivered, but the goosebumps were at a minimum. Heather Johnson had been dead for fifteen years. She was killed in a hit and run on the way to school, and they never caught the driver. Alex suspected that was why she stayed. Never hurting anyone, Heather would ride the bus from her parents' house to school every day. He tried to help her a few times, but she wasn't ready to cross over.

They pulled up to the bustling school. He stepped off the bus, his comfort level immediately decreasing. Alex wasn't the biggest lover of high school. It was just a pit stop to get where he really wanted to be—college. He was hoping life would be different there. Maybe he could fit in better because no one would know him. Not that being someone who could hear and see things from the other side didn't make life interesting, but it had its difficult moments. And when he was younger, he didn't deal with things as anonymously as he learned to as a young adult. Since most of the kids went to grade school with him, they carried their opinions to high school. They still taunted him about the time he saw the ghost of a teacher that had died twenty years prior. She was skulking around the hallways, opening and shutting doors. One day, he became frustrated with her and started having a conversation that resulted in a shouting match. His mom was not happy that day. She had to go pick up her eight-year-old son from school because he had been put on suspension for two days. The teacher's ghost didn't leave, and Alex had to learn to ignore her.

Margaret was waiting for him by the bleachers with her friend, Cadence. The girl had been a West Coast transplant. Her wealthy filmmaker father decided Los Angeles had grown boring and lacked in cultural stimulation. He uprooted his family, and they moved to Garden City, Long Island—home of the front lawns that went on for miles and English Tudors you could land a plane in. Cadence attended their school while she stayed with family. Her father was renovating their house to make it livable. Alex tolerated her.

The smirk on Cadence's face cleared the path for what followed. "Hey, glad to see you were able make it on time, Alex. I was just telling Margaret we need to leave for class with or without you. But you're here now, so all's right with the world again."

"Cadence, knock it off." Margaret glared.

"When is your house supposed to be done? I'm sure you're anxious to start the school in your district," Alex said sarcastically.

"Jeez, you two. Enough with the drama," Margaret snapped.

"Margaret, I need to talk to you. Cadence, can you give us some time alone?" He knew that would burn her butt. Cadence furrowed her brow and huffed off.

"You know you pissed her off, right?" Margaret looked up at him, eyes narrowed.

"Yeah, I know."

"Honestly, the two of you are pains in the ass. What did you need to talk to me about?"

Alex told her about the article, then hit her with the address.

Margaret sat down on the bench.

"Yeah, I found the same article. I was going to tell you about it this morning. I nearly dropped off the chair when I read the address. But wait. How did *you* not know that something had happened in your house?"

"I don't know. It's driving me crazy. After school, I'm taking the train out to Stony Brook to see Gram. Do you want to come?"

"Uh, hell yeah. Someone needs to watch out for you. Besides, I'm hoping your grandma made some of that killer cheesecake she's always baking." She rubbed her belly.

"Good. And by the way, it's watch out for each *other*." He leaned onto her shoulder. "Right?"

Margaret got closer. Locking eyes with him, she softly replied, "Right."

His body tingled; the soft bow of her lips was intoxicating. He wanted to kiss her. He bent his head toward hers and . . .

"Hello, are you two done yet? Margaret, we have to get to the science lab if we want to use the space before the next class starts," Cadence shouted from the other side of the bleachers.

"I'd better go. I'll see you after school, okay?"

"Sure. See you then."

Alex gazed at Margaret as the distance between them grew. *What the hell are you doing? She's your best friend, damn it. You could risk everything. Stop, McKenna. Just stop.* Alex's head buzzed with self-inflicted torture as he closed his eyes and took in the fragrance of cinnamon and sugar—the lingering signature scent Margaret chose for the Fall.

WHEN THE LAST BELL RANG, Alex placed the call to confirm their trip to Stony Brook. His grandmother was going to fix dinner for the three of them, and yes, she had cheesecake. Alex smiled to himself. Margaret was going to be happy.

The L—short for the Long Island Railroad—was on time. They needed to change trains in Huntington, and a delay would throw off the entire schedule. After they reached the station, a short ride from Anytime Taxi service would complete the journey.

Normally when he made the trip with his mom, the drive was under an hour. But the train ride was going to take double the time. Alex didn't have much patience. Margaret was trying her best to occupy his mind by rehashing the recent events and history he was able to uncover, but he didn't want to tell her that it just gave him more anxiety. Not knowing something so devastating had happened in the house he lived in was not only perplexing—it was disturbing. It meant his senses had failed him.

Over the years, it hadn't been easy knowing things. Seeing things that others didn't wasn't exactly a conversation opener, but he had grown comfortable with his ability. And now, to think it might not be reliable or something else had the capability of masking it made him shudder. He decided to close his eyes and listen to some music. Maybe it would take his mind off of everything for a while. He held up his MP3 to Margaret. Putting an ear bud into his right ear, he handed the other one to her. She placed it in hers and laid her head on his shoulder; only an hour and a half more to go.

AS THE TAXI rounded the last corner, he could see his gram waiting on the porch. She was sitting in her usual thick pine chair, bundled in a bulky green coat. Alex swiped his debit card and added a tip for the driver before emerging from the back seat and under the midnight blue sky. A little white puff floated in the air from his breath. The temperature had dropped considerably since they had left Floral Park, and he wished he had worn a heavier jacket.

When Mary spotted them, she stood up with open arms and exclaimed, "Bonzetta, Bella Mia! Come, come!" Alex looked around to see if anyone else was outside. Nope. Sometimes his family's flamboyance embarrassed him. Margaret quickened the pace, and Alex wasn't sure if it was because she was so happy to see Gram or the fact that she was really close to the cheesecake. He cupped her hand, and with a few brisk strides, they were standing on the front steps. As in most Italian families, they greeted each other with hugs and kisses—a tradition that Margaret loved. *When your family is stoic and distant,* she had once said to Alex, *the change was nice.*

"Come, get inside. It's freezing. I fixed you both a nice dish of spaghettini."

Alex crossed the threshold of the front door. His ears were lulled with the melody of his gram's favorite song, *Come Back to Sorrento,* while his nose smacked into the tantalizing aroma that filled the air and teased his taste buds. He loved Italian food, especially his Gram's. Tomatoes, basil, and garlic were some of the best smells ever.

They took their coats off and hung them up in the little hall closet behind the front door. The dining room table was already set with dishes and silverware. In the center was grated cheese, salt, and crushed red pepper. Margaret and his gram liked to spice up their spaghettini, but Alex preferred just a bit of salt. After all the plates were filled with food, they sat down. The first few minutes were a symphony of flavor and clanging as their forks twisted pasta into the muted floral dishes. Alex tried to wait until they had finished eating to ask the question that had been plaguing him all day, but he couldn't.

"Gram, there's something that's really bothering me. There was a fire in our house over eighty years ago. Two people died—a mother and daughter."

"And you're wondering why you didn't feel anything from the day you moved into that house?"

"Yes. It's so weird. Normally, I would have gotten something right away. But there's nothing. I've seen some activity, but nothing dark. Definitely nothing about the fire. Gram, what the hell is going on? Did I lose my ability? I mean, I don't think so, because like I said—still seeing crap. But then could this thing, whatever it is, have control over me? Enough to alter my senses and hide the truth? I'm telling you; it's driving me crazy."

Margaret shook her head in agreement. "He's obsessed with this. Couldn't sit still the entire ride over here."

"I know this is not what you want to hear, but I haven't heard of an entity that could mask itself so well it could stifle our ability to feel it. This will take some looking into, because it's not only fooling you. Your mother lives there, and your aunts and I have been in that house on many occasions. Maybe some sort of protection spell has been cast to hide the true nature of the entity. But that would mean it has a human counterpart helping it. I'm hoping that's not what we are dealing with."

"Why? How could that make this any worse?"

"Because, Bonzetta, humans are capable of horrors that don't have the restrictions the dead do.

I did discover something about our Halloween theory, though. It was in one of my mother's personal journals she brought with her from Naples. There was an incident that happened in her village when she was just a young girl. The circumstances of the actual killings were different. The people there were burned beyond recognition. But the countdown— every six days until Halloween—was exactly the same."

"Do you think it could be the same entity?"

"Not the same entity, but it could be the ritual that is being used is similar. Once again, that hints toward a human accomplice. The manner of deaths being so different—one extreme heat and the other freezing temperatures—gets my senses feeling two separate evils perpetrated these deaths."

Margaret chimed in, "Besides one was in Italy and the other here in the States. And the years are so far apart from each other."

"Oh, Bella Mia. That does not mean anything to an angry or evil spirit. It can travel across oceans in a mere blink of an eye. And since they're not of the living world, time has no boundaries for them, either. But still, I'm sensing the entities are definitely different."

"So, what do we do, Gram? If we're right, we only have five days until the next killing."

"I'll continue to go through my mother's journals, and you need to see if you can uncover any more information on that house, you're living in. See if you can find out the cause of the fire and why the husband couldn't save his wife and daughter. If it were in the middle of the night, they should have all been sleeping. His wife would have been beside him. Did they split up to get the children? We need some answers about that night."

"Okay. I'll get started tomorrow. We better get going; it's a long trip home."

"Why don't you call your mother and tell her you're both staying over. You can catch an early train in the morning. It's too late to leave, mi preoccuperò. Margaret, do you think your parents will be alright with that?"

Margaret nodded in agreement.

His gram reached for the phone receiver from the kitchen wall and pulled it through to the dining room, handing it to Alex. He didn't argue; he knew better. While calling his mother, he looked at the long, stretched-out phone cord.

Everything in the house was like an homage to the seventies. The couches still had plastic on them, and lace doilies accented every side table. She refused to buy a new phone when the one she had worked perfectly fine. And the last time any new furniture passed through the front door was out of sheer necessity, when she had to buy a new mattress. The previous one had so many lumps it was affecting her sleep.

After Margaret finished her call, they helped clear the table and wash the dishes. When they were done, Alex asked if he and Margaret could look over some of the journals. Gram disappeared into her bedroom and returned with an armful of books before saying goodnight.

Margaret reached into her pocket and pulled out an elastic band. Running her fingers through her hair, she pulled it back into a ponytail. A few loose strands framed her face, and she tucked them behind her ears. Alex gulped to push back the lump in his throat. *She's so beautiful,* he thought.

"Hey, everything okay?" Margaret asked.

"Huh? Yeah, sure. Why'd you ask that?"

"Because you were staring at me. I thought maybe you were gonna say something."

"No, I wasn't staring. I was thinking." Alex fidgeted nervously with the books. "Let's get to researching."

It was nine o'clock when they started flipping through the pages, looking for something that might be helpful. At midnight, Alex glanced up toward the clock on the wall.

"Damn. We'd better get some sleep. It's late." He set the journal down on the coffee table amongst the menagerie of other information. He arranged them in a neat pile to appease his gram's slight case of OCD and turned off the light. They sauntered upstairs to the guest rooms. Margaret was in the first room at the top of the stairs, and Alex, the far room at the end of the hall.

"Well, I guess . . . goodnight." Alex patted Margaret's back.

"What am I? A dog?" She hugged him.

"No, I just thought—never mind. I'll see you in the morning." Alex started toward his room.

"Hey, McKenna," Margaret whispered. "Sweet dreams."

I will if they're about you, he thought to himself.

He flipped the light switch on. It was his grandpa's room when he was a kid. Blue and beige striped wallpaper covered three of the walls, and seventeenth century sailing ships accented the wall with the bed. Another room frozen in time.

He took off his pants and hoodie, flopped down on the mushy bed, and rolled onto his side. He clutched the comforter and wrapped himself up like a burrito. His eyes weighed heavily from exhaustion as he studied the ships on the wall. He had been in this room probably a hundred times growing up, and yet, he never noticed there were words blended into the background. *The man who experiences a shipwreck shudders at even calm seas.*

ALEX WOKE to the sound of steam knocking its way through the pipes—another piece of modern technology his gram wasn't quite up to speed with. She preferred the iron box radiator over the newer, quieter methods of heating a home. She said it gave a house character. Alex would bet it was because she didn't want to spring for the cost of a whole new heating system. For as long as he could remember, she'd had the kindest heart when it came to her family and friends. No matter what the cost, if someone she loved was in need, she'd find a way. But not for herself. When it came to her own material possessions, she was very frugal. He found that quality both endearing and frustrating at times, but there was no arguing with her. The room was freezing; radiators were definitely slower to heat.

He psyched himself up enough to throw the blankets off and quickly slipped his pants and hoodie on. He and Margaret had agreed to leave early, so he waited to shower. As he briskly walked down the hall toward Margaret's door, the clatter of pans from the kitchen wrapped a hug around his heart. The aroma carried to the second floor, awakening his childhood memories and stimulating his palette. Fresh Focaccia bread.

He knocked on Margaret's bedroom door twice.

"Hey, ciucciamia, you up?" Alex waited at the door for a response.

"Yeah. Just don't want to get out from under the covers. It's freezing in here!"

Alex grinned to himself. "I know. I had the same lack of motivation. But trust me, it's better if you do it quickly. Thinking about it just seems to make it colder."

He heard some rustling, then a thud. "You okay? Can I come in?"

"Sure."

When he opened the door, Margaret was sitting on the edge of the bed.

"What are you doing?" He couldn't help but smile. Even first thing in the morning, she was the hottest girl he'd ever seen.

"Well, I was putting on my jeans until I lost my balance and fell back onto the bed. And now I'm really cold. What did you call me when you knocked on the door? Cio . . .?"

"Oh, nothing." Alex cleared his throat.

"Nooooo, not nothing. You said something in Italian. What did you say?"

"'Good friend.' You know, "Hey, good friend, you up?' You know how it slips out sometimes." Alex looked away.

"Oh, okay. Well, *good friend,* I'm starving."

"That's good, because I think my gram is baking up a storm in the kitchen."

They ambled into the bathroom and brushed their teeth with the help of an index finger, and then followed the ribbon of aroma to the kitchen.

His gram sat at the table, skimming over the newspaper, a cup of coffee nestled in her hands. The bread was on the counter with a large stick of butter softening next to it. Sunlight was beating into the bright yellow kitchen, warming Alex and bringing a welcoming calm to his chilled bones. Pouring a mug-sized cup of joe, he pulled off two large pieces of bread and slathered the butter on. The dough was soft, and the golden goodness seeped into the heat, drizzling off the sides into the crisp brown edges. To Alex, a slice of his gram's homemade bread was the closest thing to heaven on earth.

"Hey, Gram, I was thinking last night about the family from the 1930's. I wonder if the son is still alive. He'd be in his nineties by now, but if we could find him, he might remember what happened. I mean, he was only seven, but I don't think a memory like that ever leaves you. I'm going to see if I can find him. Fingers crossed he's still local."

"That's a good start, but be careful, Alex. This one is exceptionally dangerous. I wanted to talk with you about Wilby. If he isn't showing any signs yet, he could be, as I said last night, a late bloomer. But there is the possibility he favors your dad's side of the family. If that's the case, he is in more danger than either you or your mom. Keep him close and try not to let him spend time alone in the house. I've been doing some thinking of my own, and this time, I'm very worried." She reached her hand out to Alex's face and pinched his cheek —something she hadn't done since he was small. Alex felt the prickly bumps glide up his back and arms. If his gram was worried, they really were in trouble.

A beep from the horn of the taxi meant it was time for goodbyes.

With a few tight hugs and a brown sack packed with cheesecake (that Margaret guarded like it was filled with large, rare diamonds), they hopped into the cab and headed to the train station. Alex propped his head on the window. All of those people in their warm homes going about their business, not knowing the things he did. Never making a connection with the other side. He tried to imagine for a second what it would be like, but he couldn't. He had been born this way, and this was his normal. As much as he hated the thought, he would have to clue his mom in when he got home. Wilby could be in real danger, and she needed to stop denying the truth and get involved.

ALISTER'S GHOST

He wasn't surprised when he came home to an empty house. It was like that more and more lately. It was good, though—he didn't need to worry about Wilby too much if he wasn't there. He wasn't sure how or why, but he felt like they were not targets, just the unlucky inhabitants of the house. Although he couldn't prove anything yet, he felt sure somehow the victims were all connected. The families affected had lived in Floral Park for generations, and since his own was relatively new to the village, it was more likely that, as long as they were away from the house, the danger was minuscule.

His mom moved them from Queens right after the divorce, and although it wasn't very far from where he used to live in Bellerose, it was considered Long Island. She told them it would be a fresh start. Alex was eight. After nearly nine years, he knew the only thing dividing them from Queens was a ten-minute car ride. Floral Park was nice, with all the trees and landscaping, but their problems just followed them. Nothing really changed. Their dad was still MIA with a new family, and his mom was still in denial of her family history.

Alex felt as alone as he always had—until Margaret, that is. She changed everything for him.

For the first year of high school, he thought for sure he'd be alone for the duration. But there she was one day, sitting next to him in science class. Margaret was unlike anyone else he had ever met. Never once did she make him feel insecure about his true self. Now, a year later, he couldn't imagine life without her.

After a long, hot shower, he made the executive decision to skip school that day. *Mom will be pissed,* he thought, *but it's worth the wrath.* He texted Margaret, who had come to the same conclusion. The matter of dead bodies piling up and the possibility of more danger lurking in the future trumped calculus. For today, anyway. Margaret suggested she stay home and run a separate search. Maybe she could track down one of the family members. With any luck, someone was still alive and kicking. Alex agreed: divide and conquer.

He started with the articles he had been reading the day before. *A child and mother found dead after a devastating house fire. Carol Bishop and her young daughter, Ester, perished when a fire started by faulty wiring swept through the family's home while they were sleeping. Mr. Jim Bishop and his seven-year-old son, Alister, were rendered unconscious from the smoke when their home at 55 Geranium Ave. went up in a blazing inferno. Thankful to the heroics of his neighbor, Michael Kirkpatrick, they were pulled from the fire and survived. The grieving Bishop was quoted as saying, "This house was supposed to be our beginning for a new life. Residing in Brooklyn, we thought the kids would have a better life in a house with a yard and quiet streets. What have I done?"*

Without warning, Alex felt heat rise from the bottom of his feet, rushing through his legs and torso, engulfing his head. He leaped from his chair and ran to the bathroom. Turning on the cold water to the shower, he jumped in fully clothed. As he stood under the rain shower, he shivered. The cold replaced the heat that, only a moment ago, was unbearable. It had simmered down as quickly as it had come. He let the water run over his face a few more seconds, hesitant to step out and reap the outcome. When he was feeling brave, he wriggled out of the drenched clothes and ran to his bedroom.

Opting for some heavy sweats, he went to the kitchen to make a cup of hot chocolate. He grabbed a bag of tiny marshmallows and set them down on the counter. The microwave dinged, and he took out the cup of hot water and poured in a packet of sweet, chocolatey, powder goodness.

"Now for the best part," he muttered. He turned to grab the bag. It had disappeared. "What the hell?"

The echo of a child's laugh resonated from upstairs. Alex knew Wilby wasn't home, and there weren't any other kids . . . *Ugh.* "Jacob! Bring back my marshmallows, now! Just because you're dead, it doesn't mean you get to be rude." Alex waited —nothing. Finally, he gave up and went back to his research.

Whatever entity caused him to feel the fire must have been trying to connect, but until it revealed itself, he had no choice but to wait.

He had the name of Alister Bishop and, fingers crossed, he would still be alive. Alex typed in the name and then "Floral Park." Three Alister Bishops came up. One was a pastor at the Lutheran church and appeared to be in his thirties. Another one was born last month. Clearly not him. Alex sat glaring at the monitor after reading the last entry. Alister Bishop, age eighty-nine. Resides in Floral Park Nursing and Long-Term Care facility. It was only a fifteen-minute walk away. His stomach fluttered and his fingers tingled with excitement. *Could it be this easy?* He picked up his phone to text Margaret but hit dial by mistake.

"Hey, what's up?" Margaret yawned.

"I think I found him. I'm not positive, but I think Alister is still alive and living right here in Floral Park."

"What? When are we going? I'll come and pick you up."

"Whoa. Hold on. It's the nursing home. I'm only about fifteen minutes away. I can walk."

"And go without me? Alex, have you been drinking some of your mom's wine?"

"My mom's wine . . . Oh, I get it. You were trying to be funny. Okay, come and get me."

"Smart guy. I'll be there in twenty minutes."

Alex put the phone down and pulled out some jeans from his closet. As he was dressing, he twisted his binder back in place. He hated when it shifted. It could really be uncomfortable on his chest. Which reminded him, his shots had been making him nauseous lately. He decided to keep it to himself, though. His mom would just worry, and the doctor said that could be a side-effect. This time, he grabbed his heavier jacket, a printout of the article on the fire, and his keys. He stood out on the stoop, waiting for Margaret. He was too anxious to sit still and being outside made it seem like he was getting somewhere.

The dark green Hyundai pulled up, and Alex leaped off the top step, landing on the concrete walkway. He slid into the passenger seat and glanced at the side-view mirror.

"Jacob, go back in the house. You can't come with me."

Margaret's head spun around to the back seat. "Who the hell are you talking to?"

"Jacob. He's a six-year-old boy that seems to think it's more fun tagging along with me than taking the light."

"So, this is new. When the heck did this happen? You didn't mention him."

"A few weeks ago, when I picked Wilby up from school. Jacob could tell I saw him, and he followed us home. Been there ever since. He hides from my mom, and Wilby can't see him, so it looks like I'm the one he's bonded with. I've been coaxing him to cross over, but he's scared."

"Poor little guy. It's okay, Jacob; if anyone can help you, it'll be Alex."

"Don't encourage him. He'll be with me 24/7."

"Well, it's true. We both know that's what's gonna happen."

"Yes, I will help him. But right now, we have a bigger issue to tackle. Jacob, please go home. I'll be back soon. Promise."

Alex turned back around and laid his head against the window.

"Is he gone?" Margaret shifted the car in gear.

"He's gone from the car, but I'm sure he'll be home waiting—along with my marshmallows." Alex sighed.

"What?" Margaret questioned.

"Nothing, never mind."

"I can't believe you might have found Alister. That was easy."

"Yeah. It will be if it's really him. Although, getting in to see him might not be as easy as it was finding him. They're pretty strict over there. My grandpa was there for a short time after his stroke. My dad wanted to keep him home, but it was too difficult with the care he needed. Anyway, I tried to go and see him a couple of times on my own. They wouldn't let me in without my mom. You have to be over eighteen. So we might have to get creative once we get there."

"Hmm . . . Sounds like it might be tricky. I love it." Margaret reached out and grabbed his hand and squeezed. "We're in this together. Whatever you need."

"And that's what makes my life just a little bit easier."

"Huh. Only a little bit? I thought I was your BFF? The one who really got you, and who you'd be lost without? "

"Laying it on kind of thick?"

"Actually—no." Margaret laughed.

The structure of the nursing home was designed to give the visitor a welcoming experience. It reminded Alex of an old southern mansion. He had driven to Disney World with his mom and brother two years ago. Their route took them through both Carolinas, Virginia, and Georgia. He loved the architecture of the south. Big pillars, a circular driveway, and a plethora of gardens. Large windows and cascading ivory complimented the brick building. But Alex knew what was on the inside, and it was as far away from the warmth and hospitality of the old south as you could get. The nursing home had a reputation in the whispers of their residents—a truth his family discovered after his grandfather's stay.

The doors were on a handicap motor, so entering unnoticed was fairly easy. Access to the rooms was another story. They waited patiently until a group of scrub-adorned caregivers walked in, then they quickly followed and ducked into a nearby lobby area before the receptionist at the front desk had a chance to see them. The facility had two floors, each one containing about twenty-five rooms. It would have been an impossible task—searching aimlessly to find Alister among an ocean of residents. Alex, anticipating the difficulty, made a call on the drive over, pretending to have a floral delivery for Mr. Bishop, and his charm had won out. Kim, the woman at the front desk, had no idea that, somewhere in the conversation, she had slipped that Alister was in room 214.

There were several other people waiting to see family members, sitting on the plush couches and chairs the facility provided—another facade to appease the outsider. Alex nodded toward the couch, and they sat down for a few minutes to wait for the right time to escape up the stairs. The moment came quicker than anticipated when a disgruntled visitor started to make a scene about the condition of his loved one.

After a few tense words, Alex could make out it was the

man's mother. He had been concerned the last few visits because she had a sore on the backside of her left thigh. His anger was escalating, and the director of the nursing home had been summoned. By the time she had gotten there, it had escalated from loud voices to threats. Alex saw their chance and took it.

He tugged Margaret's hand to get her attention, then looked toward the stairs. They both stood up and proceeded to their destination as if they had borrowed Harry Potter's cloak of invisibility. No one turned a head to notice them. When they reached the landing of the second story, there were three hallways. They checked the numbers on the doors; the hallway on the far right was where they needed to go.

"Alex, were you listening to the guy downstairs? He was really angry, and I don't blame him. How could they allow that to happen to his mother?"

"It's like I said, this place has a bad rap with the residents. Most of the time, they manage to cover up what they're doing —or not doing. But occasionally, a family member is more inquisitive, and they get caught. Some of these people have been hospitalized with severe bed sores, and others have had numerous falls, failure to thrive . . . all kinds of crap. What kills me is that no one does anything. It's not only the staff, but the administration running the facility. They always manage to walk away with no real consequences. That's why my dad has so much guilt about my grandfather. Once he found out the things they were doing, he got him out of here, but it was too late. He had gotten so depressed, he never recovered. He just slipped away after that. My dad tried to do everything he could to expose them, but in the end, they just got a slap on the wrist."

"Horrible people." Margaret's complexion glowed with anger. "Your grandfather knows you guys tried. You know that, right?"

Alex just nodded. He couldn't have this conversation now.

"Room 214. Here it is." He listened at the door to see if he could hear if there were others in the room with Alister, but all he heard was laughter. Alex pushed the heavy door open, and he and Margaret slid through. An elderly gentleman was sitting in a recliner in front of the television, watching an old rerun of Gilligan's Island.

Gingerly, Alex approached the man. "Excuse me, sir, are you Alister Bishop?" The man didn't answer and kept watching his show.

Margaret leaned in and whispered into Alex's ear. "Maybe he didn't hear you."

Alex raised the volume of his voice and tried again. "Hello. Are you Alister Bishop?"

The man grabbed the remote for the TV from a side table and muted the volume. Pushing the chair forward to an upright position, he cautiously stood with the aid of a cane that had been hooked on the arm of the chair. He turned to face them, squinted his eyes, and knitted his brow.

"I am. But who are you and why are you in my room? If you're another one of my so-called relatives, get out. There is no estate, no hidden money—and certainly if there were, you would not be getting your claws on it."

Alex widened his eyes with confusion.

"No. We're not your family. And we don't know anything about any money. We just need to talk you about your house. The one on Geranium Ave. in Floral Park. Where you lived as a boy."

The color of the old man's face turned from red to pasty white. He shuddered, tilting him off balance. Narrowly, he grabbed the arm of the recliner in time to topple backward and into his seat. Alex and Margaret lunged to help, but he was safe before they reached him. Standing next to him, Alex could see the years mapped out through the deep wrinkles in his face. The old man looked up and glared. Then he lowered his head as if he were hiding a shameful secret. Alex crouched down beside him.

"Alister . . . It's you, isn't it?" He kept his voice soft.

Alex pressed his hands into his burning ears to ease the migraine that had seeped into his brain. Reading the emotions of others had its good and bad points. Today, not so good. The man was suffering from mental anguish. He just needed to find out the cause. Taking several deep breaths, he gained enough control to calm the pain. An unwanted side-effect of the *know*.

"What do you want from me?" the old man mumbled. "I haven't lived in that house in over eighty years. I sold it over fifty years ago. How could I possibly help you with anything regarding Geranium Ave?"

"I live in that house with my mom and brother."

Alister put his head in his hands and began shaking it back and forth. "No. You mustn't stay there. Please. Listen to me. You get your family out of that house. It isn't safe. Go and leave me alone. I can't remember that night again or the horrendous years that followed. Please . . . Leave."

The old man began sobbing and shaking so badly that Alex reached out and held him. Alister stopped and pulled back. "You know."

"Know what?" Alex reached for a glass of water from the table and handed it to him, but he pushed it away.

"You've seen her. I know you have. I can tell. Once someone sees that monster, the others know."

"Monster? What monster?"

Anxiety flooded his body and squeezed his chest like a vice grip. Getting the information from Alister was slow, and he didn't want to upset him anymore than he had to, but he needed answers.

"My mother . . ." Alister pushed forward and steadied

himself until he was on his feet again. Then he shuffled over to the window and faced outward. "She died with my sister in a fire when I was seven years old. My father tried, but he couldn't get to them. The smoke was too much for him. He collapsed trying to rescue them. If it weren't for our neighbor, we would have died too. He ran in and dragged my father and me out. My mother was the sweetest person you'd ever want to know. But her spirit—that's something else. I think rage took her over that night. But I don't have to tell you. Who are you? You're different. I felt it when you touched me."

"Why do you say that?" Alex didn't want to go into his family history, but he was curious how Alister knew.

"Don't try to fool me, kid. I told you. Once you see her you know each other, we're somehow connected. You can feel it. Like a charge of electricity running through your veins. But with you, there's something else. This isn't a surprise to you."

Alex reflected to last night when he felt the heat burst throughout his body and the flame ignite and consume him. He shook.

"Yes. I can see certain things that others don't. But I haven't seen anything. More like I've felt it. How did you know that about me? Most people don't have a clue."

"I've been this way since the night she and my sister died. I see things—people. I tried to tell my dad, but he thought it was trauma from the fire. So did the countless doctors he took me to. They were so sure it would go away with time. But it didn't. Nearly drove me to insanity in my thirties. I couldn't take it anymore, and I left the States. I thought if I got away, maybe they'd stay here. I was wrong. It's not the place. It's me. She comes to me from time to time. At first, she was sweet and looked just like I remember. But then she changed and became something that is pure evil. Nothing I've ever tried has stopped her. I thought if I sold the house, she'd leave, but she stays in that house, terrorizing every family who has ever lived there. I've come to realize there's no escape. It has been more peaceful here, though. Maybe she doesn't like this place, because she rarely visits me here. Given the disgusting behavior that goes on, it's no wonder." Alister sighed.

Alex wasn't sure how to approach this. He wanted to find out more about Alister's dad, but clearly the man was shaken, and he didn't want to cause him additional pain. But on the other hand, people were dying, and if they were going to save lives, he needed to push.

"Alister, you said she changed. Did you see her physically do this?"

"What do you mean?" Alister turned and faced them.

"Does she switch from bad to good in front of you?" Alex wasn't sure where he was going with this, but it seemed important.

"No. First I see her, and then she disappears for a moment, and then reappears as this horrible thing. It's really quite frightening. Its eyes are cold, almost demonic. Pure black masses in its sockets. You can feel the rage. All of my hair stands on end, as if I've put my finger in a light socket. Pure evil energy. It's hard to believe that thing is my mother."

"What about your father? Did he ever see her?"

"Once. But he would have never admitted to it if I hadn't been standing beside him. It was the early 1950's, right before I put the house up for sale. I was twenty-five, and he had given me the place to do with what I saw fit. He hadn't been inside in years. He tried after the fire to have a life there for us. He had it completely restored, and we stayed in it for a while, but the pain became unbearable. He would live deaths night over and over again. Finally, we just left. It stood empty for several years while I was growing up. Anyway, we went there early one evening to see what had to be done to put it on the market. I was in the kitchen opening the windows, and he was upstairs getting the bedrooms, when I heard him scream. It was spine-tingling. Here was my father, a bull of a man, and he sounded more like a child who was frightened for his life. I ran to his room and saw him standing—motionless. As I walked through the doorway, it became very clear why. There she was on the other side of the bed in front of the windows. Her piercing dark eyes and icy halo on a hovering shell that once was my mother."

"Wait. What? An icy halo? You didn't mention that before."

"I didn't? Yes. She always has a ring of ice surrounding her head. I grabbed my father, and we fled. I shouldn't have sold that damned house. I truly believed that she would follow us and leave it alone. I was foolish. He never spoke of it—or her—after that. I'm not sure he believed it was her. But I did and still do. I think she became consumed with anger over the fact that he couldn't save her and my sister."

"But then why come to you?"

"What do you mean?" Alister's eyes widened with confusion.

"If she blamed your father, then why not appear to him all those years? She came to you, not him. Just that once? It doesn't make any sense." Alex felt more frustrated than when they had started this conversation. He thought he was getting answers, but instead, he had more questions.

"I don't know. It never occurred to me. I think I've been so wrapped up in my own terror all this time that I never questioned it. Maybe it's because of how I can see things since the accident. Or maybe there's a part of her still there, and she starts off with her motherly love, but the rage takes over. I don't know. This is all tiring me out. I never wanted to revisit any of this. Please, I need to rest."

Alex knew if he ever wanted to be welcomed back for more questions, they needed to leave. He hesitated though and asked one last one.

"Alister, we're going to go, but I hope we can come back and see you soon. I have one quick question and we will leave."

Alister huffed. "What is it?"

"How did your father die? I can't find any information on him after 1988."

"He passed away in 1990. Imagine all those years living with that guilt. You couldn't find anything on him because after 1988, he became a recluse. He never left his house again. He had bought a small home in New Hyde Park when I was fifteen, and that's where he died. Two months prior, his longtime friend died in his sleep. He was the last one still around from the old era. My father was heartbroken. I think it just did him in."

"Thank you for talking to us." Alex extended his hand out. The sensation of a sharp needle pierced his palm, and he abruptly let go. Rubbing his hand with his thumb, Alex took one more glance at the old man—he was hiding something.

"Please, get out of that house before something awful happens to your family."

Alex nodded. He knew his mom was not about to move them out, but he also knew that Alister didn't know about his grandma and the extent of his own capabilities. He and Margaret had some serious research to do in a short time, and then, they would be back for round two with Alister.

After they pushed through the doors to exit the facility, Alex rubbed his hands through his hair.

"Damn. He's not telling us everything; I know it."

Margaret's forehead wrinkled when she knitted her brows. "I don't have a *spidey sense,* but I felt like he was holding back, too. He hesitated too many times. I know you don't want to hear this, but I think we need to tell your mom. Lives before pride."

"I thought about that earlier. I know it's a risk because her attitude the past few years has been, 'if we don't talk about it, then it's not happening.' She knows I'm still involved, so the whole thing is sort of ridiculous."

"Another thing I was thinking about is Jim Bishop. The fire, and everything about it, seems off. I think we need to really focus on this guy; find as much as we can about him. Dig deeper. I think we just scratched the surface."

"Let's go to my house. We can bring my mom up to speed and hope she doesn't kill us." Alex chuckled.

"We have a plan. But before we go home, let's stop off for a sandwich. I'm starving." Margaret rubbed her stomach.

"Village Pizzeria?" Alex smirked. It was his favorite place to get a sub.

"Always with the Pizzeria. Yes. We'll go there. But later, we hit the bakery. I've got a sweet tooth."

"You still have half a cheesecake."

"I know. But I'm feeling some black and white cookies. So, I'm thinking Butter Cooky Bakery on Jericho Turnpike. You know they're the best, and I know you want nothing less for me."

"This is true. Why else would I give you the gift of me as a friend?" Alex glanced sideways.

"Well, if it gets me my cookies, believe what you will, but everyone knows it's me who's the real gift here." She stuck out her tongue.

"Ciucciamia, that's something I tell myself every day." He smirked.

She gave him a hug. "Aww, you're my good friend, too."

Alex rolled his eyes. *If she only knew what the word really meant.* As they got into the car, he took another look at the facility Alister called home. *What really happened all those years ago?* He couldn't get the question out of his mind.

A MEATBALL HERO for him and an eggplant parmesan for her—both loaded with mozzarella. Chips and two sodas sat on Alex's desk, waiting for them to devour. Margaret had to use the bathroom, and he didn't want to start without her. The aroma of the garlic and seasoned meat flooded the air and made his resistance waver. He tore a piece of the bread and popped it into to his mouth. It was laced with some of the sauce from the meat, and the flavors melted over his tongue, leaving him with a want for more. He was still chewing when Margaret sat down.

"Their sandwiches are huge. I love that about this place." She picked up her sandwich with both hands and widened her mouth to move in for a bite.

Alex loved watching her eat. The way she curled her tongue to lick her bottom lip when she thought no one was watching. *Get a hold of yourself,* he thought.

Margaret did have a real passion for food—and sweets. She made everything she ate look so appetizing. Even if it was eggplant. She had been a vegetarian since the second grade after watching a documentary on animals being slaughtered for meat. Alex—not so much. A carnivore through and through.

"I wish my mom would get home soon. This waiting to tell her feels like an ax hanging over my neck. My stomach's doing flip-flops."

"She'll explode for sure when you first tell her, especially when she hears we ditched school. But you know your mom; she'll eventually calm down and listen. She loves you too much to stay angry. So, eat your sandwich. It'll calm your stomach. You know how you get when you don't eat. The volcano erupts inside that belly of yours."

Alex nodded in agreement. Margaret knew him—really knew him. She took another bite, and a droplet of sauce landed on her chin. He grinned. *Could she be any cuter?* White-knuckling the desk, he pulled back the urge to nibble her chin clean, and instead reached for a napkin.

"You've got a little . . ." He reached out to wipe her chin. "Oh, thanks." Margaret leaned in closer to him.

Alex gently wiped the tomato sauce from her chin, his hands shaking. There was definitely something riling his stomach, but it wasn't lack of food.

"Ahem . . . There you are, all clean." He scooted back.

"My hero." Margaret grinned.

"You know, I've been thinking we do need to look harder at Jim Bishop, but there's someone else we're forgetting." Alex started typing on his keyboard.

"Carol Bishop." Margaret took another bite of her sandwich.

"That's why we're partners in crime; you're brilliant."

"You're so full of it, Alex McKenna."

"We've been focused on the husband, but there's so many unanswered questions about that night, and she's definitely a key player. Why didn't she get out? I keep thinking of something my gram said. It was late at night. They were all sleeping. Or at least, that's what Bishop told the fire department. So, how come Carol and Ester didn't make it? Carol should have been right beside Jim in their bed, and Ester's room is right next to Alister's."

"I agree. Even if the couple split up and each went for a child, they should have all made it out. If Jim got Alister out, what stopped Carol? Why didn't Jim grab both kids? We've got a lot of questions. Time to find some answers."

He finished off the remaining bites of meatball and then resumed typing—Carol Bishop. "Okay, here we go. Damn. There's a lot of them."

"Well, I'm pretty sure we can rule out anyone living. Whatcha think?"

"Sarcasm. Sometimes endearing, and sometimes—not so much." Alex shot her a glare.

"And today?" She smirked.

"Endeeeeeeearing?"

"Smart."

"So, let's go back to original article about the fire. Maybe they mention a family member for Carol that I might've missed. Nothing—damn."

"That's it?"

"I don't see anything else. This crap is so old. I really hope we don't run into a dead end."

"Don't be so quick to surrender. Here, let me have it."

Margaret scooted in front of the monitor, slipped out her elastic band, and pulled back her hair. Alex studied the fluid motion of her wrist looping the band around her glistening strands.

"Now, let's see what we can come up with."

"Alex? Are you home?" His mom called from downstairs.

"Yeah, Ma, I'll be down in a minute."

"Are you ready?" Margaret pushed the chair back and got up.

"Not really, but let's go light the fireworks anyway." Alex pulled an imaginary noose around his neck.

"A little dramatic, McKenna."

His mom, Gina, was waiting in the living room, sitting on the couch.

"The two of you have a seat." Her tone was stern.

Alex raised a brow. She already seemed pissed off, but they hadn't said anything yet.

"The school called me at work today. It appears you weren't there, Alex." His mom's eyes narrowed.

"I can explain. We needed—"

"We? Don't tell me you skipped also, Margaret?"

"Ma! I can explain if you let me get a word out."

"Alex, I swear if you shout at me again, this discussion will definitely end with you going to your room. Maybe you should go home, Margaret."

Alex pleaded. "Mom, please let me explain before you make her leave. I'm sorry I shouted; there's just something really bad happening, and I need to explain."

His mom sawed in a heavy breath and crossed her legs. "Tell me."

Alex stuck to the facts about the fire, the series of deaths, and everything else they'd uncovered. He felt the need to explain quickly before his mom changed her mind and sent Margaret home. After he was done, he waited. His mom's silence was like a black cloud hanging above him. At any moment, the storm would rage and pour down on his head.

"I'm not going to lie to you, Alex. I've felt things lately. A veil has been broken, and I'd hoped it would weave itself back together, but I can see now it's not going to happen. For most of your life, I've tried to keep you out of this part of our world. I thought if I turned a blind eye, then you and Wilby would be safe. But I know you've been working with Gram, and I also know your abilities have been growing stronger every year."

"Mia madre, I'm not trying to hurt you or go against your will. I can't deny the piece of me that is such a large part of who I am. Ma, I just need your help."

"I know, mio figlio. I just wanted to protect you. But you must understand that you can't just go off and do what you want. There are boundaries and consequences to your actions."

"I'm really sorry."

"Me too, Mrs. LaBoccetta," Margaret interjected.

"Margaret, you practically live at this house. I think you can call me Gina."

"Okay, Mrs. La . . . Gina," Margaret said softly.

"Now, before we get started, I want to be crystal clear. No

more decisions to miss school without speaking to me. I mean it, Alex. My goodwill will only allow for so many excuses—got it?"

"Yes, no more secrets. No more surprises."

"Good."

"Something's bothering me; you said you've felt things. I haven't been able to pick up on anything other than the normal spirit here and there. I mean, these headaches have been clouding my thoughts, but still, I should have been able to get something."

"I haven't seen anything. It's more like there's something out of place. I thought it was because I was out of practice. Now I'm thinking there might be a darker reason. Alex, you're very strong with your gift, but remember, your mother has been around a little longer, and I've had time to develop skills before you were born. Although, I know you will eventually surpass both me and your grandmother. For now, it could just boil down to experience. But I will say this: I can't home in on anything specifically. It's like I got up to get something and can't remember what. It's gnawing at me."

"Has this ever happened to you before?"

"No. Not even when I tried to tuck all of this away. I still saw and felt everything—I just didn't discuss it with you or your brother. Maybe that wasn't the best way to handle it, but I thought I was doing the right thing at the time."

"Margaret and I were talking, and we think we should check further into Bishop's wife, Carol. Also, Bishop himself. The circumstances surrounding the fire are weird, and the deaths in Floral Park lately . . . I feel like they're all connected."

"I agree. Oh, crap, I've got to get Wilby. Your dad called earlier and said he can't pick him up from school. So typical."

"We can get him, Gina," Margaret chimed in.

"Thanks, honey, but I need to stop at the store on the way

home. I'll be back shortly. Margaret, are you staying for dinner?"

"I wish. I gotta get home. My parents came back from Florida today and my mom wants a *real* family dinner. Like she has a clue what that means. Oh . . . Sorry, Gina. I didn't mean to sound disrespectful. It's just, if they stayed home more often, family dinner wouldn't be a special occasion we have to schedule."

"Oh, ragazza dolce, you don't need to apologize. You know you're always welcome here."

Margaret smiled and dropped her head to the gaze at her shoes. Alex knew she was both embarrassed and enamored with his family's show of affection. Time to rescue the girl.

"Come on, I'll walk you out to your car." Alex opened the door. Margaret eagerly followed him.

When they reached the car, she slid into the driver's side and turned the key in the ignition. Alex hung on the open door.

"You're lucky, McKenna. I know they embarrass you sometimes with their loudness, but they love you so much, and show it all the time."

"That they do." He grinned. "I'll talk to you later. Good luck with the family dinner thing."

"I need more than luck. See ya."

Alex stepped onto the stoop in front of his house and sat down. He heard the creaking of the garage door shutting, and moments later, his mom came around the corner in her 2005 Nissan Altima. She waved to him as the car slowly passed by. Alex soaked up the aroma of maple, ash, and pine. Floral Park was definitely a menagerie of horticultural delight for the senses. A bold squirrel trotted along the sidewalk, and then nervously scurried up a tree after spotting Alex.

"I know you're here, Jacob." Alex glanced to his left. The

boy manifested two steps up from Alex. "Where's my marshmallows?"

The boy giggled.

"And while we're at it, Wilby's baseball, my mom's favorite bottle of perfume, and the television remote? You need to bring those things back. Why do you keep taking them, anyway?"

"I don't know. I get alone." The boy's lower lip curled.

"You mean lonely?"

"Uh-huh. I miss my mommy."

"I know you do. Listen, buddy, remember what I told you about your mom? She was in the car with you during the accident. She's crossed over into the light. I'm sure she's waiting for you right now. You just have to walk through it, Jacob."

"I'm scared, Alex. What if she's not there?"

"Was your mommy a good person? Did she love you? Take care of you?" Alex used a soothing tone.

"All the time. She was the best mommy in the world." The boy peered up.

"Well, then, there you have it. She is most definitely waiting for you. Good mommy's only go to one place."

"Heaven?" Jacob questioned.

Alex hesitated. He hated labeling the life after this one. He really didn't believe in an absolute. He felt heaven was a manifestation of what people needed to believe not to fear death. He knew there was good, and he knew there was evil. And if everyone needed to label the separation of those two truths as Heaven and Hell, who was he to argue? But he knew better.

"Yup. Your outstanding mommy is waiting in the light to walk you right through the big golden gates of Heaven."

"Can you take me, Alex? Please?"

"Oh, little man, I wish I could. But only those who are

ready can go, and my soul has things to do first. But I know if you . . ."

"Hey, weirdo, who the hell are you talking to?"

Alex whipped his head around—Kyle Branders. The bully had relentlessly terrorized Alex in the ninth grade. That was until the beautiful day that Margaret punched him in the face. Alex was tempted many times to fight back, but he figured his weirdness label was bad enough without adding troublemaker to the mix. Besides, his mom was just starting to feel normal again after the divorce. It took her several years to achieve a level of comfort where she could breathe again, and he wasn't about to rob her of that.

But when Margaret took matters into her own hands and knocked the five-foot, ten-inch sophomore on his ass in front of half the class, he had to admit it felt fucking awesome. He glanced back at Jacob; the little boy was gone. Alex sighed. He was relieved the frightened child didn't have to add "encounter with a huge asshole" to his list of shitty things that had happened to him.

"What the hell do you want, Kyle?"

"Nothing. I was just walking to my friend's house, minding my own business, until I saw you. The biggest freak at school having a conversation with himself. Oh, wait, I know what you're doing. You're talking to one of your ghosts, aren't you? Good thing they have you to help them out. Lord knows how they would ever find their way without you. I just wonder about all the poor souls who died before the great Alex McKenna was born. Are they all just wandering the earth aimlessly, searching for you? What is that, like a gazillion people? Sounds to me like you might need some help. Who ya gonna call—ghost busters!" Kyle roared.

"You know, Kyle, it's a shame intelligence isn't determined by the amount of garbage one person can spew out of their pie hole. Because you'd be a damn Einstein."

Alex knew as soon as the words left his lips that he was in trouble. Kyle lunged, taking the front lawn in three steps. Alex jumped up in time to meet the fist that had found his gut as a target. Spiraling backward, he slammed into the brick steps, the air pushed from his lungs. Kyle reared his right fist back and sent it sailing right for Alex's jaw. Alex winced waiting for the inevitable, but nothing happened. Kyle's face turned pasty gray and his eyes widened the size of golf balls. His fist, suspended and lulling inches away from Alex's face, was fighting to pull away from the unseen force that held him back.

"Jacob?" Alex struggled to focus.

The little boy held onto Kyle's arm, pulling it back. "It's okay; you can let him go."

"He wants to hurt you."

"I'll be okay. Just release his arm."

The boy listened and let go. Kyle rose up and ran to the edge of the property before stopping to catch his breath. Hunched over with his hands on his knees, he looked back at Alex, fear dripping from his face. Straightening up, he gasped one long breath in and then ran down the block.

Alex smirked. He knew it wasn't right to take joy in someone else's misery, but he couldn't help it. The guy was a creep, and he deserved it.

"Come on, Jacob, let's go inside. You're pretty awesome, dude. Thanks for the help."

Alex was thankful, but he was also confused. Jacob was very young to the celestial world, and it took a lot of energy for a spirit to interact with the living to the capacity that the little boy did with Kyle. Stealing a bag of marshmallows is one thing, but to grip a corporeal being and hold on—that took real practice. Jacob hadn't been dead that long.

Alex closed the front door behind him and went into the kitchen. Jacob followed, just as he thought he would.

"You know, little man, I meant it when I told you it's okay to go. I appreciate what you did for me, but you should be with your mom."

"Alex, your brother Wilby is cool."

Alex chuckled. "Yeah, he's okay. You hang around him?"

"Sometimes. But he doesn't see me. Your mom's nice, too. I think she sees me. I try to hide from her, but I don't think it works."

"That's because she's like me. But you got us off the subject of you. Jacob, I'm real busy now, but when this case is over, we're gonna have to solve your problem. Okay?"

Alex stepped closer to the little boy, who was hovering a few inches above the floor. "I promise we'll fix this."

"Thank you, Alex. I'm glad . . ." Jacob jumped up abruptly, flew toward the ceiling, and disappeared.

"Jacob? Where'd you go?"

"Who's Jacob?" Wilby came into the kitchen from the back door. He was carrying two brown paper bags filled with groceries.

"No one."

"Alex, we could use a little help," his mom called out from the driveway.

"Coming."

After all the groceries were unpacked and put away, Alex made a small pot of coffee for himself and his mom. Wilby had gone to his room to do homework, and it was the perfect time to share some thoughts about the case with his mom.

She had gone upstairs to change. She ambled back into the kitchen after swapping her business casual for fuzzy socks, loose sweatpants, and an oversized sweatshirt.

"Is that coffee I smell? You're a godsend. I can't get warm; it's freezing outside."

"It is getting nippy. I love it, though." Alex gave a thumbs-up.

"Mio bel ragazzo, I know you do. Ever since you were a bambino, your body ran warm. I used to bundle you up to go out and play in the yard, and when I turned my head for five minutes, you'd have your coat, hat, and gloves thrown on the ground. You'd be twirling free. It was a challenge to keep you clothed." She nodded and rolled her eyes.

Alex grabbed two mugs from the cupboard and poured each of them a cup of Joe. Putting a drop of almond milk in his mom's and dousing his to a warm beige, he set the cups down on the table. Alex sat down and propped his feet up on the chair next to him. His mom crumbled into her chair and leaned back. Letting her head fall backward, she stretched her arms toward the ceiling before wriggling into her seat.

"I spoke to Gram while I was out. She called me because she was concerned. I told her you had told me everything. She sounded relieved. We discussed the Bishops. I think we can all agree that we need to find out as much about them as we can. Since you've already found Alister, I think focusing on Carol might be a good idea. We can delve further into Jim, but let's get some info on her first. Gram gave me a great idea—the il vecchio in Little Italy."

"How can he help?"

"Gram hasn't found anything yet that explains how this spirit can numb our senses. We need to know what we're dealing with in order to get prepared. Think about it, Alex. If the recent deaths trace back to the Bishops, and if the vision we had is connected, then that means this ghoul goes back decades. Maybe he can point us in the right direction. Bella mia, I've tried concentrating—nothing. Just little feelings like I told you about earlier. That and these terrible headaches."

"Me too. On both counts. The headaches make me nauseous, and when I try to concentrate on something that might be hiding itself here in the house, all I get is a bigger headache."

"It'll be an adventure, and we'll eat dinner. It's been a long time since we've been there. Do you think Margaret would like to go?"

"That's a loaded question. Of course, she'd love to go. In fact, I bet she'd get pissed if we didn't bring her. That girl loves her food almost as much as researching all the weirdness in our lives." Alex laughed.

"It's already kind of late, and Wilby has a load of homework. Let's go tomorrow night. We can leave after I pick up your brother from school. I'll come home, change, and then out the door we go. Ask Margaret tonight so she has time to get permission from her parents."

Alex sighed. "I'll tell her, but have you met her parents? They couldn't give two shits if she's home or not."

"Ragazzo, watch your language. That's not true. They wanted her home tonight. Maybe they're not as involved as our family is, but they care about their daughter."

"The only reason they wanted her home tonight was for appearances. Their cousins are up from Connecticut. They're really richy-rich. Margaret's mother didn't want any family whispers at the dinner table."

"Oh, I'm sorry. I had no idea."

"It's okay, no one does. Margaret doesn't run around blabbing about her family issues. She only discusses it with me."

"You two are very close."

"We are. She saved me. I mean, at school. You know how rough it was in the beginning. People like Kyle—they made it almost unbearable. But she set all that straight. Until today, at least. I hadn't heard a word from Kyle all year. He really threw me off-balance earlier."

"What happened with Kyle?"

"Nothing more than the usual."

"Faccia bella, I pray to the universe and everything in it,

that one day in your life, things will be different. But for now, know you're loved . . . so much." She reached out and squeezed Alex's hand.

"I know, Mom. I do."

"Speaking of love—what's up with you and Margaret?"

"Maaaaa! We're best friends, that's it."

"You lie, my boy. I see the way you look at that girl. And I see the way she looks at you. Why don't you speak up and tell her?"

"Because for me, it's not that easy. I know who I am, and Margaret's never judged. But it's one thing to be my friend; it's another to have me as a boyfriend. I haven't gone through any surgery . . . I'm not . . . "

"Stop right there. Do you think so little of this girl that you assume to make up her mind for her? Margaret is special; I know you see that. But so are you. You will take your journey when the time comes, but until then, it doesn't change who you are. You are Alex McKenna—my son."

Alex peered up toward the ceiling, tears trickling down his cheeks. He wiped them away with the back of his sleeve. "Thanks, Mom. Ti amo. But I'm not ready to find out yet."

"Okay, baby. When the time is right, you'll know. Ti amo anch'io." His mom stood up and wrapped her arms around Alex. He slumped into her protective shield. He was grateful every day for having his family. The universe had smiled on him.

VICTOR

Alex shot out of bed like a cannon. Beads of sweat nestled above his upper lip, and he wiped away the saltiness with the back of his hand. He stretched his arms out in front of him; the goosebumps were at full attention. The dream was so real, the malevolent figure with an icy halo around its head. He couldn't see its face, which was cloaked behind a veil, revealing only enough to make Alex's heart pound at a frenetic pace. He wasn't sure if this was the know, or if his mind was creating the pictures from Alister's words about his deceased mother. Either way, the fear he felt was very real, and he chose to take it as a warning. Treading carefully was his new mantra.

The plan for the day was school, then he and Margaret would meet his mom and Wilby at his house. From there, they were going to Little Italy. When he called Margaret the night before to ask if she wanted go, his eardrum nearly shattered when she replied in an octave, he'd never heard from her before. To say the girl was excited was an understatement.

He sat on the edge of the bed and ran his fingers through his hair. The thought of Margaret first thing in the morning woke up more than just his memories of last night. *Dial it back, McKenna. There's shit to do today.* His thoughts didn't cooperate; she remained vividly in the front of his brain. A shower would help wash them away and give him focus—he hoped.

After a long, hot shower, his mind had cleared. The dark spirit in his dream started to feel more like a message rather than a composite drawn from his imagination. Over the years, Alex had learned to distinguish between warnings and dreams. But once in a while, if a spirit was strong enough, it could confuse him. He needed time for the emotions to settle so he could sift through them and pull out the parts of himself he knew were responsive to the situation—fear.

Fear is a strong emotion for anyone, but for him—like everything else—when it was ignited, it was ten times stronger than a person without his abilities. Alex had learned to use it to his benefit. His goosebumps were a direct link to that fear, and one he cultivated to work for him. The stronger the bumps, the bigger the problem. Since they had been his warning beacon since he was a child, he had time to feel comfortable enough to let them guide him. When he'd first woke up that morning, the bumps had completely covered his arms and legs. His fear was real, which meant so was the thing in his dream. He was getting a warning—or worse, the darkness found a way into his thoughts.

He dressed quickly; he wanted to catch his mom before she left for work.

He turned the dining room corner into the kitchen; Wilby sat at the table, crunching on cereal.

"What's up, fratellino? Do you know where Mom is?"

"She's in the basement, getting laundry. She said to tell you don't leave. She wants to talk to you."

"Well, that's funny, because I want to talk to her, too. So, how was Dad's? Did you have a good time?"

"It was okay. Mom said we're going to Little Italy for dinner tonight. I'm getting a meatball sandwich."

"Cool. Margaret's coming too. You good with that?"

"Sure. I really like her. She's different than other girls. She likes to kill zombies with me."

Wilby's favorite video game was about the post-apocalyptic world that had been overrun by zombies. He played it every chance he got.

"Yeah, she is pretty cool." Alex grinned.

"Oh, there you are. I need to talk to you about a dream I had last night," his mom interrupted.

Alex froze. This was not good.

"A dark spirit with an icy halo?" Alex asked.

"Yes. Did you see it too?"

"I woke up in a cold sweat. At first, I wasn't sure if it was because of Alister's description or something else. But now that you've seen this apparition in your dreams too, I think it just confirms my fear."

"Which is what?"

"This spirit—or whatever it is—got in our heads. Almost as if it's taunting us. Telling us that it can see us, but we can't see it. Has this ever happened to you, Mom?"

"Never. Hopefully, we'll get some answers tonight. Is Margaret coming?"

"Yeah, we'll meet you here after school. I gotta run." He grabbed a granola bar off the counter.

"Don't you want a ride?" his mom questioned.

"I'm taking my bike. I need to think."

ALEX TEXTED Margaret that he was heading to school early. Luckily, she knew him well enough to understand what that meant without any further explanation on his part. She understood his need for alone time. He often used the empty high school campus as inspiration for his thoughts. Aside from a few dedicated teachers and some earthbound teen spirits, the grounds were open and quiet.

Gliding through the streets canopied with orange and gold, the scent of pine and ash pulled him into the landscape of Floral Park. Alex held his face to the wind, allowing the cold air to sting his cheeks. He imagined the victims—overcome with fright, the terror of the freezing temperature seeping into their brain and encasing their heads in a helmet of ice. He shivered. The lush green of maintained lawns had turned into a depository for all the leaves that had died and feathered their way to the ground. All part of the cycle. What about the victims of this new string of murders? Did they feather their way to the next life? Or were they trapped somewhere between the worlds, waiting to be set free? He knew that, on more than one occasion, if a spirit had a particularly abrupt and painful death, they could become confused. Never taking the light, never connecting to someone like Alex to help them.

Alex pulled the bike over to the sidewalk. Setting it on the kickstand, he sat down on the curb. *So many souls needed help, how could he ever rescue all of them?* He placed his head on his knees. His life could feel overwhelming sometimes, and no one could fix it for him.

He turned his head slightly. A familiar sound interrupted his thoughts. Raking the lawn two houses down was one of those lost souls. An elderly gentleman, whose apparition came only in the Fall, and only as long as there were leaves to rake. He wouldn't talk to Alex, or even look at him. He'd been coming back every Fall for the past seven years.

Knowing it was useless to try and make contact, Alex looked away. It hurt him to know he could help but was restrained by the man himself.

A large, gloomy puff in the dismal sky caught his

attention. Hung on a steel gray canvas, in the distance, charcoal tentacles were creeping closer, devouring little morsels of light leftover from the sun's attempt to pierce the barrier. He hoped for a thunderstorm. Alex enjoyed a good lightning show, and it had been a while. Slipping his phone from his pocket, he glanced at the time. He needed to get moving. The remaining ride, he concentrated on Carol and Jim. According to the neighbors in the article, they were a loving couple with two beautiful children. But Alex couldn't stop the pang in his gut—the one that he had trusted all his life. And this time, it was deafening with alarm bells.

The parking lot was nearly empty, just as he'd expected. He locked his bike up and headed to the bleachers in front of the football fields. He sank down to his usual step; it had become his unofficial possession and a place to meet Margaret. The ground was wet with dew, and it crunched under his Chuck Taylors. He liked the sound. It reminded him of his little brother. Wilby was a cereal fanatic.

Unfortunately, the dew had taken the bleachers as well. He leaned over the chain-link fence separating the watchers from the players. The team was out in full color, practicing the latest moves to optimistically prove them champions for a second year. Alex appreciated the span of the football field. He could be spared the uproar of innuendos flung by the coach to motivate the eagerly receiving jocks. It was like watching a silent movie. He used to hang out on Sunday mornings with his dad before the deconstruction of their family. His dad is a huge fan of Douglas Fairbanks—a passion he passed down to his son. Most guys his age might not even know who Douglas Elton Thomas Ullman was, but to Alex, he was one of the best parts of childhood.

His mind wandered to the conversation he'd had with his mom earlier. He still felt going to Little Italy would waste precious time. If his gram was right, there were only a few days left before another murder. The time traveling into and out of the city could be spent here, where the story unfolded. It was freaking him out that they didn't know what was causing the interruption of flow with their abilities, but he felt strongly that the search should focus on Carol and Jim. That's where it all starts. His gut was telling him they would lead him to the cause. Although, there was a giant plus to going. He'd get to see Margaret's reaction to Little Italy. The aromas, the culture —she was going to soak it all in like a sponge. Her parents never exposed her to anything that the average aristocrat would deem to be *below standards.*

A surge of electricity coursed through his veins. "Hi, May." Alex remained focused on the team.

"Good morning, Alex. Margaret's not here today?" The voice echoed softly.

"Not yet. I need some time to think, but she'll be here shortly."

"You look tired. Are you feeling alright? Maybe a nice cup of tea to pep you up?"

"I'll be okay. Just deep in thought. I got a rough case."

"Oh, you mean the freezing murders. Everyone in the realm are abuzz."

"Really? What are they saying?"

"I'd rather not repeat the muttering of ill-advised ethereal students. My mother always said, 'If you can't say something nice, don't say anything at all.' I miss her."

"It's okay, you can tell me."

"They're saying this one might be too much for you. This could very well be the case that will bring Alex McKenna to our side of the veil."

"Do they, now? Well, you tell everyone that I'm much stronger than their opinions of me."

"Well, I know that. They're just bored, always gossiping about someone. And you, dear boy, seem to be their favorite subject." May gazed out toward the running players. "I've watched many changes over the past eighty plus years. Some good, some not, but the football team's new uniform pants are alarmingly tight."

Alex laughed. "I bet you have seen a lot."

"Indeed. Well, I will let you have your time. Please do give dear Margaret my regards."

"I will. And May, be careful. Whatever this is, it's strong."

"Duly noted. Thank you." May faded out.

Alex pulled the article about the fire up on his phone. *The neighbor saved Jim and Alister, but when he tried to go back in after Carol and Ester, the smoke was too thick. Where were they? Why didn't they follow Jim and Alister out?* He read the news article five more times. The words stuck in the back of his throat. *And what does this fire have to do with the murders? Does it have anything to do with them, or is all just coincidental?* The longer he pondered that night, the more questions he had.

"Hello!" Margaret came from behind. Alex jumped.

"Crap, you startled me."

"How's the think-fest going?"

"It sucks. I just keep adding more questions." He furrowed his brow.

"Well, maybe we'll get some answers tonight. Who is this old man?"

"Il Vecchio. He came to the States from Naples a long time ago; nobody really knows when. He has special abilities, different from my family's. He can see the past."

"What do you mean? See it how?"

"My gram explained; he sees the events of the past like a movie projected onto the screen. He can focus on an event, and then it appears. He's really old, too. Gram thinks he's over 150 years old."

"Okay, that's impossible. Isn't it?"

Alex shook his head. "I don't know, but she believes it . . ." His voice was meek.

"You seem down. What's going on?" Margaret sounded concerned.

"I'm worried. We're running out of time. We could be looking at another victim in a couple of days. I just think we need to focus on the house and what happened instead of taking a trip to the city."

"Stop damning it before we even go. If you guys can find out what's suppressing your *spidey sense,* then you can fix it."

"You make it sound so easy." Alex smiled.

"Let's just say I have complete confidence in your capabilities." Margaret rested her forehead on his shoulder. "It's gonna be okay; you'll figure it out. You always do." She lifted her head and grinned.

"It seems the teen spirits think this will be my last case." Alex looked up and squinted.

"Why . . . Wait, how do you know that? Was May here?"

"Just before you came. She said to tell you hi. Apparently, they think this is going to be the one that will be the death of me."

"What the hell? You're not taking them seriously, are you? We both know their propensity to spread doom and gloom."

"Oh, I'm not letting it get to me. I was thinking about the fire again . . . Where was the fire department? The station is literally five minutes from my house."

"Remember the time period we're dealing with. You just didn't grab your cell and dial 911. Things had a much longer process. And maybe the weather played a part that night. It was winter; could've been snow on the ground."

"You are the smartest person I know."

"You're pretty smart yourself for realizing that." Margaret giggled.

Alex tightly crossed his arms, resisting the urge to brush

away loose locks from Margaret's face. May was wrong: it wasn't the case that would kill him; it was this girl.

"The bell is about to ring. We'd better get going. I'm gonna skip lunch today and go to the library. I'll meet you at your car after fifth period."

"Okay, see you then. And try and stay clear of the opinionated dead. It'll just make you crazy."

Alex chuckled. "I'll try." *If only the dead complied,* he thought.

The morning flew by surprisingly quick. On his way to the library, Alex spotted Kyle. Luckily, the hulk of no brains and extra anger didn't see him. The library was another place Alex could seek solace. With all the noise in his head from the dead and the living, every chance he got to steal away to somewhere peaceful was his idea of heaven. Aside from a few earthbound souls, the library was empty. Not the most popular place to eat lunch. The bleachers were probably packed, which is why he preferred them in the morning.

The school library had a small section dedicated to the history of its town. Floral Park had been the first incorporated village back in the 1920's, and its history was rich with colorful residents. He was hoping one of the books might contain more information on the Bishops. They were one of the first to buy into the promises of green lawns, safe streets manned by the town's private police force, and the construction of what the mayor touted as the best schools in Nassau County.

As he flipped through the pages of the second book he grabbed, his eyes narrowed, and his mouth gaped. Halfway into the history of local businessmen to settle in the town was a picture of Jim and Carol Bishop. They were standing in front of their new home at 55 Geranium Ave. Standing beside them were their two children, Ester and Alister. Alex leaned closer to the picture to get a better look. Alister was so young, maybe five or six. Ester's smile lit up the page. A wave of sadness crashed into his core, drowning his heart. They were so happy and unsuspecting.

You're not looking close enough. The unvoiced words stunned his ear.

Alex's flesh stung with the sudden outbreak of goosebumps. He knew who it was. This soul had a particular gift for manipulating his will. He communicated with thought. A plus for Alex. If someone walked in, they wouldn't see him talking to himself—a regular occurrence that freaked out most of his fellow students.

Hello, Victor. What havoc are you creating today?

Victor's most pleasurable enjoyment came from seeping into students' heads and planting ideas they wouldn't otherwise think to do. Every once in a while, it became very dangerous. Last year, Victor nearly killed a kid when he convinced him he could Parkour across the rooftops at school. The kid fell, but luckily May was there to catch him. She set him down in a nearby oak tree. The students thought he escaped death by hitting the tree, but Alex knew his friend had been the real hero.

I have not engaged in any foul play, if that's what you're asking me. My days have been quite dreary since that unfortunate event last year.

That was a little more than just unfortunate; you could have killed that kid.

But he's fine.

Yeah, because of May. You would've let him plummet to the pavement.

This is a waste of time. It's over. My concern, dear Alex, is that you're not seeing what you're looking at.

Stop the riddles, Victor. I don't have the time or the patience.

Boy, take a closer look at the photo.

Alex dropped his chin and widened his eyes.

Like I said, nothing.

You are trying my patience with your lack of detail. Direct your gaze to the right of the little girl, standing behind her.

What the hell?

Alex held the photo closer. The light in the library was for reading; he needed a spotlight. Pulling his phone from his jean pocket, he tapped on the camera icon and took a shot of the photo. Manipulating his fingers across the screen, he enlarged the area, focusing in on Ester. Hovering behind her was—something. It clearly had the young girl in its sight, its head practically resting on the child's shoulder.

Victor, do you know what this is?

I'm afraid I don't. But whatever—or whoever—that is, the little girl appears to be its sole focus.

Thank you, Victor.

You're welcome, young Alex.

Why did you help me? That's a bit out of character for you.

Gossip is, this case will end you. I'm just trying to avoid that from happening.

Why? You never cared about me before.

Because, my young man, if you die, there's a large possibility you'll stay around. You won't leave the souls that need you. That'll mean you will make death miserable for me. It's hard enough having you around, but if your soul shed the constraints of the living, staying in Floral Park would be unbearable. I rather like it here.

Okay, Victor. Whatever your motivation, I'm thankful.

Alex wriggled as a light breeze tickled the back of his neck. Victor was gone. He hastily gathered the books and put them away. He couldn't wait to show Margaret what he had uncovered.

He tried to make it to the small patch of grass Margaret claimed as her spot for lunch each day, but she was already gone. The clang of the bell made him wince—he'd have to wait until the end of the day.

The afternoon didn't fly as quickly as the morning, and Alex found his mind drifting. His dad had called him last night, inviting him to dinner next week. Alex had declined. It was tough enough dealing with the split of his family but having the facade of father and son bonding time, in the middle of a huge case, just irked him. Besides, his birthday was at the end of the month. He'd see his dad then. A day had already been planned by his stepmother. Another obstacle, for another time.

When the bell went off at the end of fifth period, Alex hauled ass out of the classroom. Margaret was waiting by her car, talking with Cadence. Fortunately, the girl was gone by the time Alex reached her.

"Hey, you're gonna want to hear what Cadence just told me. Her dad knew one of the victims. He said the police are not releasing all the information. Not only were their heads frozen, but all of the families went back for generations as residents here. You know what that means?"

"We found a common thread. The killer isn't randomly picking victims. They're all connected somehow. I've got some news, too. Check this out. It's a photo of the Bishops. Look behind Ester."

"What the fuck? We have to find out who that is."

"You said 'who.' Why do you think it's a person? I couldn't tell; it looks undefined."

"No, it's pretty clear. Look at the curvature of the body. Here's the torso, the neck, and the head. Sure, it's blurry, but I think this is definitely a who and not a what."

"I didn't see that. Neither did Victor."

"I thought you were going to stay clear of the creepy dead for today. Victor being the number one creep of them all."

"You know it's not that simple. Besides, he's the one who pointed out the apparition. Come on, we gotta go. My mom will be waiting."

Once they were out of the parking lot, Alex relaxed. The school was like a magnet for the earthbound teens who had died in Floral Park over the past eighty years. Their collective energy often drained him.

Margaret parked in front of the house and they briskly headed inside. His mom was finishing a phone call in the living room.

"You hungry?" Alex asked Margaret.

"I could use a cookie or two." She grinned.

Alex disappeared into the kitchen and returned with a box of peanut butter cookies. They sat down on the couch and shared a row of cellophane-wrapped goodies. When his mom was done with the call, he told her about the photo and Margaret's information about the history of the murder victims.

"All the more reason for us to drive into the city tonight. The old man knows more about New York's history than anyone else. Bring the picture. I want to show it to him."

"Is Wilby up in his room?"

"No. Dad picked him up about thirty minutes ago. I thought it might be better if he didn't come. There's a lot of people, and given the reason we're going, it seemed safer."

"Poor little man. He really wanted a meatball sandwich."

"I promised him we'd bring one back. He can have it tomorrow. Let's go."

What should have been an hour-long drive dragged on for two. The rush hour traffic plastered on the parkway was filled with tired drivers eagerly trying to make their way home to their families. Alex cracked the window for air and let the overpowering aroma of gasoline, burning rubber, and oil seep into the sedan. Two cars had collided, and the drivers hobbled over to the side of the road. An officer was on the scene, assessing the situation. Alex noticed an older woman standing by his side. Maybe his mother or grandmother? The policeman had no clue he had a companion.

He turned to Margaret in the back seat but caught himself before he spoke out loud. She had closed her eyes and leaned her head back, resting it on the seat. A sudden blare of a random car horn startled her, and she jumped up and hit the top of her head on the roof.

"Oh my god, are you okay?" Alex reached for her.

Margaret was rubbing her head. "Yeah, I'm okay. It scared me more than anything. I don't feel a bump."

"We're almost there. You getting hungry?"

"I think my stomach is saying yes. Those cookies have outlived their purpose." She chuckled.

The car pulled off at the next exit. His mom drove around for a few blocks, looking for the parking garage she and his dad used to frequent when they would have a night out in the city. After the car was safely tucked away, snug in its stall, the three of them started their hike to Manhattan's Mulberry Street—the hubbub of Little Italy.

More than a century ago, Italian immigrants settled in the area of Manhattan that would eventually be known as the world-famous Little Italy. Once stretching from Canal to Houston Street, between Lafayette Street and the Bowery, in modern times, it had been reduced to the blocks surrounding Mulberry Street. What was once lined with carts filled with vegetables and fruits for sale, had grown to shops that sold anything from delectables to trinkets representing the heritage.

Margaret's eyes grew when they reached the beginning of a world she had never visited. Alex took pleasure in her awe. He loved sharing his culture with her.

Everywhere you turned, green, white, and red decorated the outside of the buildings. The streets were packed with tourists, and instinctively, Alex clasped Margaret's hand. She nervously met his eyes and clutched tighter.

"Stay close, you two. We have to go about halfway down in the middle of the block."

Alex had been there too many times to count. It was a favorite family destination when he was a kid. Wilby was just a baby, and his parents would take them on Saturdays. They came for lunch and stayed through dinner. Sometimes his gram came, too. They were good memories.

Since the divorce, all weekend family time changed to mom's house or dad's, Alex hadn't been back. Now, the richness of his heritage was flooding in. Part New York, part Italy, it was the perfect blend of both worlds. The air was familiar as he walked through the streets again. It was thick with the bouquet of olive oil and garlic, and he felt at home. Alex never experienced a sense of family anywhere else that was this strong, with the exception of his own house.

The six-story brown and red brick tenements bore the stories of all the immigrants who once called them home. Over a hundred years ago, the buildings were buzzing with families speaking no English or broken English, all living together and working for a better tomorrow. The weathered stone told the story of children playing handball, carts propped up against the walls, and the wear of generations passing through. The fire escapes were newly painted, but still held the secrets of lovers stealing away a few minutes from the watchful eye of their families.

Alex lifted his chin and inhaled—the smoky scent of peppers and onions frying left a trail of imaginary breadcrumbs to a small restaurant with an outdoor patio for dining. The savory scent of warm mozzarella melting into sweet cream butter on top of a warm crust lured him into the menagerie of perfumes designed to awaken the taste buds. Moistening his lips with anticipation, his nose captured the allure of garlic, basil, oregano. and fennel—sweet sausage.

"There's a lot of people," Margaret exclaimed.

"I know. The city is so different than Floral Park, but this is nothing. You gotta see it around Christmas. It's packed. They string the decorations across the street, like something out of that old movie, *It's a Wonderful Life*. It's so cool. The sidewalks get so crowded, you can barely walk. I don't know, you think all the noise and motion would get to me, but it doesn't. I love the culture."

"I think it's because it reminds you of your family. That's what I'm loving about it tonight. It's like a huge dinner at your gram's house, with every relative you have in the state showing up." Margaret beamed. "I'm going to soak in the whole experience. When do we eat?"

His mom interjected, "Let's go see Il Vecchio first. Then I'll take you to the best little ristorante on Mulberry Street. There!" His mom pointed.

She brought them to a tiny bakery smack in the middle of the block. The brick on the tenement above the business was painted red, white, and green, symbolizing the Italian flag. When Alex opened the door, a little brass bell dinged the announcement of new customers. He and Margaret glided to the glass showcase filled with delightful rows of homemade pastries, cookies, and cakes.

"I think we found Margaret's favorite place." Alex chuckled.

She gently tapped her fingers on the glass, her eyes rolling back and forth, trying to decide which to choose.

"I think I'll have one of everything." She bit her lower lip.

"Business before pleasure. Let's see if we can get some answers first."

Margaret frowned. "Sure, I get it. But Gina, before we leave . . ."

"How can I help you?" An elderly woman speaking broken English emerged from the back.

"We came to speak with Il Vecchio. Is he here, please?" Gina said in a polite tone.

"Who are you?"

"Could you please tell him Gina LaBoccetta is here? Mary LaBoccetta is my grandmother."

The elderly woman studied Gina, and then Alex. "Is this your son who's not a son?"

Gina tightened her jaw. "This is my son."

Directing her gaze back to Alex, the old woman spoke. "We know much about you and your fondness for the dead. You spend a great deal of your time with them. You see many things. Your future will be tested. Hold true, Alex McKenna."

"Hey, over here." Gina snapped her fingers. "I'm trying to be polite, but you need to leave my kid alone."

"Such a good mama, always watching out for the special one. Wait here."

After the woman left, Alex confronted his mother. "What the hell was that? How did she know my name?"

"Well, they know Gram, so I'm going to guess they probably know about all of us. The LaBoccetta bloodline goes way back."

The woman shuffled through the door connecting the bakery with the kitchen.

"You can go back and speak with Il Vecchio. He is waiting for you."

The three of them moved toward the door but were interrupted. "Not her." She pointed to Margaret. "Lei non appartiene. No alieni in the back."

"What did she say?" Margaret blinked.

"She called you an alien."

"What the hell?"

"What she means is no outsiders." Alex shook his head. "Mom, I'm staying with Margaret."

"No. You must go with your madre. Il Vecchio wishes to meet the boy," the old woman insisted.

"You two go ahead. I'll be fine." Margaret half-smiled.

"Stay right here. We'll be back in a few minutes," Alex whispered in her ear.

The elderly woman waved them to follow. They were led through the kitchen, where no one was baking. She brought them to a thick, steel door, pushing down on the handle, which she struggled to pull open. Alex goosed his neck to peer in and get a better look before entering, and his mom latched onto his arm.

Dairy items such as ricotta, eggs, milk, whipping cream, and mozzarella were neatly placed on shelves of steel racks lined up on both sides of the room. The temperature was cool —slightly uncomfortable, but not freezing. Sitting in the center of the room on a wooden folding chair was a small-framed, elderly man. Alex guessed if he stood up, he might be about five feet, five inches. Slender in build, his hair was snow white, framing a weathered face with piercing, light blue eyes. His stare gave Alex the shivers.

The woman pointed to two empty chairs off to the side. Alex slid them across the cement floor and placed them in front of Il Vecchio.

"Aspetterò fuori," the old woman stated. Il Vecchio nodded in agreement.

Alex struggled to tame the pounding in his chest. Not knowing what to expect from this man, his nerves were recklessly messing with his brain. He sucked in a few deep breaths, but the pounding continued.

"Non aver paura." Il Vecchio looked at Alex.

"I'm not afraid. I just don't understand why you wanted me here."

"Alex, speak Italian," his mom instructed.

"There's no need, Gina. I understand English," Il Vecchio professed.

Alex was stunned. Not only did the man understand English, but he spoke it perfectly, with no trace of his native tongue.

"I was curious to finally meet the boy who's turned the ethereal plane on its side. You've helped many spirits find their way, Mr. McKenna."

His mom intervened. "I understand your interest in my son, but we don't have much time. Murders are occurring . . ."

"I know about them. Evil has befallen your town. What do you need from me?"

"Answers. Why we can't see this creature, or sense its presence in our own home? What kind of spirit has this capability?"

"This is a creature spawned from darkness. I know of only a few other instances where this was possible. Gina, your ability is strong, but your son's is something we rarely see. Cultivated, over time, he will become a leader amongst those in our world. This entity is very powerful to hide from him. But we're clever and have the light on our side." Il Vecchio reached into his pocket and pulled out a string of red beads. "Take this rosary. Place it on the front door of your house. When you leave, my sister will give you a prayer. After the rosary is secure, recite the prayer three times. This should lift the cloak the spirit has used to hide itself. Alex, it will go after you. Evil only knows one thing—destruction. You are the light directly in its path."

Alex took the rosary and nodded. "Do you know what we're dealing with? Why this is happening?"

"When I felt you were coming, I looked to the past for answers. But all I could see was a tunnel of darkness. The events in that house are hidden, just like the spirit. Tread carefully, my young friend. Vai con la luce."

"Grazie." Alex nodded.

"Thank you for seeing us. Gram said to tell you molte grazie." Gina stood up. "Time for us to go."

The man slightly nodded and summoned his sister. The elderly woman entered with a piece of brown parchment, rolled up and tied with a red ribbon. She handed it to Alex. The two of them followed her back to the front of the store.

"That was strange how that guy spoke perfect English," Alex remarked.

"I swear, growing up in this family, very little surprises me anymore. But that was definitely one of them."

"I can't wait to get Margaret and go eat. I'm starving."

They pushed through the double doors leading to the bakery—it was empty. Margaret was nowhere in sight.

Alex turned to the elderly woman. "Where's the girl?"

"Non lo so. I left her right here." The woman pointed to the pastry case.

Alex ran for the door and, ripping it open, raced out to the sidewalk. His mom was right behind him. His body stiffened when a shrill scream pierced his eardrum. A woman a few feet away was pointing across the street.

Alex whipped his head around to the right. A sinister silhouette had Margaret in its grip. The beast was dragging her as she fought to pull away.

"Alex!" Margaret screamed.

"Ma! There she is!" Alex pointed just as the obscure figure pulled Margaret around the corner.

"Hurry Alex, before they get too far away!" His mom bolted.

Alex clenched his fists and took off. Passing her up, he rounded the corner and saw Margaret being pulled through the door of a darkened building. He ignored the burn searing through his thighs. He raced to reach her.

Catching the door right before it shut, he could feel the

negative energy from the villainous shadow fill the air. This was dark magic for sure. He closed his eyes and relied on his gifts. He saw Margaret's face in his mind and let it drift like smoke from a fire. His heart skipped a beat when he found her. Each person has a signature, molecules that come together to form who they are. The molecules leave a trail like breadcrumbs. One of Alex's developing talents was to be able to see those breadcrumbs in his mind's eye. Once he locked in, it would lead him to his quest. In this case—Margaret.

Her trail was dripping with terror. He whiffed in the sour smell of rusty, damp pipes, and his stomach roiled with bubbling acid. He coughed and pushed the nauseating smell from his senses, concentrating only on Margaret.

A door slammed in the nearby vicinity, and Alex stopped in his tracks.

"Alex," his mom whispered.

"I'm here. Follow my voice," he spoke softly.

"It's so damn dark in here. Do you have a flashlight on your phone? Mine's not working."

"I do, but I was trying not to announce our whereabouts," Alex hissed.

"Listen, you stay behind me, do you understand? No more wildly running off. You have no idea what we're dealing with," she snapped.

"I'm faster and stronger. You were lagging behind. I didn't want to lose them."

Alex realized what he had said as the words passed his lips.

"I'm telling you, kid, I know you're worried, but we're not getting into a pissing contest. Our focus right now is getting Margaret back. I'll deal with you when we get home. Stand the hell behind me and tell me which way to go. You have her trail?"

"Yes. We need to go straight. It's still pretty strong. I think they're close."

Cautiously stepping through the dim passage, Alex struggled to suppress the emotions that weaved in Margaret's trail. Fear was the most heightened, but sadness, despair, regret and . . .

He took a quick breath. His pulse throbbed in his temples, fighting back the screams of his beating heart. He felt her—love.

"Get the fuck away from me, you son of a bitch! You have no idea who you're dealing with. The LaBoccettas are going to have your soul for breakfast!" Margaret roared.

Gina pushed back, stopping her son mid-stride.

"Do you remember that holding incantation we used when you were nine? That confused spirit thought you were his son, and he held you captive in your room. Gram and I sort of hand-cuffed him until she could whip up a spell to cross him over."

"Oh my god, yes. You pinned him to the ceiling until he could be sent to the next life."

"Do you remember the words?"

"I think so. Mom, you're brilliant. But wait, how are we gonna find out who it is?"

"Right now, I'm more concerned with getting us home alive."

"Good point."

"You ready? Once we turn this corner, we better be on our toes," his mom murmured.

Alex nodded in agreement.

With Gina using her body as a barrier between her son and the entity, they steam-rolled into the room. Margaret was bound with both hands tied to a beam above her head. Her hair was soaked with moisture from a dripping pipe. The entity blended into the darkness, making it difficult to spot.

"Alex! It's in the corner." Margaret directed her gaze to the left.

"Now, Alex!" his mom shouted.

Looking away from the creature, which was now floating toward them, they shouted the words to bind its unholy soul.

"Ti lego, bestia, dal fare il male e il danno contro le altre persone."

Gina shouted, "Again!"

"Ti lego, bestia, dal fare il male e il danno contro le altre persone."

The creature froze, and Alex swung his arm into the air, slamming the beast into the wall.

His mom rushed to Margaret and untied her.

"We have to go now! I have no idea how long that will hold it."

Rushing to get out, Alex held his breath until the first rush of cool air hit his face. The door banged shut behind them, and they swiftly navigated through the streets, straight for the car.

"Everyone in, hurry." His mom put the key in the ignition. "You two good if we skip dinner?" The sarcasm dripped from her lips.

"Just get us the hell out of here," Margaret howled.

The car ride was quiet on the way home. Alex had no words, and he was fairly certain neither did Margaret. That was the first time she had been in that much danger. Normally, her contribution was the tireless research she helped him with. His gut was queasy. He feared this might be the dose of reality that would break them apart.

When they reached the house, Alex was surprised when Margaret followed them inside. He thought for sure she would make a quick exit and drive away, never looking back.

Gina set her purse down on the couch. "Alex, can I have the rosaries and prayer we got from Il Vecchio, please?"

"Now?" He rubbed the back of his head.

"Yes."

Alex handed them to his mom and stepped back as she tied the rosary to the handle of the front door. Pulling the ribbon open, she unraveled the scroll and said the prayer out loud.

"The shield of the Archangel Michael is above us, the shield of Michael is below, the shield of Michael is beside us, the shield of Michael is before us, the shield of Michael is behind us. The fire of Michael surrounds and defends us."

"What next?" Alex inched closer.

"I'm not sure but I don't feel any change. The darkness that blinds us to this entity is still here."

"Yup. Wait. Look at the rosary." Alex pointed.

The beads were spinning in a circle around the lever growing faster and faster until they exploded and scattered to the ground.

"What the hell? Ma, what does that mean?"

"It means whatever this is, II Vecchio's prayer couldn't penetrate it. We keep looking for the right one."

Exasperated, they all went to the kitchen, and his mom made a pot of coffee. While they were sitting around the table, waiting for the black gold to brew, Margaret was the first to break the awkward silence.

"I don't know what that was. I looked right at it, and its face was . . . not a face."

"What do you mean, not a face? Like it was missing?" Alex leaned his elbows on the table.

"No. Like, it was there, but really blurry."

"A deceit spell." His mom got up.

"What's that?" Margaret scooted closer to Alex.

"It's a spell that can be cast to deceive someone's perception of what they're looking at. In this case, it blurred out the creature's face."

"It didn't feel like a creature. I mean, it looked really weird, but when it grabbed me, it felt solid. And no electrical charge.

Like when May touched my arm at school that time, Alex, I could feel a surge coming from her. This thing tonight didn't have anything like that."

"Well, now this really got interesting. I'll call Gram in the morning, and I'm going to tell your dad to hold on to Wilby for a few days. This is an entirely new monkey wrench being thrown into the mix." His mom poured a cup of coffee and went upstairs.

"You hungry?" Alex asked Margaret.

"No, I think my appetite is officially shot for the evening."

"You want to take our coffee up to my room?"

"Sure, that'd be good."

When they got to Alex's room, he shut the door behind them. Margaret collapsed on the bed and he sat on the chair at his desk, trying to give her space.

"What was that trick you pulled tonight?" Margaret sipped her coffee.

"What trick? What do you mean?"

"Don't play stupid, Alex. You know what I'm talking about."

"You mean the pushing the thing into the wall?"

"The very same."

"I don't know. I've never done that before."

"It was so awesome!" Margaret screeched.

"It didn't scare you?"

"It startled me, but how could anything you do scare me? You're my best friend. I trust you."

The calm captured the fear that had been raging through his limbs. He was sure she'd leave, so sure he had lost her.

"You're okay with all of this?"

"I wouldn't say I was okay with being kidnapped and tied up, but with you? Sure." Margaret smiled and laid her head on the pillow.

Alex got up and plopped down on the bed beside her. In minutes, they both succumbed to the heavy weight of sleep.

FLORAL PARK, New York 1929

CAROL BISHOP WAS busy directing the movers. She had labeled each box specifically with the room they would be placed in. *It's the most efficient way of getting everything done in a timely manner,* she had told Jim. Carol knew he wouldn't argue. He hated unpacking, and anything that would move things along quickly was perfectly fine with him.

The two children were in their rooms, putting away clothes—another decision Carol had made. She figured if the children's furniture got there first, it would keep them busy and out of the way. She was right. They were so excited about their new rooms; she hadn't heard a peep from them in quite a while. She had asked Ester to help Alister. He was only four, and although very smart, he would need assistance. She decided her own unpacking would start with the kitchen. It was the biggest job, but that didn't matter. She was so excited. They finally had a formal dining room. She could unpack the good china they had received as a wedding gift. The hutch Jim bought her was due to arrive tomorrow, and everything was falling into place perfectly.

She took a moment to take it all in. Growing up, never once did she think she could afford such a lovely home, but here she was, starting a wonderful life. Looking around the kitchen, she imagined Alister running in trying to steal cookies, the aroma of fresh pumpkin baking with hints of cinnamon and brown sugar drifting throughout the house. A stew would be cooking on the stove, blending a ribbon of carrots, potatoes, and brown gravy into the tantalizing smells of the bread.

Her vision was interrupted abruptly. Someone was screaming, and it was getting louder. She loosened her grip and dropped the heavy box. It made a loud thud as she ran toward the penetrating pitch. It was Alister.

Carol took the stairs as if she were gliding and reached the first landing in seconds. She could see her son lying face down in the hallway. She hurried up the remaining staircase and ran to his side.

"Alister!"

She rolled him over. His skin was as white as the first winter snowfall. His eyes were closed. She pressed her head to his chest, heard a strong pulse, and let out a sigh of relief.

"Alister, honey. Wake up. You're scaring Mommy."

The boy started to wriggle, and his eyelids flickered back and forth before slowly opening. He saw his mother and reached out, folding his tiny arms around her neck. He began to cry.

"My dearest boy, what happened? Did you fall?" Carol scanned around the hallway, looking for boxes or anything he could have been standing on. There was nothing.

"Ester! Ester, where are you?" she screamed.

Ester came out of her room. The door had been shut.

"I asked you to watch him! Didn't you hear him scream?"

"Yes. But I thought he was fooling around. He kept coming in and running around my room. I asked him to get his things unpacked and put them on his bed and I would be in after I was done with mine. I shut the door, hoping he would listen and do what he was supposed to. I had no idea. Is he alright?"

Ester knelt on the wood floor beside her little brother.

"Hey, kiddo. What happened?" She gently rubbed the top of his head.

"The lady tried to grab me. She said she wanted me to go with her."

Carol slid her arms under his little body and lifted him to her chest. She stood up and started circling around the hallway like a ballerina in a child's music box.

"What lady? There was a stranger in the house? Where did she go?"

"I don't know." Alister started to shake. "Mommy, she was so scary. Her face was like this." He scrunched his face up and pulled the skin back with his tiny hands.

"Ester, ring the doctor. Your brother is in shock." Her eyes filled with tears. "My poor boy. I should have never left you to do such a big job. You've imagined this horrible woman because you were overwhelmed."

"No. Mommy, I saw her. I swear."

"Alister, language! Shock or not. Let's run you a hot bath, and then afterward, I'll make you some hot chocolate. Ester, never mind with the doctor. I know what your brother needs. I'll take care of him, and I want you to tackle his room as soon as you're done with your own." Carol gave her a quick, piercing glare.

"Yes, ma'am." Ester got up and went into her room.

Alister pressed his small mouth up to his mother's ear and whispered, "She's coming back."

Carol squeezed her son close and brought him into the bathroom to run the water.

***

THE NEXT MORNING, Alex sat hiding out in his room while he waited for Margaret to finish in the bathroom. He could go downstairs and hang out in the kitchen, but he was avoiding confrontation with his mom. He knew his words were out of line last night, and his mom promised she would deal with him when they got home. But exhaustion overruled discipline, and he had temporarily escaped her wrath.

To add to the impending sentence that would be executed by his mom, all he could think about was what happened to Margaret last night. He nearly lost her. The thing used his feelings for her to lure him in. She was now more vulnerable than she'd ever been on one of his cases. The thought disgusted him.

Margaret came barreling through the door and interrupted his thoughts.

"Hey, you doing okay?" She took a small brush from her purse.

"I'm good. You feeling better? I know last night was . . ."

"Stop. Last night happened, but it's over. Time for us to move on."

"There she is, the kick-ass girl I lo—uh, you know what I mean."

Alex fidgeted with the zipper on his hoodie.

"I do. Come on, we need to go waste a day at that place with the books and whiny teens."

"I don't think I've ever heard that description of school before—I like it. But I was thinking of ditching school. We're too close to losing the next victim."

Margaret sighed. "You're mom's gonna be pissed, but I totally agree."

Alex gingerly stepped down the stairs, trying desperately not to alert his Mom. The plan was, once they reached the door, he'd announce their departure and quickly slip out.

"Bye, Ma. See you later!" He hoped she'd let it go at that.

"Good try, kid. Get your ass over here. And you too, miss. I want to speak to the both of you."

Almost made it, he thought. "We're kind of in a hurry. Can we talk tonight?"

"Not a chance."

Gina came walking in with that look on her face that only mothers could have—their superpower. With laser-like intensity, she glared, and then nodded toward the kitchen.

Alex slumped his shoulders; he knew when he was defeated. "The both of you, sit." His mom slid the chairs out. "Here we go. Fresh cinnamon rolls. I baked them from scratch. Your aunt Ella gave me the recipe." She set the plate on the table.

Dumbfounded, Alex turned to Margaret. She shrugged her shoulders and widened her eyes.

Maybe it was the last meal before execution.

Alex hesitated. "Are you alright, Ma?"

"I'm great. I have a son who acts before thinking, his friend who follows without question, a demon ghost we can't see, and oh, yes, a multitude of murders that we have no way of stopping. But with all this going on, we still have fresh cinnamon rolls, so yeah, I'm pretty damn good." His mom narrowed her eyes and tightened her lips.

Alex froze. He didn't know what to do with this new approach his mom was taking. Was it the calm before the storm? Had she snapped? He wiggled in his seat and played with the cup of coffee in front of him. He knew the next words out of his mouth were crucial. They could mean the difference in being grounded for life, or just a few days.

"I'm really sorry. I don't know what got into me. I was so heightened with all the anger surging, I couldn't think." Alex hoped he could play the *gifted* card.

"Don't give me that load of bullshit. Let me remind you— you're turning seventeen. I'm your mother. You have rules, and I make the rules. Disrespect will not be tolerated, especially in a life or death situation where my years of experience are trying to help you. I know you have talents but using them before understanding them will get you killed, and possibly others you love." She shot a glance at Margaret.

"And you, how was it that spook got you in its clutches? The bakery is under a protection spell. No dark forces can enter."

Margaret bit her lower lip, and she blinked to hold back the tears. "I got bored, so I went outside to check things out."

Alex swiveled in his chair. "What?"

"I'm sorry. I didn't think . . ."

"That's my point. You didn't think. Margaret, you've been doing this with Alex long enough to know the dangers of not paying attention. I need you to hear me. If you do something like this again, you will not be allowed to participate in any future cases. No research, no nothing. Am I clear?"

"Yes." Margaret lowered her head.

"Listen to me, the two of you. I'm not trying to be the bad guy here, but you have got to understand the scope of what's going on. Gram and I, we don't say things just to hear our own voices. It's our job to guide you and keep you as safe as we can."

"I really am sorry, Mom."

"Me too, Gina."

Gina's eyes darted back and forth between the two teens. "Okay, now we move on. Mangiare! Aunt Ella's recipe is the best. Oh, I also wanted to tell you, Alex—Doctor Freeman's office called. Your blood work is in. They made an appointment for Friday the 29th. I know it's your birthday, but I'd like to get the numbers and make sure you're on track. How are you doing with the shots? Any side-effects?"

Doctor Gerald Freeman was a well-known pediatric endocrinologist that specialized in transgender youth. Alex adored him and had been a patient since he was about nine.

"No. I've been fine." Alex rolled his eyes and bit into the warm cinnamon bun. He hated when his mom asked about his shots. He did them, end of story.

"Mmm, Gina, they're awesome." Margaret closed her eyes and smiled.

"How has school been? Any more issues, Alex?" His mom waited for an answer.

Alex nodded; his mouth was full from the last bite. "Hmm." He nodded and then swallowed. "School's going. Nothing new." He opted to leave out his little run-in with Kyle the other day.

"Good. I spoke to Gram this morning. She was shocked Il Vecchio couldn't see the past for this house. She's very concerned—especially for Wilby. She suggested letting your brother stay at his dads until this blows over. I'm inclined to agree with her."

Alex tried to settle the locomotive running through his veins. He hated having his little brother in harm's way, but he also hated leaving him someplace where they couldn't watch him, either.

"I get what you mean, but it bothers me we can't keep an eye on him. Do you think we could wait until we have a better understanding of what—or who—we're dealing with?"

His mom rested her elbows on the table, hands clasped. "I'll think about it. I don't need to say anything to your dad until later today. He's picking Wilby up from school. Gram also told me you've been training him behind my back. And before you get upset with her, she told me out of concern. Like I said, she is very worried. What have you been showing him?"

Alex sighed. "Just basic stuff. Being aware of what's around you. Not looking at the world with a blind eye like most people do. I'm worried, though. He doesn't show any signs of having any abilities. Or like Margaret calls it, the *spidey sense.*" Margaret punched his arm.

"Ouch. Not so hard, girl."

Margaret ignored him and began clearing the dishes off the table.

"We'll just have to wait and see."

Alex cleared his throat. "I'm really happy you're back practicing."

"I wanted to keep your life easy. I thought by denying who we were, it would be the solution. But now, I see it only added to the danger. When I get home from work, I'm going to meditate. Reconnect my emotions. Are you coming home right after school?"

Alex knew that if he wasn't upfront with her, this newfound partnership would be reduced to a solo act very quickly.

"Actually, I wanted to talk to you about that. Me and Margaret aren't going to school today."

His mom's eyes narrowed, and the corners of her mouth dropped. He hated that look.

"Before you freak, let me explain." By then, Margaret had the dishes dried and put away. She sat beside Alex for support.

"We don't have any connection yet with the Bishops to the murders. The only thing we know is two people died in a fire eighty-six years ago, and now bizarre murders are being committed. If Gram's right, and this is a countdown to Halloween, then time can't be wasted. And after what happened last night, we know whatever is doing this wants us stopped."

"I agree." Gina got up from the table.

"You agree with what?" His brows furrowed in confusion.

"That school is not high on the list today." Gina smirked.

"Really? Thank you."

"So, what are your plans?"

"We've kind of hit a wall. We talked to Alister. He told us his mother Carol had been visiting him since her death. He said her spirit can sometimes change into a dark entity. It scares the hell out of him."

"Are you focusing on Carol?"

"We thought we'd try to look into her, and also Jim, the husband. The entire night of the fire doesn't fit together. If the neighbor hadn't rescued them, we might have been looking at four deaths instead of two. Kirkpatrick was definitely a hero that night."

"Kirkpatrick?"

"Yeah, Michael Kirkpatrick was their neighbor. He lived across the street back then."

"Alex, I know the Kirkpatricks. Michael's son is Bobby. I used to go to school with his granddaughter. I've been in his house a few times when I was younger. He lives fairly close, in New Hyde Park."

"What? This is awesome. Do you think we could talk to him? He could fill us in on exactly what happened that night. I know he was just a kid, but he must have seen what his dad did."

"My friend and I have kept in contact sporadically over the years, but I do still have her number. Let me try calling and see what I can do. Now, how do I say this to her without sounding crazy?" his mom retorted.

"I'm not sure, but I think leaving out the part about a sinister ghost and murders might be wise." Alex grinned.

His mom shot him a sideways glance. "Helpful," she said sarcastically.

Gina had worked a little LaBoccetta magic. She told her friend that Alex was doing a paper on the history of Floral Park for his English class. She'd remembered the Kirkpatricks used to live across the street from their house, and her grandfather was a bit of a hero. Her friend agreed to call and ask her grandfather if he'd speak with them.

After an hour of pacing, they got the answer they'd hoped for. Bobby Kirkpatrick agreed to see them that afternoon.

"I'll need to reschedule my appointments this afternoon," his mom said as she scrolled through her phone.

"You're going with us?" Alex asked jubilantly.

"Hey, kid, we're in this together." His mom hugged him.

AS THEY PULLED up to Bobby's house, Alex hesitated.

"Mom, I think Bobby is connected to this somehow. I mean, not just because of his dad."

"What makes you say that?" She grabbed the door handle and pulled it open.

"Something I'm feeling. Not sure exactly what it is. Like he's a part of them but removed at the same time. It's confusing. My *ability* is telling me we need to look deeper. The connection is not as obvious, but it is waiting for us to find it."

"When we go in, don't corner him with questions. We'll get more information if we're casual about our visit," his mom instructed.

Standing in front of the two-story colonial, Alex was surprised to see it was so well-kept. It was small, but a clean white with dark gray trim. The lawn was still a luscious green and hadn't begun its winter sleep yet, and pink azalea bushes trimmed the walkway. He placed his hand over his chest for a second—his heart pumped so fast; you would have thought he had just finished a marathon.

His mom approached the door first and rang the bell. When the door opened, Bobby greeted them. Alex studied the deep lines carved into the man's face. He bore all the weather of a lifetime ending. Hunched over with a cane in his right hand, he hobbled out to greet Gina.

Following a brief exchange of words, Bobby extended his hand and invited them into his home.

His house was just as well maintained on the inside as the out. Each piece of furniture was pristinely preserved as if it hadn't been sat on—ever. The tables were clean—not a speck of dust—and the air smelled like fresh Christmas pine.

Bobby showed them into the dining room, where they all took a seat around a heavy mahogany table. He excused himself and went into the kitchen to make a pot of coffee. When he returned, he had a pink box in his hand. Margaret's eyes lit up, and Alex swore he could hear her stomach doing leaps of happiness. Bobby set the box in the center of the table and laid out small dessert plates and forks. As the lid was lifted to reveal the treasure, the sweet scent of powdered sugar, almonds, and vanilla tickled the senses. Cannoli's—one of Alex's favorites. After everyone was served pastry and coffee, Bobby sat down.

"Little Gina LaBoccetta. I haven't seen you since you graduated high school. And look now. You have your own family. Has time been kind to you, Gina?"

"Yes. Well, I'm divorced, but my life is good."

"I'm happy to hear you're doing well. My granddaughter told me you're interested in our family's history in Floral Park. Alex, you have a school paper to write?"

"I do. I was so surprised when Mom said she knew the previous neighbors. I found out there was a fire in our house when the Bishops lived there."

Alex paused for a moment to play his questions out in his head one more time.

"Could you please tell us a little bit about that evening? It must have been huge news back then." Alex bit the cannoli.

"I was only seven, but some memories stick with you. I do remember my father rushing out of the house after hearing screams come from the Bishops' place. I opened my bedroom window, which faced the street. The entire house was engulfed in flames. Black smoke bellowed from everywhere; it was difficult to breathe."

"You said your father raced over. Then what?"

"He broke the glass in one of the panes to the French doors in the sunroom along the side of the house, opened it, and went inside. Next thing I saw was the front door opening, and he was carrying Alister. He laid him down on the lawn. By that time, I could hear the sirens of the fire department in the distance. He ran back in, and then, minutes later, he dragged out Mr. Bishop. He tried to get back in to save Ester and her mom, but it was too late. Smoke had consumed the bottom floor."

Alex knitted his brows. "How do you know it was filled with smoke? Did you go across the street?"

"No. My mom wouldn't let us out of the house. My father told me later. He was devastated he couldn't save them."

"How was your father afterward?"

"I think it consumed him. He and Mr. Bishop never spoke again. Or at least as far as I could tell. Which I always thought was strange. You'd think Mr. Bishop would have been indebted to my father for saving the lives of both him and his son. In fact, there was a savage fight between the two of them shortly after the night of the fire. But my father never spoke a word about it."

"We didn't know that. I'm sorry. It must have been so difficult for your family."

"Mostly on my sisters, because they were older. They remembered how he was before all of that started."

"Your family was financially well-off, right?"

"We were until the stock market crashed. It devastated our wealth. My mom said that father tried a few investments over the years—you know, trying to get back what they once had, but nothing really panned out. It made him bitter. I don't understand what my family's finances would have to do with your paper."

"I'm sorry, I don't mean to sound like I'm prying. I was just trying to get a picture of everyone's state of mind back then. I mean with the crash and Depression; I was trying to figure out how that directly affected the residents of Floral Park. It seemed to be such an exclusive place to live back then. I was only curious."

"Like I said, the crash destroyed my family, and many others. A lot of folks tried to keep up a good front. Truth was, they were all as broke as most."

"Did your dad ever mention anything more about the fire over the years?"

"Well, that would have been difficult for him to do."

"How so?" Alex inquired.

"My father killed himself not too long after the fight with Bishop."

"Oh, Bobby, I'm so sorry. I had no idea."

Alex glanced at his mom. She shook her head in disbelief.

"I think we've used enough of the man's time, Alex." His mom stood up. "Thank you so much for speaking with us. It was so nice to see you again."

"Yes, thank you, Bobby. This will really help with my paper."

"Good. I'm happy to hear that. I don't talk much to family, and most of my friends are gone. It was nice to see a face from the past. Gina, you have a lovely family."

"Thank you."

"Um, I have a one question before we go, if you don't mind."

Alex nudged her shoulder, but Margaret ignored him.

"Well, the quiet one speaks. Margaret, is it?"

"Yes."

"What would you like to know, little lady?"

"You said your mom wouldn't let us out of the house." Margaret inched closer.

"My three older sisters."

"Do you think they might be able to help Alex with some more information?"

"No, I'm sorry. The two eldest are gone a few years now, and the baby of the three, Greta, is not very sociable. She stays away from most people, including me."

"Okay, you two, let's go before we overstay our welcome." Alex's mom put a hand on each of their backs.

After another minute of goodbyes at the door, the three of them loaded into the car and pulled away.

"What do you think about Bobby, Mom? Do you think he told us everything?" Alex turned his head to face his mom.

"I do think so. I didn't get the sense he was hiding anything."

"What about his sister? Greta, I think he said."

"You know, for now, I think we should focus on the people we know are directly involved. Let's not run in all directions. Michael Kirkpatrick performed a heroic deed, and Bishop rewards him by getting into a fight and cutting him out of his life. Doesn't sound Kosher to me. In fact, it makes me think Jim Bishop was hiding something."

"That's exactly what I was thinking. What was that fight about? Why was Bishop so angry? He couldn't possibly blame his neighbor for not rescuing Ester and Carol. That wouldn't make any sense." Alex furrowed his brow.

"What about Bobby's dad committing suicide?" Margaret chimed in.

"He must have been so riddled with guilt. You heard what Bobby said; he couldn't deal with not being able to save Carol and her daughter." Alex leaned his head back.

"Yeah, poor man, he must have been tortured." Margaret sighed.

"So, once again, all roads lead to the Bishops," Gina added.

THE ENCOUNTER

In the evening, Alex's mom ordered pizza for the three of them. A much-needed round table was put into action to lay out the facts and discuss past events. With Wilby at his dad's, it made things a little easier. Margaret phoned her mom to tell her she was spending the night. It never appeared to be an issue. Her parents often went out on the weekends.

"Good pizza. Thanks, Gina." Margaret caught a string of cheese on her lip.

"You know you're part of this family, right?"

Margaret swallowed hard. "I, uh . . . Yeah, I do."

Alex's mom smiled and reached her hand out, clutching Margaret's forearm. Her smile quickly faded. "Alex, did you feel that?" His mom stood abruptly.

"Yeah." Alex turned his head, dropping his chin to his chest. "I felt it, but I don't hear anything."

Alex pressed on his gut; a hundred butterflies simultaneously circling his insides tickled his senses. He reached for the back of his neck. It was soaked. He looked down at his arms—goosebumps were everywhere. "Did you hear something, Ma?"

She shook her head no.

"Alex, what's going on?" Margaret scanned the kitchen, pivoting around in her chair.

"There's a hollow feeling in my chest, and the air just got a lot cooler. I think we should get you out of the house." Alex grabbed Margaret's hand.

"Honey, grab your coat and wait for us in your car. One of us will come out in a few minutes." His mom hurriedly wrapped Margaret's coat around the girl's shoulders and guided her toward the back door.

Alex stood with his eyes closed, listening.

"No. I'm not leaving the two of you. Forget it." Margaret huffed.

"Margaret, please go. We'll feel better if we know you're safe. Something is here," his mother pleaded.

"I said forget it." Margaret pulled away from her and darted to the center of the kitchen.

Alex's eyes opened abruptly. "Ma!"

"I feel it. Alex, give me your hand."

The temperature plummeted to freezing, making the kitchen feel like a meat locker. Mother and son clasped hands and stood back to back.

"Margaret, if you're going to be stubborn, then come over here and hold my mom's hand!" Alex demanded.

His mom whispered in his ear, "No. Have her hold onto you. You're the stronger of the two of us. I'm a bit out of practice."

"Tesoro. Come here. Grab my hand instead." He extended his arm, and Margaret leaped toward it. She cupped it tightly, and he squeezed back, creating a snug bond. "When it appears, do not look at it. Okay?"

Margaret stared into Alex's eyes.

"Margaret! Do you understand?" Alex spoke firmly.

"Yes?"

Alex knitted his brows.

"Sorry. Not knowing what to expect here." She pursed her lips.

"I know. Me neither. Just close your eyes, please," he said softly.

A discordant melody filled the room, much like a violin with missing strings.

"What the hell is that sound? It's hurting my ears." Alex turned his head. "Ma, it's here."

"I know. I see its reflection in the microwave."

Alex remembered that, at first, his mom had hated the huge stainless-steel microwave when her ex-husband had brought it home. *It was a great sale;* he had told her. She scoffed at the size because it took up half the counter. Now, Alex was sure she was glad to have the monstrosity in the kitchen.

The shadow flowed in from the wall, separating the kitchen from the dining room. Alex pivoted Margaret around so her back faced it. He squeezed her hand tighter and repeated his last instructions. "Remember what I said. Do not open your eyes."

He leaned his head into his mom's. "Can you make out what it is?"

"Not yet. Can you believe how cold it is? The closer it gets, the worse it becomes." She was shivering. "I'm willing to bet we're in the presence of what's been killing everyone in Floral Park."

"Yay for us." Alex pressed Margaret's head into his chest.

"Alex, I'm okay. I've got my eyes closed." Margaret's voice quivered.

"I know you do. This is for my peace of mind. Okay?"

Margaret nodded her head. "Your mom's right. It's freezing in here."

"Ma . . ." Alex had lowered his voice to a whisper. "We're

in real deep shit. If this thing is what we think it is, we're seconds away from becoming permanent popsicles."

His mom scanned the kitchen and focused on the canister of salt on the counter near the spices.

"I've got an idea. Alex, do you remember the prayer that Gram taught you when you kept seeing the shadow man?" His mom started inching toward the counter.

"Yeah. Where are you going?" Alex pressed his back to his moms to tighten the bond.

"I'm going to grab the salt and circle it around us. As soon as the circle's complete, say the prayer with me. Okay?"

"Yes." Alex could feel his hands going numb from the cold, but he didn't risk moving them away from Margaret.

Gina broke free from her son's side and dashed toward the counter. She grabbed the salt canister and, ripping off the lid, quickly poured the white crystals on the floor, sealing them into the circle. She set the canister on the floor and backed up to Alex, grabbing his free hand. They squeezed tightly and both began chanting in Italian.

"Nel Santo Nome di Gesù, sigillo me, i miei parenti, questa casa, e tutte le fonti di approvvigionamento del Preziosissimo Sangue di Gesù Cristo."

Alex translated the words in his head. *In the holy name of Jesus, seal me, my relatives, this house, and all the sources of supply of the most precious blood of Jesus Christ.* His grandmother had been teaching him protection prayers in the language of their ancestors for a few years. He never understood why she chose to give the lessons in Italian. Now, hearing the words resonate through the room, a powerful reinforcement squashed the fear that was building, igniting a burning in his chest and strong beating of his heart.

Alex opened his eyes and glared directly into the black sockets of the malevolent spirit. Although its face at one time might have been human, it was now an amalgamation of open sores and misshapen parts, with a head much too large in proportion to its body. It bore very little resemblance to anything of this earth.

They repeated the prayer again.

"Nel Santo Nome di Gesù, sigillo me, i miei parenti, questa casa, e tutte le fonti di approvvigionamento del Preziosissimo Sangue di Gesù Cristo."

"It's not working. It's just hovering here!" Alex exclaimed to his mom.

"It can't cross the salt circle. That's why it's hovering. Just keep saying the prayer with me," his mother pleaded.

"Nel Santo Nome di Gesù, sigillo me, i miei parenti, questa casa, e tutte le fonti di approvvigionamento del Preziosissimo Sangue di Gesù Cristo."

The spirit's jaw dropped releasing a loud, shrill scream. Margaret collapsed at the waist.

"Margaret, get up. I know it's painful, but don't break our bond. I think we're pissing it off." Alex squeezed her hand.

Continuing to lock eyes with the spirit, Alex squared his shoulders and glared back, unwilling to look away. He was not wavering.

Alex leaned into his mom's ear and whispered, "It's got me locked in a stare. Whatever it does is not affecting me, and I think I'm getting it frustrated. Good for us."

Gina nodded and closed her eyes as she continued with the prayer. The spirit tried moving closer, but the salt barrier held strong. The ghostly presence circled them like a wolf to a cornered deer. Luckily, with Margaret and his mom out of the picture, the only one it could work on was Alex. Hovering as close to him as it could get, its cracked ridden lips parted, blowing out a cloud of icy gray air. The cloud moved toward Alex. He gasped as the dust particles floating in the stream of sunlight froze. Once again, the salt barricade proved impenetrable. The cloud hovered, leaving Alex unscathed.

His mind broke through any fear and allowed the strength of who he is and what he's capable of to take over. His chest filled with a searing power that coursed through his veins and ignited a strength that had been simmering. This time, he shouted the prayer from the depths of his belly and let it rise through the room. His voice filled every crevice of the kitchen and seeped through all the rooms in the house. Like a series of well-placed speakers, it encompassed the entire dwelling and consumed the spirit. The apparition wailed in pain and flew back and up toward the ceiling.

With every word, Alex felt stronger, more confident and powerful. He held its glare, not wanting to risk breaking his hold. With one last verse, he sent a wave so loud, the beast let out another shivering screech and dissipated. Black and gray clouds trailed like a jet stream until no evidence of evil remained.

"It's gone," Alex said wearily.

Loosening his grip on Margaret and his mother, he dropped to the floor. He was exhausted; his legs were no longer able to hold him up.

"Alex, are you okay?" Margaret crouched down beside him while Gina did a walk-through of the first floor.

"He'll be okay, Margaret. He just needs time to rest," his mom shouted from the hall.

"Are you sure, Mrs. L? He doesn't look good," Margaret said nervously.

"I've seen this before with my dad. It's draining when encountering a spirit of this magnitude." The older woman walked back into the room and stood next to her son.

Alex reached out and grabbed Margaret's hand. "I'm fine. I'm going to go and lay down on the couch for a few minutes."

Margaret helped the weakened Alex stand up, and they both hobbled over to the living room.

His mom went back into the kitchen and put a pot of coffee on. She turned on the oven and proceeded to slice some bread, and then grabbed a cookie sheet from one of the cabinets and placed the slices on the sheet and put them into the oven. Opening the lower cabinet, she removed a container of sugar and three plates.

"Alex, do you want butter?" His mom's voice echoed into the living room.

"Yeah, Ma! Hey, do we have any of that chocolate syrup left?" Alex shouted.

"I think so; let me check! Yes! You want some in your coffee?"

"That would be great, thanks!"

Margaret sat down on the floor next to the couch and leaned in. "What the hell was that thing? Did it look as bad as it sounded?"

She nestled closer to him.

"Worse. If that thing was a person at one time, I don't think there's anything left that is human now." Alex turned to face Margaret. "When I looked into its eyes, I could see nothing but rage and evil. No compassion or connection other than the need to kill us."

"We have to get you guys out of this house." Margaret stood up.

"No. We can't leave. This thing isn't just attached to the house. You know that. The people that are dead are proof of that fact. We aren't going anywhere. Besides, the connection starts here. I need to figure this out."

"First of all, *we* need to figure this out. You're not on your own with this," Margaret said firmly.

"I can't risk you getting killed. So, for this one, yes, I am," Alex insisted.

"Bullshit, Alex McKenna. You have no power to tell me what I can and cannot do. In fact, I'm staying right here until this thing is over." Margaret distanced herself by walking across the room.

"The hell you are. I can't protect you here all the time."

"I don't need protecting. You told me not to look at it, and I won't. But you also said just a second ago that it doesn't matter whether you're here or not, because its killing extends to everywhere. So, big man, if you want to protect me, how do you plan on doing that if I'm at my house?"

Alex glared at her. He had nothing. As much as he hated to admit it, she was right.

He surrendered. "Fine."

Margaret left the room and sauntered toward the kitchen.

Jim Bishop is definitely the key, Alex said to himself. *But where are we gonna find information on him? Hell, that's going back nearly ninety years. We've been lucky so far,* he thought. *I need to figure out a new approach to this. Maybe check into more of his financials. That might be available in some of his business records. That is, if there are any.*

He was interrupted by his mom and Margaret coming into the room with the toasted bread and hot coffee. Alex sat up and reached for a cup of the soothing black liquid and a serving of warm bread. As he took a bite, the butter oozed into the tiny nooks of the bread and spilled into the crust, running over the top and down the side. He licked his fingers, lapping up the golden goodness.

"Margaret tells me she'll be staying here with us until this is over. I think that's a good idea. I also thought about what you said, Alex— I'm going to speak with your dad, see if he'll keep your brother for a few weeks. I know it's not completely safe, but at least he doesn't live in Floral Park."

Their dad lived in nearby Bellerose. And although it was only a few minutes away, it was not Floral Park. After the divorce, he wanted to separate himself from Gina, but still be in close proximity to his kids. He once told Alex he thought it was a good compromise.

"Ma, you don't think I should still be training him? Especially now." Alex dunked his toast into the cup of coffee.

"Yes, I do. But I think keeping him away outweighs any lessons right now. You can teach him to look for signs, but until he can fully understand the feelings associated with that, he's better off detached."

Alex reluctantly nodded. He glanced over at Margaret and smiled, but inside, he was holding nothing but fear for her safety.

"I think tomorrow we need to go to the library and see if we can get more information on Jim Bishop."

"We sort of hit a wall last time. Didn't we get everything there was?" Margaret laid back and pressed her head onto the billowy couch.

"We did. But we weren't delving into his business. I think we need to look further back into those records. Maybe there will be something else there that could lead us to other contacts. It's a long shot, I know, but I think we should at least try. Even if we find one more name leading us to a source that might know something about Jim's past, it would be more than we have now."

Margaret sighed. "Can't we just do a search on your laptop?"

"We can. But I have a feeling we're not gonna find much. This is all local information we're after. Remember all the data we found on the ghost haunting Mrs. Fletcher? The library gave us a stack of material we didn't find in our Google search."

"Oh . . . you're right. We found a pile of stuff."

"Yup. So why don't we do a preliminary search tonight, but if we don't find out anything useful, tomorrow we'll head to the library."

"Good idea."

Margaret called her mom and, just as she thought, her parents had no issue with her spending a few more nights at the McKenna/LaBoccetta house. Agreeing they were too tired, and it was too late for her to go home for clothes, they retreated to the bedroom.

Margaret borrowed one of Alex's t-shirts and slipped away to the bathroom, while he plopped down on the bed and gazed up at the ceiling. Something was gnawing away at his thoughts about Jim Bishop. He seemed like the perfect guy with the perfect life, up until the fire. His iPad went blank just as he reached for it. He'd forgotten to charge it again—a bad habit that eluded correction.

Damn, he thought. Rolling over and off the bed, he ambled to his computer. He typed in the name "Jim Bishop," along with, "Floral Park, 1925." He decided to go back further before the Bishops moved into the house. Nothing. He broadened his search and changed "Floral Park" to "New York." He soon figured out, after scrolling through several pages of information, that Jim Bishop was a fairly common name. To narrow the search, he weeded out the ones who were not the right age. Out of the thirty-something names he originally started with; he was down to five.

The bedroom door breezed open to reveal Margaret standing in the archway.

Alex's leg nervously shook, tapping his heel on the floor. He folded his hands behind his head and attempted to casually lean back in the chair, but he pushed too hard and nearly fell backwards. Scrambling to save face, he swiftly switched to a question. "Uh, the shirt fit okay?"

"What do you think?" Margaret coyly replied.

"It's great, good. I'm glad it worked for you. Come here and look at this." His eyes darted back to the screen, and he fumbled with the mouse on his desk.

Margaret rolled her eyes, then proceeded to scoot a chair over from the corner of the room. "What are we looking at?"

"I found five Jim Bishops that are close to our guy's age. I figure we check into each one and see if we can find the right one."

Searching for aspects that would eliminate each contender, it took about an hour for them to feel confident they had found their man.

"It looks like Bishop used to live in Manhattan. That's weird."

"Why?" Margaret laid her head on the desk.

"If we're right and this is that Jim Bishop, then the stories don't match. This clearly puts him in the city at the same time he was supposed to be living in an apartment with his wife in Brooklyn. Don't you remember the news article about the fire? He was quoted as saying he and Carol had moved from an apartment in Brooklyn— they thought it would be great for the kids to have a backyard. "

A line in the article caught Margaret's eye. *Catherine Bishop was killed in a hit-and-run on Tuesday, October 31st, 1922.* She reached over Alex and navigated the mouse.

"Look at this. I think this might be the something you've been feeling."

They huddled closer, soaking in the words.

Prominent heiress Catherine Bishop was struck down by an unknown vehicle late yesterday afternoon as she and her daughter were walking home from the park. Witnesses were horrified to see a black, four-door, touring automobile plow into her while narrowly missing Mrs. Bishop's five-year-old daughter, Ester. Witnesses went on to say that, if Ester hadn't been distracted by a nearby balloon vendor, she would have surely perished with her mother. Private funeral services will be at St. Patrick's Cathedral on Saturday, November 4th at 11 a.m. Catherine Bishop is survived by her husband James and their daughter, Ester.

New York Times, Obituaries

Alex stared at the screen.

"Oh, jeez. He was married before. Ester doesn't even belong to Carol Bishop." Margaret waited for a response. "Alex? Did you hear me?"

"Yeah. I was just thinking. We need to find out more information on the first Mrs. Bishop. I've got that feeling."

"Oh . . . I love your *spidey sense*. And normally, I'd say let's keep looking for more, but I'm beat."

"Me too. How about we pick this back up in the morning?"

Margaret whispered in his ear. "Definitely."

Alex wriggled his neck; the little hairs at the nape were standing at attention. He traced the bow of her lips with his eyes—they were plump and delicately smooth.

"Uh, you can sleep in Wilby's bed since he's not home."

She tilted her head and played with the ends of her hair. "I'm fine here. Your bed's big enough for the both of us."

His hands trembling, he shut down the computer.

Margaret crawled into bed first, near the wall, and then Alex scooted in, hanging on the edge.

"I think now I know why my mom and I have been getting headaches. That was our reaction to this thing. We just didn't realize what was happening." Alex yawned.

"That makes sense. You were worried you weren't feeling anything. It was just a new radar that went off." Margaret wriggled tighter under the comforter.

"Hmm. I like that. A new radar."

"Go to sleep. We can talk more in the morning." Margaret rolled over on her side.

Alex envisioned enveloping the girl of his dreams in his

arms, caressing the back of her neck with his lips, and closing the gap between them. *If only he could tell her.*

THE LIE

A warm beam of gold and orange crept through the room, laying way for a new day. Alex fluttered his eyes; the room was bright. Crossing his forearm over his brow, he lay thinking about Jim Bishop. *Who the hell was this guy?*

He knew by the whisper of Margaret's breath she was still sleeping. Not wanting to wake her, he quietly slid off the bed. The past couple of weeks had been pretty rough, and the events of last night had drained all of them. He pulled on some sweats and a hoodie and headed for the kitchen. The rich aroma carried throughout the house as he descended down the stairs. It was a strong blend of a Brazilian fusion. His mom had received the rich beans from a close friend who had vacationed in the exotic location. Alex had never tasted anything so good. He went straight for the pot and grabbed a mug from the cupboard. He glanced at the fridge and saw a note from his mom. Snapping it out from under the small, *I Love N.Y.* magnet, he read it before tossing it in the trash.

Alex settled back into the comfort of the kitchen table,

chuckling to himself. The kitchen—a common gathering place for most families. It didn't matter what was wrong with you, it could all be healed with food. He loved that, and everything that went with it. His family was big, loud, and for every cliché they represented, they had genuine love for each other. Family—at least on his mom's side—was good.

"Morning!" Margaret glided into the kitchen.

"Hey. You okay?" Alex got up and grabbed another cup, filling it with the liquid gold. "Here you go."

"Thanks. Yeah, I'm good. I must have been wiped out. I don't remember anything after my head hit the pillow. Have you been up long?"

"Na. Just a few minutes. My mom went to see Gram."

"Huh. It's early." Margaret clasped the warm cup and blew on it.

"I know. But I think, after last night, her parental meter is on high alert." He smirked. "It's been so long since the two of them got together on anything like this. I'm hoping they work some magic."

"I'm not sure, but it seems that your mom thinks you're the magic- maker in the family. And so does your gram."

"I know what they think. I also know there are a few things I'm able to do that they can't, but you never saw them work together. I mean, they are strong when they're a team. Don't let either one of them be underestimated."

"So, are we off to the library?"

"I'm not so sure we have to. Let's see what else we can dig up online. Apparently, Catherine came from a wealthy family. Maybe we'll get everything we need here."

"You still want to look into Bishop's business dealings?"

"Yeah. But it seems to have taken a turn. We need to redirect our search. He bought this house with Carol in 1928. But maybe he also kept a residence in the city for a while. One that Carol didn't know about. Catherine died in 1922. That gives Jim ample time to re- establish his life with wife number two. We also need to see if he inherited any money from his first wife's death."

"You're looking for motive, aren't you? You think Catherine's accident was more than that?"

Margaret got up and tore a piece of bread off the loaf on the counter. She started to take a bite.

"No."

"No? Then why . . ."

"Yes. I do. No, don't you want butter?"

Margaret laughed. "What are you, the bread police?"

"I just mean it's good with butter." Alex reached for the knife.

"Well, it's good without it, too." She took another bite.

Alex lowered his head as if he was frustrated. "You know there's a pain in my heart with every bite you take."

"Get used to it, bread boy. This is how I'm eating it." Margaret grinned.

"You're killing me. Okay, why don't we bring this upstairs so we can get started?"

Margaret nodded.

"Mm. Wait. I want to grab another piece."

She took a dish from the cabinet and tore another piece of bread off the loaf before wrapping it back up in the brown paper bag. A heater on her coffee, and they were both ready for the fact-finding mission. Margaret set the cup and dish down on the desk and scooted over the extra chair. Dunking her bread in the coffee, she cupped her hand under her chin and slurped, clearly trying her hardest not to get any drops on the desk. Alex glanced at her with a smile.

"What?" She wiped her mouth with her hand. "It's good like this."

"I know."

"Whatever." She rolled her eyes.

"I wonder why Bishop didn't mention to anyone that he had been married before. I mean, obviously Carol knew. She was raising Ester. I think I'll give Bobby Kirkpatrick a call. Maybe he knew but didn't think it was important."

"Yeah. It is all kind of weird. If you're right about Jim, why would he still keep an apartment in the city when he was married to Carol? Oh, this crap is getting confusing; and tomorrow is the sixth day. What the hell, Alex?" Margaret raised a brow.

"I'm hoping my mom comes back with some news from Gram. Let's keep looking. There has to be something." Alex ran his fingers through his hair and grabbed several strands in exasperation. "We just need to find it."

Engrossed in the search, they were startled when they heard the front door slam.

"I'm home! You two up there?" His mom set two armfuls of groceries on the kitchen table.

Alex and Margaret went barreling down the stairs. "Oh, there you are. How was the library? Any luck?"

Alex started unpacking the bags. "We didn't go. We found out that Jim Bishop was married before."

"I know." She glanced over at Alex.

"You know? Did Gram tell you? Did she find out more stuff?"

"Yes, she did. In fact, when I pulled up, she said she was just getting ready to call us. Let's get this done and sit down. Is there any coffee?"

"Yeah. Almost a full pot." Alex pointed toward the coffee machine.

"Good, because I stopped somewhere else on the way home."

Alex's mom went out to the car and emerged with a pink box.

"Butter Cooky!" Margaret's eyes widened, and the corners of her mouth raised in a half moon.

"I thought you'd be excited."

"Ma. You do know that's her fave, right?"

"Hence the box. Get six plates down, and napkins too."

"Why? There's only three of us."

The chiming of the doorbell answered Alex's question. He raced to the front room and opened the door.

"Hey, what are you guys doing here?" Alex stepped aside to let his family in.

Piling through the door, from his mom's immediate side of the family, were both her sisters—Carla and Jennie—and her brother Nick.

"Your mom thought maybe we should have a little pow-wow to discuss what's been going on lately."

"Cool. She's in the kitchen."

The group traipsed through the dining room.

"Hey, why doesn't everyone sit around the dining table? There's more room," his mom yelled out.

"I'll help with the coffee," Aunt Carla trumpeted.

"Where are the plates?" Jennie shouted.

Alex responded, "I'll get them, Aunt Jennie."

Uncle Nick sat down next to Margaret. "So, how's my nephew treating you? All good?"

Margaret blushed. "Everything is a-okay."

"Because if he's not, just say the word. I'll take care of him."

"Uncle Nick!" Alex roared. "Leave her alone."

"Ah, forget about it. It's all good, Margaret; he'll catch on sooner or later." Uncle Nick winked.

Alex's cheeks glowed like a ripe red delicious apple.

"Alex, grab two extra chairs from the hall closet." Aunt Jennie sat down and started serving coffee.

"Okay, Aunt Jennie," Alex acknowledged.

"I'm here, I'm here." Alex's mom sat down at the end of the table across from her sister, Carla.

Alex was impatient. "So, what did Gram tell you?" he asked.

"Apparently, he was married to Catherine, and she died in a hit-and-run." Nick bit a cookie.

"We know. Ester is her daughter, not Carol's." Gina sipped her coffee. "She also said some of the neighbors back then thought there was more to the story, but nothing has ever been proven. This is just hearsay from generations passed down, but Gram said they were pretty adamant that the night of the fire left too many questions."

"Yeah, no kidding," Nick said sarcastically.

"Wait, how do all of you know this?" Alex asked.

"Your mom called me a couple of days ago for help, and you know this family—you tell one, you tell all." Aunt Carla stirred her coffee. "Did you know that Jim inherited a substantial amount of money after she died? Or that he was in trouble financially before she died? He had an accounting firm in the city. He started off doing very well, but apparently got involved with heavy gambling. He owed a lot of money to all the wrong kinds of people. Remember there was no Atlantic City back then. Everything he did was underground and run by gangster types."

"Ma, how come you didn't tell me you called Aunt Carla?"

"We were kind of busy, kid."

"Do you think Bishop had Catherine killed for the money?" Alex inquired.

"That would make sense. We talked about this on the way over. Greed is usually the simplest and most common denominator when it comes to the ugliness inside us," Aunt Carla responded.

"But don't forget, that means he was willing to risk his own child. Gina, you said the girl was with her mother when she was run down, right?" Jennie interjected.

Gina grabbed a napkin from the holder on the table. "It seems that way. But Gram's going to keep sleuthing. She knows so many people who lived in the neighborhood back then, and many of them are still in contact with her."

Nick spoke up. "He was a special kind of evil."

"Alex, you said last night that we needed to see if there was an insurance policy." Margaret took a bite of a black and white cookie.

"You did?" His mom was apparently surprised.

"Yeah, something I was feeling. It just seems to make sense. Don't you think it was more than coincidence that Ester wasn't hit? I know what the witnesses said—she was distracted by a balloon vendor. But why would a mother let her five-year-old wander off? She would have been holding her hand and been by her side. What really separated them?"

"I agree. There would have been no way you or your brother would get away from me in a large city like that. It almost sounds coordinated. Doesn't it?"

"What kind of man risks his family just for a pay-off? I never get those kinds of idiots." Uncle Nick shook his head.

"Desperate ones," Alex replied.

"You're so right, nephew. You're so right." Uncle Nick patted Alex's back.

Both Alex and Margaret nodded in agreement.

"Let's run this through again. Bishop has a successful business in New York. He marries Catherine and they have Ester. Then he gets in trouble gambling. The kind of trouble that could get him killed. So, knowing he's the beneficiary on his very wealthy wife's policy, he has her killed." Alex turned to the window. The sun was disappearing behind an ominous cloud.

"I think that's the gist of it." His mom sat back in her chair.

Alex raised his brows. "But then how does all of this connect to the killings? *Does* it connect to them? If so, why freezing? Damn. I think for every question we answer, ten more crop up."

"And remember, every six days until Halloween. What's the importance of that? I mean—" Aunt Carla was interrupted.

"Yes! Also, six is the sign of the beast." Aunt Jennie lowered her voice before speaking the next sentence. "Maybe this is a Devil thing."

"There she goes again," Aunt Carla blasted. "There's no reason to believe we're dealing with the Devil. Every time you see a six, you go there. Cut it out, Jenn."

"Yeah, Jenn. Carla's right. Cool your heels," Uncle Nick retorted.

Aunt Jennie pushed back from the table and crossed her arms.

"Alex, you still gonna make that call?" Margaret touched his hand.

"What call?" Alex's mom perked up.

"I was thinking of talking to Bobby Kirkpatrick some more. Maybe there's something he's forgetting or might not think is important."

"That's a good idea, but why don't we see if he'll meet us for lunch? If he's available, I'll book us a table at Russo's. I'd rather we met out of the house, given what happened last night."

"Good idea." Alex smiled.

"Oh, good idea going to Russo's for lunch. Entice him with some good food." Aunt Carla laughed.

His mom poured more coffee. "Thanks for coming over, you guys. This information really helps, but I think we still have too many unanswered questions."

"That may be, but I think we can all agree the man had an agenda, and a diabolical one at that. Let's see what Gram uncovers and let us know if you get anything new from Bobby. In the meantime, we're here if you need us. Salute!" Aunt Carla held up her coffee cup.

"Salute!" The family's voices echoed through the dining room.

Russo's, on the Bay in Queens, was about twenty-five to thirty minutes away. It had the best food, and they were Gina's cousins, so it was pretty much their go-to place for lunch and dinner.

ALEX CALLED BOBBY. It took a little convincing because he really didn't travel any distance from home, but eventually, he caved. They agreed to pick him up at his home; Bobby had recently stopped driving.

When they arrived at the restaurant, Bobby's relaxed demeanor changed. With pursed lips and a stiff body, he was more statue than man in his seat. Alex reached over and patted Bobby's shoulder. His abilities drained a portion of the tension from the weary man—a gift only Alex possessed in his family.

"You're gonna love the food here. It's just like my gram makes." Alex smiled.

"It looks fancy." Bobby kept gazing at the dual cherry

doors with etched glass inlet, crowned with antique brass chandeliers hanging over each side.

"It's okay." Alex gave him a wide grin. "They're family." Hesitantly, Bobby stepped out of the car. Alex enjoyed the scent of garlic, tomatoes, basil, and fresh-baked bread gliding through the restaurant. He glanced over at Bobby, who grinned while turning his nose up to the banquet of aromas. His posture relaxed. After the waiter seated them, they took ample time to review the menu before placing their order.

Alex was the first to commence with conversation.

"Bobby, did you know that Jim Bishop had been married before?" He forked a piece of the Caprese salad and tapped it on the dish to remove excess olive oil. "His first wife was killed."

"Yes. My father didn't discuss it much with us kids, but over the years, my mother made a remark or two about it. Why?" Bobby placed a cloth napkin under his chin.

"The circumstances seem strange—the way she died. Are you familiar with the story?" Alex sipped his water.

"It was a hit-and-run. Ester was with her, but she was fine."

Alex interjected, "Bobby, do you think Carol resented Ester?"

"It sure seemed that way. Jim had the girl call Carol 'Mom,' but I don't think Carol cared for her much. My mom often commented about how she ignored the poor girl, and when she did acknowledge her, she'd be yelling. Alister was her prized possession, for sure."

"Did your dad know Jim's first wife, Catherine?"

Bobby squirmed a little in his chair and turned away from the table.

"Uh. Yes. I believe he did. They were friends for a long time. You need all of this for your paper, Alex?"

Alex looked at his mom, who nodded. "Bobby, have you read about the recent murders in Floral Park?"

"Yeah, I've been following it on the news. Tragic."

"Well, my family is sort of caught in the middle of them. We think they have something to do with what happened to Bishop's family."

"What? How does something that happened eighty-six years ago have anything to do with the murders now?"

"It's a really long story. You know my grandmother, Mary LaBoccetta?"

"I know what they say about her. My mother used to tell us she was a witch." He laughed.

Alex hesitated. "That's sort of true. It kind of runs in the family, and we need help."

"You're saying, what? You're a witch? Gina, what's the boy talking about?"

"I'm sorry, Bobby, but it's true. And we need your help. People are dying, and we are also in danger because of that damn house. Can you help us?"

"Please excuse me. I need to use the restroom." Bobby got up abruptly.

"Damn, Mom, maybe we shouldn't have told him. I think he's spooked."

"Give him a few minutes to process what we said before judging."

Moments later, lunch arrived, and Alex sat tight until the waiter was finished serving their food.

"Ma, I feel like Bobby is holding back. I know we shocked him with the witch thing, but he was antsy before that. What do you think?"

"Yes. I'm not sure what he's hiding, but whatever it is, he's very uncomfortable." His mom frowned.

"I think it's guilt." Alex glanced back toward the restroom.

"Why would you say that?"

"I feel it."

"Hey, he's coming back." Margaret tilted her head.

Well, he didn't run out on us. That's a plus, he thought.

Each of them took a bite from their lunch, and when Bobby reached the table, they had a good reason not to talk. Alex figured it would give him more time to feel calm and digest the information they had shared. Whatever it was that Bobby was hiding needed some coaxing.

Alex took another bite of his veal parmesan. It was really good, but his gram made it better. Most restaurants never got the veal thin enough, but she could pound it until it was thin as paper. This made the meat mouthwatering tender, and with the right amount of breading and frying time, the edges were a little crisp. He loved it that way.

When they were finished, the waiter asked if anyone wanted dessert. Even Margaret was too full, which tickled Alex. Now was the time to get some answers; he focused on Bobby.

"I'm sorry we dumped this insight into our family on you; I really am. But we need help if we're going to stop the murders. The information we have so far leads us to believe there might be another killing tomorrow. We are really pressed for time."

Bobby sawed in a heavy breath and nodded in agreement.

Alex tread softly. "You said your dad knew Catherine. Did he talk much about her?"

"Some."

"Was there trouble with Jim and Catherine before her death?"

"I . . . I'm not sure. Maybe."

"It's okay, take your time. Is there anything else you can remember?"

"Nothing. I'm not supposed . . ."

"Bobby, tomorrow is coming very quickly, and we have no way of knowing who the next victim is."

"I want to help. I really do. But I made a promise to my dad years ago. If I betray that promise, then she wins."

"Who, Bobby? Who wins?"

"Carol." Bobby fiddled with a sugar packet.

"Carol's been dead over eighty years; I don't think you have to worry about her." Alex knew he sounded harsh.

Margaret squeezed his hand under the table. She leaned in and whispered in his ear. "This is rough for everyone. Give him a chance."

Alex had the ability to see and hear things from souls that had passed. But when it came to seeing his own way, sometimes his judgment was clouded and fueled by impatience. Running most of the time on high emotions left him little room for finesse.

Alex softened his tone. "I'm sorry, Bobby."

Bobby placed his head in his hands and muttered under his breath.

"I'm sorry, Dad." A tear trickled down his cheek. "Jim Bishop didn't have any money. It wasn't until he met and married Catherine that he gained a place among the prominent society. Since Catherine's family was so rich, he was introduced to all the affluent people. He liked it—a lot. But there was one very huge problem. He didn't like Catherine. He felt she was too overbearing. He liked his women to be more submissive. And my dad said that Catherine was everything but obedient."

"How so?" Alex was intrigued.

"She was well-educated. Her own woman. So, although they had Ester, she continued to work. She had a job at her father's newspaper and wouldn't give it up. It infuriated Jim, but he couldn't do anything about it without risking the loss of all her money. So he started, you know."

"No. I don't know, Bobby. What did Jim start doing?"

"He . . . Oh damn, I shouldn't be saying any of this out loud. I promised." Bobby tapped the table with his fingers.

"Please. What did he start doing?" Alex pleaded.

"He started dating other women behind Catherine's back. That's how he met Carol."

"What? We thought he didn't meet Carol until a few years after Catherine's accident."

Bobby started shaking his head in disagreement. "No. She was the reason that Catherine was killed. So that Jim could keep all the money and Carol, too."

Alex stared at Bobby. He had been right. The man had been holding back. Alex clenched his jaw; the fire burning in the pit of his stomach was growing. Luckily, Margaret caught on and started rubbing his knee. She leaned into him, and he calmed down a little. His mom was another story.

"You knew this the other day when the kids came to see you, and you said nothing? Bobby, how could you be so callous about this? Our neighbors are dying."

"Ma." Alex grabbed her arm.

His mom pulled back the attack. "I apologize. Please forgive me. I know this must be difficult. When family's involved, everything changes."

"Bobby, the more we know, the more we can connect the dots and have a better chance of stopping this darkness. I know you made a promise to keep quiet. How old were you when your dad told you all of this?" Alex inquired.

"My teens."

"So you've been harboring this secret for over sixty years? It must have been torture."

Bobby looked away from the table and then directly back to Alex. "You have no idea."

"You said Carol wins. What did you mean?"

"She wanted everyone to know that Jim left Catherine for

her. He kept it quiet for obvious reasons, but she felt slighted. You see, Carol was the opposite of Catherine. She grew up poor, with parents who were immigrants from Poland. Meeting Jim and his lifestyle . . . Well, she thought she had hit it big. She wanted to be just like Catherine. Fancy clothes, house, car—whatever she could get her hands on. Dad told my mom that she was very sweet to everyone and put up a good front of the doting wife, but really, she was just interested in Jim's money."

Alex grinned. "Kind of funny, right?"

"What's that?" Bobby's eyes widened.

"Jim married a female version of himself."

"You're right. That's irony for you," Bobby agreed.

Alex was sorting this new information out in his head. The pieces were there, but still something was missing.

"I'm curious, Bobby. Did your dad happen to mention why Jim built a house in Floral Park? I mean, with all that money, why not some mansion or stay in Manhattan?"

"That's the biggest joke of all. After Catherine's death, her family didn't believe it was just an accident. They never really trusted Jim. And when he made his relationship with Carol public, they were infuriated. Catherine's father hired the best attorney in the city. He got the life insurance policy overturned, and all the money went into a trust for Ester. She couldn't touch it until she was twenty-one. Jim wound up with nothing. And Carol saw all her dreams of being in high society go down the drain."

"So, if all the money was in a trust, and Ester died in the fire, what happened to the money?"

"I'm not sure. My guess is, it went back to the family."

"We thought Jim Bishop lost his ass in the stock market crash." Alex shook his head.

"Nah. That was just what he told everyone. I guess he didn't want the world knowing his dirty secret."

Alex turned to his mom. "I'm not sure where we're going with this, but now we have something to work with. It sounds like Jim and Carol weren't very good people. I think we got our focus. Do you agree?"

"I sure do. I think we need to go to Gram's and put our heads together." His mom reached for her purse to leave a tip for the waitress.

"Listen, Bobby." Alex reached out and placed his hand on Bobby's arm. "I'm sorry you had to do this today. But what you did helps us more than you know. I think your dad would understand."

Bobby inhaled a deep breath and lowered his head. "I think it's time to go."

Alex's mom paid the bill while the rest of them went to the car. Alex started the engine and put the heat on. It was getting pretty nippy out. He turned to the back seat, where Bobby was sitting with Margaret.

"Bobby, one thing you said still doesn't make sense to me," Alex said.

"What's that?"

"You still didn't explain what you meant by 'Carol wins.' How does she win?"

"Like I said, she wanted the world to know that Jim chose her over the perfect Catherine. If this got out, then she would get what she wanted all along."

"But they would also know about the affair and Catherine's death."

"Yeah, well, I never said she was sane. Mom said she could be downright mad at times. She had a way of covering it all up when she was around folks."

His mom got into the car, and they were soon on their way back to New Hyde Park. After they dropped Bobby off, they headed home. After parking the car in front of the house, they all lingered outside.

Alex sat down on the top step, and Margaret scooted next to him. He looked up at his mom, who was staring at the French doors to the sunroom.

"Ma, did you see something?"

"Not sure. I'm gonna go in first and check it out."

"Uh, no you're not. Strength in numbers, remember?"

"You know what trumps that?"

"What?"

"Me. I'm the mom and what I say goes. So, once again, wait here."

Alex rolled his eyes, but he knew there was no arguing with her when she made up her mind to do something—another trait he seemed to have inherited.

"Okay. Let us know when to come in. It's starting to get really cold out here."

His mom widened her eyes. "Get your tushes off the cold bricks."

Moments later, he and Margaret heard a scream. They went racing through the front door. Standing in the living room were his mom and Wilby.

His mom was holding her chest.

"Damn, Wilby, you scared me. Why are you home? You're supposed to be with your dad."

"Dad had to go to California for work. They called him late this morning. He tried to reach you. He said he left a lot of messages. I tried also, but you weren't answering your texts, either."

Alex's mom pulled her phone out of her purse. "Crap. I put it on silent when we went to the restaurant. I forgot to check it."

"Okay, so Dad went to California. Why didn't you stay and hang with Shea?"

"The rest of the family was going to the country for the

weekend. They asked me to go with them, but I'd rather be home if dad's not there."

"I really wish you had gone, kid." Her voice fractured.

"Why? What's going on here?" Wilby looked at the three of them for answers.

"Nothing for you to worry about. We got it handled," Alex chimed in.

"No. Alex, if he's here, then he needs to know the whole story. We can't keep him in the dark any longer. Not after that thing we saw the other night. Wait . . . Maybe he can stay with Lisa." His mom started dialing.

Lisa lived five blocks over. She used to babysit for them occasionally when she was in high school.

"I'm tired of all of you trying to keep everything from me. I'm not a baby. And I'm not staying with anyone else. I'm staying home." Wilby's cheeks beamed a bright red. "Tell me!"

His mom ended the call.

Alex knew she was going to tell him, because he felt she was thinking just like he was. Wilby was growing up. To shield him from this would be to deny who he was and where he came from. Even if it never kicked in for him, he was still a part of the weirdness.

His mom tapped the cushion next to her and motioned for Wilby to sit beside her. She told him everything, saving the worst for last— the frightening encounter they'd had in the kitchen the night before.

At first, Wilby was quiet. Alex figured it was because he was soaking it all in, but he was wrong.

"If this Mr. Kirkpatrick knew all of this, why didn't he tell the police or something? I don't understand." Wilby's eyebrows raised with the question.

Okay, so he's fine, Alex thought.

"Good point." Gina hugged her son. "Let's go to Gram's before it gets late."

Alex excused himself and headed upstairs. His binder had twisted, and it was annoying him. Sometimes, after wearing it for several hours, it would stretch a bit. Luckily, he had two. He quickly grabbed his spare from the top dresser drawer and took off his shirt. Right about then, Margaret opened the door. He gave her an exasperated look.

"Here, let me help you with that. I had a feeling this is what you were doing."

"You did? How?"

"I saw you tugging at it during lunch."

"Ugh. Sometimes I really hate this thing."

"I know. Lift your arms."

"Uh, no, it's okay. I've got it." Alex's voice shook.

"Come on, it's me. I can help. What the hell are friends for if you can't use them?" She blinked.

"I don't think . . ."

Before he could finish the sentence, Margaret had grabbed the top of it and wriggled the garment up his waist and over his chest and his head.

"There you go," she said proudly.

"Thanks." He turned and faced the wall. Slipping the spare down his torso, he shimmied it into place, then tugged on a t-shirt and turned around. Margaret stood with her head half-cocked.

"Are you embarrassed in front of me, Alex McKenna?"

"No. Why do you say that?"

"Well, you face the wall like I'm a firing squad."

"I just like a little privacy, that's all."

"Oh, okay. Sorry. I was just trying to help."

"I know."

His eyes gazed into hers. He wanted to take her into his arms right there and kiss her pouty, cherry cola-drenched lips. But he couldn't—rejection from her would crush him.

Alex cleared his throat. "Come on, let's go downstairs." Margaret hesitated.

"We good?"

"We are." Alex smiled.

FLORAL PARK, New York 1932

CAROL ORDERED the little girl to go to her room and stay there. Ester cried, but she knew it fell on deaf ears. Carol didn't care about her. In fact, she hated her. That was okay. She could still talk to her real mom. She was there to comfort her, even if she couldn't hold her.

Many nights, she would lay in her bed, listening to Carol dote on her little brother, Alister. Ester knew it wasn't his fault. He had no idea how cruel his mother could really be, and she wasn't about to tell him. No. She would keep that secret so he could be happy.

But this night, for some reason, Carol was especially mean to her. Ester's dad had gone into the city for work and was late getting home. This must have fueled Carol's anger, she thought, because her stepmother had planned a formal dinner with the Parkers—a very wealthy family that lived in Garden City. Ester knew this because Carol had her helping in the kitchen all day. Going on and on about Mrs. Parker and her beautiful, full-length mink coat. Mr. Parker was no average Joe, either—he wore hand-tailored suits that were made specially for him.

When it was six o'clock and Jim wasn't back yet, Carol started to unravel. The Parkers were due to arrive any minute. Ester couldn't take the ranting of the insane woman any longer. She was so loud, the sound carried through the vent in her bedroom. Burying her head under a pillow, she hummed the melody of her little brother's favorite song. It was a good thing he was spending the night at his grandparents' house. The secret would be kept for another day.

This episode was especially bad and began to frighten her. She hoped either her dad or the Parkers would arrive soon. Minutes passed, but it felt like hours. A loud boom from the brass knocker on the front door instantly calmed her nerves. Pulling open her bedroom door, she ran to the top of the stairs. It was her dad. He had forgotten his key. No sooner did he take off his hat and coat than the doorbell ring. The Parkers had arrived as well. Ester felt a warmth flush over her body. No more crazy for tonight.

REVENGE

They arrived at his gram's around four o'clock in the afternoon. The sun beckoned its good-byes as they pulled up in front of her house, and the porch light glowed, welcoming their arrival. They stepped out to the abrupt chill—it was Mother Nature's reminder that October was being ushered out to make way for winter.

Halloween was usually one of the chilliest nights of the Fall. It didn't matter if the day had been drenched in sunshine and you peeled away the sweatshirt your mother made you wear before running out the door. By nightfall, you were gladly encompassing your body with sweats, jackets, and sometimes beanies to keep your ears from turning red in the plummeting temperatures. The scent of burning leaves and light of fireplaces solidified the transition from summer, and prepared families for the long winter ahead. As he steered his body toward the house, Alex couldn't stop focusing on the victims and how they died. The pain they must have felt as their flesh froze to the point of incomprehensible anguish. And their families. How do you explain something like that to them?

He caught a glimmer of a cat running across the street. Its furry gray tail was similar to a raccoon's, but far too bushy for the size of its sleek body. *Odd*, he thought. *It didn't fit. Like the story of Michael Kirkpatrick didn't fit.*

Hearing it, he sounds heroic, noble. Going there to rescue the family and emerging with Jim and Alister. But once dissected, it takes on a very different twist. Wilby was right. Why didn't Michael ever notify the authorities if he knew all about the Bishops, and what they had done? And what exactly did they do? Bobby said Carol and Jim killed Catherine. But how? Jim was at work, and Carol didn't live in the city. Maybe they hired someone? But why risk Ester, his own daughter, in the accident? Would Jim have been that heartless? Maybe the balloon vendor was an accomplice and was staged, purposely positioned to get Ester out of the way. Still, that was a cruel plan. The little girl could have been hurt or killed. At the very least, she witnessed her own mother's death.

Alex brought himself back to the cat. It had made it to the other side of the street and was perched on top of a brick wall surrounding the neighbor's house. Despite its contrast of body to tail, the creature was sort of majestic. Its chest was full and puffed out with a straight back, and the bushy tail wrapped neatly around the back portion of its body. *Things aren't what they appear to be*, he thought.

When Gram opened the door and saw Wilby, she screeched with delight. Wrapping her arms tightly around him, she kissed his cheeks until they beamed like a shiny red apple. When she released him, Wilby wiped his cheeks off with the backs of his hands.

Gram had some coffee ready for them, and she set everything up on the dining room table, along with two very thick journals. Alex recognized them immediately. They had belonged to her mother— his great-great grandmother, Loretta. Loretta was one of the strongest in LaBoccetta history. Her connection with the other side was extremely vivid. Gram learned everything she knew from her.

And now, she was sharing it with him. His gram had told him on several occasions that he was more like his great-great grandmother than anyone else in the family.

He took a sip of the hot coffee. It flooded through his body with a gentle warmth that melted away the cold that had gripped him from the night's air. Sitting back, he waited for his gram to tell them what she had found. Sitting at the head of the table, she lifted the first journal from the top. It was by far the thicker and more worn of the two. She delicately leafed through the pages, turning each one individually. Given the years, they surely would have torn easily. There were six bookmarks spread throughout, marking the pages of interest.

"Let's see." His gram found the first page and gently smoothed the paper down. "Here is the first entry that I thought might help us. Remember what I told you, Alex, the last visit you were here? About the entity? My mother called it "the dark spirit.' It was the one that killed its victims with fire."

"Yeah, Gram. I remember."

"My mother uncovered who the spirit actually was—a woman from the village who had caught her husband cheating, and he decided to enact his own solution. He killed her and then burned her body. But legend has it that the woman wasn't really dead, just comatose. It says she felt the whole, torturous death. Her screams were never heard, but they rang through her head, driving the poor soul mad in the last few seconds of life. This is why she killed her victims by setting their heads on fire."

"But how was she able to do this after death? You had originally mentioned a spell of some kind, and maybe a human accomplice. And how did she pick her victims?" Alex pried.

"One question at a time, Bonzetta."

His gram placed the bookmark back on the page she was reading and proceeded to the next.

"My mother wrote in this entry that it was difficult to figure out what the victims had in common. After prying into each family, she found that, in some aspect of their lives, they all knew the same woman. It was then the story began to unfold and make sense. It appeared each and every one of the villagers killed were either directly associated or a relative of the person connected. And they all had one thing in common—each one knew about the husband's infidelities and chose not to tell his wife. She went on to say that, after the first two murders, the families were so frightened, they made a pact. They told their relatives the truth and hoped it would keep them safe. Some of the family members fled, but it didn't help. Their fate had been sealed, and as long as the entity was able to exist in this world, they were doomed."

Alex scooted closer to get a better look at the book's contents. "Gram, it says here your mom suspected a human was helping it. You were right."

She nodded her head. "Yes. My mother found out the couple had a daughter. She was in her early twenties when her mother was killed. She blamed her father—hated him. But she also practiced a very dark side of Stregheria—Italian witchcraft."

"Wait, most of the family practices Stregheria. I've never seen anything like this our journals at home."

"No. We don't use this kind of darkness. But for every light, there are shadows lurking. And what the daughter practiced was a very dark and dangerous use of our craft. After my mother uncovered this, it didn't take her long to figure out what was going on. The daughter cast a spell to bring her mother's tortured spirit back so they could enact revenge on everyone involved. What her daughter didn't realize was the depths of madness her mother had succumbed to in her final moments. When she brought her back, she brought all of the pain with her."

His gram released a deep sigh. "The spirit did kill everyone associated with the secret, but she went on to expand her spree to anyone who got in her way. Even her own granddaughter."

Alex nearly dropped his mug of coffee. "She killed her own blood?" He wiped his palms on his jeans.

"Yes. This is the danger with this kind of dark energy—you think you have control, but it's all an illusion. The darkness is very strong. The woman's daughter paid the highest price for that mistake. She lost her only child."

"Gram, what happened? Does it say anywhere how she stopped it?" Alex was at the edge of his seat.

"It does. My mother took part in the ritual that sent the woman's tortured soul back to the abyss. Unfortunately, the spirit's daughter died as well. The loss of her own young daughter was too much for her. During the banishment, she took her own life."

"Okay, let me get this straight. Not only did the woman aid in the killing of all those people, but she lost her life and the life of her own daughter, too? This isn't very encouraging. This means whoever the puppet master is, they will die too." Alex was distraught.

"I never said they had to die, bell mia. I said she did. What happened to her was by her own hand. The ritual didn't call for her death; it was very specific. Only the elimination of the dark spirit."

"Oh, jeez." He shook his head.

"Here, read this." His gram slid the journal in front of him.

He looked down at the words on the page; they were in Italian. He frowned, but he understood them well enough to translate. He pulled the journal closer, as if this would clarify his understanding. Clearing his throat, he read the journal entry aloud.

October 31, 1908- I've gathered my sisters, mother, and aunt. We will finish this today. The circle of light is complete, and I will draw the malevolent spirit into our trap. I pray this works and puts an end to the horror that has been bestowed on our village.

November 01, 1908- We have had success in returning the spirit to its own realm. But not without cost. My sister, Lucia, suffered a break in her arm, and my mother, a severe gash on her cheek. But more painful than this was the horrifying vision of watching the spirit's daughter (and aide in the killings) take her own life. Breaking through our circle and throwing her body onto the flaming spirit, she incinerated herself. I fear her tortured soul will wander the underworld in agony until time itself stops.

Alex turned from the table. He could barely control the fear that was rising from his belly and tightening his chest.

"We need to find out who's helping this thing. Gram, any ideas?" He took a few deep breaths.

"I've been thinking about little else. Whoever it is, they would have been directly affected by the events. For that to be possible, it would mean they are long in years. Judging by what you found, Alex, this person has been doing this for a very long time. I would assume that they are probably consumed by this. Maybe even a bit mad themselves by now. However, that does narrow down our suspects."

"Great. Not only do we have a spirit who's off their rocker, but a live one, too. We're screwed. There won't be any reasoning with them if this is true." Alex put his head down on the table.

"Bonzetta, don't give up so easily. Whoever this is, they must be in a lot of pain after all these years with no satisfaction."

Margaret chimed in. "Why do you say they have no satisfaction?"

"Because they keep doing it."

"Huh. I hadn't looked at it like that. So, loony and frustrated. Alex is right. We're screwed."

Gram smiled. "Not you too?"

Alex's gram placed her hands on the table in front of the two teens. "You both need to trust your hearts. Right now, your minds will betray you. It's telling you this is impossible, but it's not. Let your instinct, and your mom, guide you and go from there. But remember, you can assuredly rule out anyone younger. This has been going on much too long. Go home tonight and take a second look at what you've got. Think about who you've spoken to, and don't let yourself be fooled. Sometimes, the easiest answer is the right one. I'll work on the spell to cast this spirit out from this world. It will take time. I don't have an understanding of the original spell, but it can be done. I'll let you know as soon as it's ready. Gina, I know you've been removed from all of this for a while, but I sense your know is getting stronger. Do you feel it?"

"I do, everyday a little bit more. I denied it for so long, but now that it's sharpening, I don't know how I could have walked away."

"Mio prezioso, you never walked away. That would be impossible. You closed your eyes for a time, but it was always with you."

Gina tightly hugged her grandmother, and Alex jolted. The electricity from their bond sent static into the air, stinging his flesh.

On the drive home, Alex couldn't help but submerge himself in the very question that he felt held all the answers: *Who had the most to gain?* He rested his head on the window. It was cold. He tilted his head toward the sky and awed at how many stars were visible—a welcome consequence of the cooler temperatures. Their sheer brilliance touched his soul. He looked beyond the obvious to the smaller, quieter stars in the distance. Their glow were mere flickers. They were almost unnoticeable. *Maybe Gram was wrong,* he thought. *What if it isn't the most obvious, but the complete opposite? Who haven't we checked out?*

Once they were home and in comfy pajamas, the teens camped out in the living room. Alex's mom had made some hot chocolate before taking Wilby up to bed. Margaret handed a mug to Alex who had his iPad in his lap. She sat next to him and leaned in to peer over his shoulder.

"What are you looking for?"

He tightened his body. "Something Gram said piqued my interest. She thought we should start with the most obvious. But what if we go about it differently? Start with someone who we never even looked at before."

"How come?"

"I was thinking that, if this person is like Gram said— worn out, frustrated, and elderly, they might be content to be more of a recluse. I'm going over the list of people who were directly involved the night of the fire, and also with Catherine's death. Then I'm checking who could still be around. Most of them would be long gone by now. So, whoever it was would have to have been pretty young at the time."

"That would leave Alister. But he didn't seem to fit the description your gram gave. And then there was Bobby, but he was helping us.

"I know, I'm still searching. Give me a few minutes. I know there's something we came across. I just can't bring it forward in my mind."

"Okay. I'll just chill with my hot chocolate while you save the day."

"Smartass."

"Well, you know what my dad always says: '"It's better than being a dumbass.'" Margaret grinned.

Alex rolled his eyes and continued searching through his notes. Alex's mom joined them after Wilby was tucked in for the night.

The dim glimmer from a standing corner lamp was the sole source of light in the room.

"It's dark in here. That corner lamp is not bright enough to read by," his mom huffed.

She flipped the wall switch, turning on the light in the ceiling fan.

Margaret winced.

"Too bright?" his mom inquired.

"Sort of." Margaret put her hand in front of the luminescent glow.

"Yeah, Ma, can you shut it off? It was good before," Alex pleaded.

She turned off the light and sat down in the large recliner across the room.

"I think I've got nervous energy. I can't seem to calm my insides." His mom sipped her cocoa.

Alex looked up from his iPad. "Me too."

The grandfather clock in the entryway chimed midnight. The three of them stared at the clock for a moment, and then at each other. Sunday.

"Ma," Alex screeched.

"Yeah, honey."

Alex picked up both arms and almost dropped the iPad. He quickly fumbled with it and then set it on the couch.

"My arms. Look."

His arms were covered in bumps. He shivered.

"Crap. Now I know why I couldn't settle my insides." His mom turned her head, panning the room.

"Alex, do you see anything?" she asked nervously.

"No."

Abruptly, Gina flew off the chair and barreled toward the stairs. "Wilby!"

"Shit." Alex followed behind her and yelled at Margaret to come with them. He didn't want to leave her alone.

His mom suddenly stopped at the landing. Alex pushed forward until he saw what was deterring her. Looming in the hallway between Alex and Wilby's bedroom was the dark spirit, an arctic halo resting above its head. The icy cold air drifted toward them, freezing up the small window. Alex pivoted around, quickly grabbing Margaret and turning her. She immediately shut her eyes. He guided her to sit down on the top stair and reinforced the *no look* rule. She nodded.

He grabbed his mom, shuffled her to the side, and squeezed past her without making a sound. She grabbed his arm to stop him, but he peeled off her fingers and moved toward the hall. Taking a step forward, Alex winced when he heard the old wood boards on the floor creek. The spirit spun around, holding Alex in its sight. Wilby's door was shut, and he knew he'd never make it to the room before the creature. He opted to get Wilby's attention another way—he shouted.

"Wilby! Wilby, wake up. Can you hear me? Wilby!"

"Alex? What's going on?" Wilby's voice was drowsy.

"Listen, buddy. I need you to do me a favor. Don't come out. Get under the covers and close your eyes. No matter what you hear. Okay?"

"Why? What's wrong? Where's Mom?"

His mom exclaimed, "I'm here, honey! Just listen to your brother. Do not open your eyes until one of us comes and gets you! We'll explain later. Do you hear me?"

"Yeah," Wilby said in a shaky voice.

"Alex, do not get close to that thing," his mom ordered.

"Had no intentions of it."

Alex scanned the hallway for something that might be useful, but all he saw were three open doors—his bedroom, his mom's, and the bathroom, which was right next to him.

"Ma. Stupid question. Does Epsom salt count as salt when we use the banishing spell?"

"Uh. No. Two different things? Why?"

"Damn. I thought we could make a line using your bath salts."

"There's salt in my bedroom." His mom pointed toward her dresser.

"I'll get it." Alex didn't move.

"I'll go. You've got this thing in a stare-down," she said.

Alex had to acknowledge the fact that she was right; he inched aside to let her pass. She slipped by without catching the least bit of attention from the thing. Alex was its sole intent. Quickly, she scurried into her room and grabbed the salt. The spirit moved closer to the teen locked in its gaze, and his mom used the opportunity to throw down a line of salt in front of Wilby's room before slipping back to the steps. Stepping down, she reached out and grabbed Margaret's shirt and told her to stand up. Facing away, she slowly backed onto the landing. Gina poured a circle on the floor around Margaret and stepped in.

"Alex, get in here with us," she directed. Alex didn't move. "Alex!"

The spirit had drawn Alex in, paralyzing him. It may not be able to freeze him, but it could hold him. Gina reached for her son and grabbed his arm, pulling him back. Losing his balance, he missed the stairs and tumbled into the two women. The three of them hit the floor, landing on top of each other. His mom scrambled to her feet to bind the circle once again, before helping Margaret back in. Alex tried to get up but fell on his backside.

"What the hell was that? Why did you knock me down?" Alex was confused.

"I didn't. That was an accident. I was trying to pull you into the circle!" his mom exclaimed.

"The circle? Where did you get the salt?"

Alex grabbed his head and winced. Relentless throbbing catapulted a tidal wave of nausea to his pit. *What the hell?*

"Don't you remember?"

"Remember what?" Alex said groggily.

He pushed off the floor with his palms, trying to stand, but weakness pulled him back.

"Forget it. There is no time for this now. I'll tell you later. Right now, we need to get rid of this thing." She wrapped her arms around her son's waist and pulled him to his feet.

Passionately, they chanted the words that had temporarily banished the malevolent spirit once before. Wailing, the dark entity fought to hold its ground. It flailed between the walls of the hallway, then disappeared in a cloud of ice-laden smoke, leaving behind a thin layer of frost.

Margaret screamed as Alex collapsed to the floor with a resounding *thud.*

"Margaret, help me get him up. Let's put him on his bed."

Margaret took hold underneath Alex's right arm while his mom got the left. They hoisted him up and hobbled his weakened body into the bedroom. They laid him down, and Margaret grabbed the comforter and pulled it up. His mom then went to check on Wilby. When she returned, Alex was in a deep sleep.

"Margaret, let's go downstairs. I need a glass of wine. Alex will probably sleep for a while."

She nodded hesitantly.

After pouring a glass of Merlot, his mom relaxed with Wilby on the couch. Within minutes, they had both dozed off.

Margaret tried not to disturb her, but her concern for Alex overrode her fear of waking his mom.

"Mrs. I . . . I mean, Gina." She shook her.

Gina pushed her lids open and stretched. Sitting up, she yawned before taking another a sip of wine.

"Everything okay, Margaret? Is Alex awake already?"

"No. I'm sorry I woke you, but I'm worried about him. Why is Alex so out of it? He didn't even remember your conversation."

"That creature was probably draining him. It had him in its stare for a while. Apparently, it was long enough to have an effect on him. This is something else I'm familiar with."

"It happened to you?" Margaret curled up clasping her knees.

"It did. I was a couple of years older than Alex. Maybe around twenty. There was a spirit that found me and latched on. He wouldn't leave. Stayed with me no matter where I'd go. He wasn't evil, just lonely. He couldn't accept his death and just wandered, trapped between here and there. Early one morning, I was up before the rest of my family. I went downstairs to fix breakfast, and there he was. He had been waiting in the kitchen for me. I sat down and began talking with him. Trying to persuade him to crossover. I think it upset him, because he stared into my eyes with an intensity I hadn't seen from him before. If my dad hadn't come down, I'm not sure what would have happened to me. He broke the connection and used the incantation that we did earlier. It worked. I never saw him again. I was completely drained, though. I went to bed and slept a full day."

"And he never came back?"

"Nope. But I do remember feeling an overwhelming sense of sadness."

"So if he never came back, then why does this thing keep reappearing? Why doesn't the prayer work permanently?"

"Because, unlike my spirit, this one is full of darkness. I also suspect whatever means were used to call it are holding it here, as well. It can't leave until the person who is controlling the strings decides they're done, or Gram comes up with a spell to break it."

"Gina, is it okay if I go up and check on Alex?"

"Sure, honey."

Margaret crept into Alex's bedroom. She took a seat on the desk chair. The room was dark except for a beam of light coming through the window. She got up and looked out. It was the streetlight on the sidewalk near the back of the yard. Everything looked so quiet and peaceful. The trees were so still, they almost looked fake. Her eyes followed the horizon up toward the nearly black sky. It was filled with stars— another sign that winter was coming. The crisper the air, the better the sky view. She glanced back toward Alex. He was stirring a little, and she grabbed the comforter and pulled it back up over his chest. *He must have pulled it down in his sleep,* she thought. She turned back to the window and heard rustling again. Glancing once more at Alex, the comforter was pulled back. Again, she pulled it up, but this time, she tucked the sides under the mattress. She sat back down in the desk chair and watched. The comforter folded itself back and off Alex's shivering body. Margaret jumped to her feet and ran down the stairs for his mom.

When the two women got there, Alex still lay in a deep sleep, the comforter pulled back to the bottom of the bed. His mom grabbed it and spread it up to Alex's neck. She stood and watched as it came off again. She noticed that Alex was muttering and tossing around. He grabbed his head and tucked it into his arms.

"There's nothing to worry about," his mom whispered.

Margaret was stunned. "What do you mean? You see what's happening."

"It's Alex. He's doing it. He's in a deep REM sleep, and whatever is going on in his head is causing the comforter to come off."

"Has this happened before with him?"

"Yes. When he was a toddler. It took us awhile to figure it out, but he can do things like this if he's in a deep enough sleep. His abilities are very strong."

"That's why he was able to slam whatever it was that kidnapped me into the wall?"

"That's the first time he was able to do anything like that when he was awake. I'm betting his fear for your safety lowered his inhibitions. Alex can have trouble with letting go and letting his power grow. Gram and I can sense his strength, but he needs to believe in it for it to reach its full potential."

The two women jumped when the bed inched away from the wall and glided to the center of the room. The shutters on the window opened and then folded shut.

"I was never able to do that." His mom latched the shutters closed.

"What about the bed?" Margaret leaned over and gently brushed his hair with her hands.

Gina smirked. "He'll move it when he wakes up. Let's just let him rest."

Alex's mom partially closed the bedroom door. A radiance trickled in from the hall light, illuminating the room around him. *We're definitely going to need some heavenly intervention on this one,* she thought.

ALEX SAW the bitter darkness that inhabited the spirit's soul. As their eyes locked, he was unable to look away. He could feel the pain that consumed the shattered ghost. The hate that resonated from it was so strong, it weighed on his chest like a cement plate. He gasped.

It wanted the cold. Needed it. The cold had become its existence, and a constant reminder of the agony of a life lost. She would have vengeance.

Shooting up in bed, Alex took in a hard gush of air, filling his lungs too quickly. He coughed uncontrollably and slithered off the bed and onto the floor. Hunching over, he grabbed his knees and drew them into his chest. Within a few seconds, it passed. That's when it registered . . . the dark spirit said *she*. Finally, confirmation of his suspicions. He had thought all along that it must be one of the two wives—now he *knew* he was on the right path. Or at the very least, he had ruled out Bishop and Kirkpatrick as the malevolent spirit.

He went to the closet and grabbed a hoodie, pulled on some socks, and went dashing down the stairs. Wilby was sleeping on the couch and Alex bee-lined it for the kitchen. Margaret and his mom were having a conversation at the table.

"We're definitely looking for a female!" Alex sat down at the table. "That evil thing referred to itself as *she*."

"What? And why are you up? I thought you'd be out for several more hours."

"I was dreaming. In the dream, I saw beyond its eyes. I remembered what affected me so much. I could feel everything. All the cold and darkness, the pain and agony. It was consuming me. We really need to know who this is."

Margaret reached for him, but they were interrupted by his mom. "Okay, I know what you're thinking. It boils down to either Catherine or Carol. Which is what we had thought it might be."

"Ma, listen. I got in its head, and if I can go further, then maybe it will reveal itself."

"No. Absolutely not. You are not locking eyes with that thing again. It's too dangerous.'

"If I don't, then we're just letting innocent people die."

"We'll find another way. This is non-negotiable, Alex."

Alex nodded his head to acknowledge his mom, but he knew the quickest way was going to be the only way. His brain started formulating the plan.

MRS. NUNCIO

It was Sunday morning, and everyone waited in Alex's house to hear the impending tragic news. Alex was especially withdrawn. He'd let another six days go by, and now, someone would die. It was about two o'clock in the afternoon when the latest victim revealed herself.

Mrs. Nuncio, their neighbor from across the street.

Alex and Margaret were sitting in the backyard on the porch. His mom was folding laundry, and Wilby was playing video games in his room. *It all feels so normal,* thought Alex. Traditionally, he'd be excited. Halloween—his favorite holiday —was only a week away. Wilby would be driving their mom nuts by changing his mind on a costume choice at the last minute, and his mom would stress, hoping she had bought enough candy.

But this Halloween felt so different. Alex knew too much to pretend it could be just another holiday. First, he heard the sirens in the distance. He looked at Margaret, who was wincing. It was the piercing alert that someone might be dead. The warning became stronger and louder. Alex stood up, walked to the back of the yard, and slipped through the chain link gate, with Margaret right behind him. He stood on the sidewalk; they were getting closer with each breath. He peered down the street in the direction of the impending doom as the ambulance rapidly took the corner and turned onto their block.

His mom came racing out of the house and stopped at his side. They both watched the paramedics get out and gingerly walk to the front door to where Carmine Nuncio was waiting. The old man was so pale, as if he'd been drained of all his blood. He was frenzied and barely understandable. Alex surmised this had to be what they were waiting for. The two rescuers walked past him and into what Alex thought was probably the scariest call they had ever received. A few seconds later, two squad cars from Floral Park's finest pulled up. The two officers searched around the property lines before heading inside.

They sat on the curb, waiting for confirmation of their fears. The gray sky cast a nod of affirmation to the gloom that was already present. Alex shivered, but the cold wasn't getting to him—it was the waiting. Time stood still on Geranium Avenue. The pressure of the unknown was driving him to near insanity. *But it really isn't the unknown, is it?* he thought. The paramedics were finding Mrs. Nuncio dead, in a horrific display of mockery to the inner circle this charade was being directed toward.

Poor Mr. Nuncio. They had no children living in New York; he was entirely on his own.

His thoughts were interrupted by a seemingly benign piece of architecture on the Nuncio house—the two pillars standing guard before the front door. Above them, two large black numbers were riveted into the peak in a horizontal display— sixty-three.

"Damn!" Alex shouted in anger. "How could I be so stupid?"

"Alex, what?" His mom reached to grab his arm, but he pulled away.

"Whose house is that, Ma?"

"Okay. Are you still having issues from your encounter? This is the Nuncios' house."

"Wrong," Alex snapped.

"I think you better get inside and lay down. You know damn well whose house this is."

"Yes, I do. It's the Kirkpatricks' house, over sixty years ago. It's been sitting right next door to us the entire time. The house that Michael Kirkpatrick owned, the house Bobby grew up in. I've been so focused on our house history. I could have saved Mrs. Nuncio."

His mom's eye teared up. "Crap . . . crap. How could we miss this?"

Margaret cried out, "We were so dumb. They were right in front of us. Poor Mrs. Nuncio."

"Hold on. Let's be sure first. Maybe it's not what it looks like." Alex's mom wiped tears away.

He shot his mom a frustrated look. "Really? You're going with that?"

"Hey, kid. Give me a break. I'm sick inside. Let's just wait and see is all that I'm saying."

He stood up once again and paced back and forth in the middle of the road until the paramedics opened the front door. They exchanged a brief conversation with the grieving Mr. Nuncio before turning to reveal wide eyes and a tight jaw. Alex knew instantly that their assumptions had been correct.

Gina glanced at Alex. "They were married for almost seventy years, sixty of which were spent in that house. No telling how long the coroner will take to get here. I'm going to go keep him company. He shouldn't be left alone."

She dried her eyes and let instinct take over, but Alex couldn't. He couldn't face the man knowing he might have prevented this. No longer able to hold back the flood gate, tears gushed, and he collapsed on the ground. Margaret sat next to him and just held him. There were no words to make this better. His mom waved them on to join her, but Margaret put her hand up.

"Alex, your mom wants us to go up there and talk with them."

"I can't. I just can't face that poor man."

"I know you're hurting. But look at it like this; there is still one more victim left this year. And then next year, the damn killings start again. You can stop that. All of it. Maybe your mom wants us to hear something that Mr. Nuncio has to say. It might be important."

Alex wiped his eyes on the sleeve of his hoodie and then cupped his hand over his mouth, taking the last of the rolling tears. He let out a deep sigh and stood.

His mom was offering words of comfort to the grieving widow when Alex and Margaret joined them. The poor man's eyes were the darkest red Alex had ever seen. His cheeks were painted with dried tears, and he could barely stand up. She was holding him on one side while he leaned into the doorway with his other shoulder. Alex took his arm, and they led him to the living room and to the comfort of his couch. Immediately, goosebumps raised their awareness, and Alex trembled. The trail of death was still fresh, along with the essence that caused Mrs. Nuncio's demise.

"She was in the kitchen at the table." Mr. Nuncio directed his question to Gina. "How this could happen?"

Gina turned to Alex and Margaret, who stood in the archway between the living and dining room.

"Her head, it was solid like a block. Like a helmet of ice. My poor Rose. I had only left her for a few minutes."

Alex pushed down the lump blocking his throat. "I am so

sorry, Mr. Nuncio. Mrs. Nuncio was always so kind to me and my little brother."

Alex's mom gently questioned Mr. Nuncio, "Did you hear anything before it happened?"

"I did. One very loud yell from my Rose. That's when I went in to see what had happened. I thought maybe she had cut her finger with the cheese knife. Silly girl was always doing that. I would tell her all the time to let me do the cutting. When I got there, she was sitting in the chair. My love was slumped over with her head on the table. At first, I couldn't make out what I was seeing. But as it became clearer, I couldn't believe it. It just doesn't make any sense."

"You two lived here a long time. You must have seen so many changes. All the families that have come and gone over the years. You witnessed a lot of history together."

Mr. Nuncio sniffled. "Yes, we did. Rose loved meeting everyone new that came to the neighborhood."

"Did you know the family that had the fire in our house . . . I think they were the Bishops. Maybe, I'm not sure."

"No, they were long gone by the time Rose and I moved in. But I believe the Kirkpatricks knew them."

"Oh, did you know the Kirkpatrick family? I went to school with Bobby Kirkpatrick's granddaughter."

Mr. Nuncio blew his nose. "I should say so; my Rose was a Kirkpatrick. Her mother's cousin gave us the house."

They were interrupted when one of the officers came over to get a statement from Mr. Nuncio while his partner interviewed Alex, his mom, and Margaret. Once he was satisfied, he thanked them and resumed his inspection of the crime scene.

"I don't want to leave Mr. Nuncio until someone comes to stay with him," Alex's mom whispered.

"Ma, I need to get in the kitchen before the morgue comes for the body. Maybe I can pick up on something."

"I don't think the officers are leaving until the body's taken."

"The paramedics are gone, so now would be the perfect time. What if I try the mind spell Gram's been teaching me?"

"Alex, you haven't been training with that very long. I don't know"

"This is my only chance."

"Okay. Try it. But be careful."

"What spell?" Margaret's eyes widened.

"Watch Alex," his mom replied.

Alex casually rose from his seat and inched toward the police officer and Mr. Nuncio. Concentrating on the officer, he imagined him *not* seeing Alex. Then, he homed in on the energy within the officer's mind. Determination and doubt were the primary emotions the officer was experiencing. Alex gently molded the emotion of determination with his thoughts, to focus solely on Mr. Nuncio. Then he snapped his fingers to complete the spell. Alex moved closer to the officer, so he stood by his side—the man never looked away from Mr. Nuncio. He needed to move quickly, because the spell only lasted a few minutes, and he had the second policeman in the kitchen to distract.

Alex cautiously approached the kitchen. Luckily, the officer had his back to the doorway. He repeated the process. This time, the officer's thoughts were consumed with fright and disgust. He used both emotions this time. Intensifying the man's state of mind, Alex was able to create the need for the cop to step outside for some air. Quickly, Alex approached the body. He stole a glance at the officer in the backyard, then quickly wiped his sweaty palms on the sides of his pants.

The looming residue of the dark spirit grew thicker, sharpening his focus. Mrs. Nuncio's body was slumped over the table, the water from the melting ice pooled up under her head. He hesitated before reaching out to touch the kitchen chair, retracting twice before gaining a firm grip. A burning sensation of cold shot through his hand. It raced along his arm and spread like a fungus before nestling in his heart. He grasped his heart—it squeezed tighter with every breath. It was freezing. Margaret entered the room just in time. With both hands, she wrapped herself around his waist and yanked. Falling to the floor, he sat stunned, gasping for air.

"Alex, are you alright?"

He put his hands over his heart and widened his eyes. Margaret crumpled to the floor beside him.

"What the hell was that?"

"Not sure. I think I just experienced Mrs. Nuncio's death." Alex coughed.

Margaret helped him to stand, and when he was steady, they rejoined his mom in the living room.

"How were you able to get past the officer in the living room?" Alex rubbed his chest.

Margaret stepped closer to Alex. "Whatever you did really worked. He wasn't interested in anyone but Mr. Nuncio."

"Excuse me, but where did you two just come from?" the officer questioned.

"I guess it wore off," Margaret whispered.

"I think it's time you leave. If we have any further questions, we'll contact you."

"I don't want to leave him like . . ." Gina turned to see who was knocking.

Father Timoney, from Our Lady of Victory Catholic Church, stood in the doorway like the priest from The Exorcist. *It would be funny if this wasn't real,* Alex thought. *But it is real, and it's not funny.*

Satisfied Mr. Nuncio wouldn't be alone, Gina suggested they go home.

They quietly walked through the atmospheric murkiness that perfectly reflected the state of the neighborhood. They stopped at the threshold while Alex's mom unlocked the front door, and Alex glanced back toward the Nuncio property.

"Ma, I think we have another big clue," Alex stated.

"What do you mean?"

"Well, Mr. and Mrs. Nuncio were connected to Kirkpatrick, but not Bishop. That means whoever called this spirit up is connected to Kirkpatrick."

"Good point. But who would be so angry at Kirkpatrick that they're killing people for all these years?"

"No. I don't think whoever is doing this is angry at Kirkpatrick. I think whoever it is might be avenging Kirkpatrick."

"Avenging Kirkpatrick? Avenging what?"

"Jim Bishop is married to Catherine. He has an affair with Carol. They plot to kill Catherine. Bishop inherits all the money, only to have it taken away. Then, suddenly, he has enough money to have this house built in Floral Park. A couple years later, the fire kills his wife and daughter, and the neighbor who saved his life and his son is treated like dirt from Bishop, instead of the hero that everyone thought Kirkpatrick was. Let's examine Michael—everyone knew his family was rich, and they assumed the Kirkpatricks fared well through the Depression, because it was what Michael wanted them to think. Truth is, they didn't."

"Yes. But that brings us back to Bishop. It was his house that caught on fire. Not Kirkpatrick's."

"But what if Bishop's house was intentionally set on fire to collect on the insurance policy? Then Bishop and Kirkpatrick would have money again."

"Oh, Alex, I doubt that would be enough to secure all of their finances."

"True. But like I said before, what if Bishop had a life insurance policy on Carol? He did it once. Why not a second time?"

"I understand where you're going with this. But it doesn't make sense. Ester died in that fire, too. You'd think if he had known what was going to happen, he'd take measures to make sure his kids were okay. He did it when Catherine was hit by the car. We can't prove it, but we all know it's true."

"I'm working on it. Didn't say it was a perfect scenario."

"And what would all of that have to do with Kirkpatrick's death being avenged? He committed suicide," his mom questioned.

"I'm thinking that whoever was up to this must have seen how Kirkpatrick went from this great guy to this broken man. I still think that it's related to him. I just need to figure out how. And Ester's death could have been a tragic misjudgment that night."

"Well, we've got another week until the finale for this year. In the meantime, get your things ready. Both of you are going to school tomorrow. Margaret, your parents will kill me if they think I'm letting you stay here and screw off. And Alex—college."

"Yeah. I know, Ma."

<hr>

LYING next to Margaret in bed that night, Alex felt Mr. Nuncio's pain all over again. The thought of losing his love and not having her in his life was suffocating. Even if they never got out of the friend zone, the loss would crush him. The Nuncios had been together for almost seventy years. How do you go on from that?

His thoughts took him to a waking dream, one where he pulled Margaret a little closer and kissed the back of her neck. She rolled over and their eyes locked. He kissed her cheeks and then her lips. Caressing her hair away from her face, he kissed her again, this time with fire. She ran her fingers over his chest and navigated to his arms and then to the back of his hair, playing with it between her fingers. The warmth of her soul spilled out to his. Margaret stirred, bringing him back to reality. Gazing upon her one more time before closing his lids, his last thought before sleep was, *I need to find a way to tell her.*

When the alarm went off, neither Alex or Margaret were ready for a day of structure. Their lives were so different than the other kids at school. Some days were harder than others.

Margaret jumped in the shower while Alex opted to lay in bed for a few more minutes. Normally, a guy would say it was because the girl took longer. Alex couldn't use that excuse with her. Margaret was a minimalist, so he just had to admit that he was being lazy. However, resting in bed quickly turned into thinking. He rolled over and plopped his feet onto the cold wood floor. Grabbing a pair of socks, he sat down at the computer and turned it on. He hated his inability to remember something so simple like charging his iPad, and yet, he had done it again.

He pulled up the newspaper article about the Bishop fire. There was the interview of Michael Kirkpatrick that he wanted to read again. Just like Bobby had said, his father ran across the street and into the burning house to rescue Jim and Alister. Alex couldn't shake the burning in the pit of his stomach. Over and over, he read the paragraph while hearing Bobby's words in his mind. He was missing something—but what?

Margaret came barreling through the door and startled him.

"You better get in the shower. I forgot I have to be there early today." She towel-dried her hair.

"Why?"

"I'm in the group in charge of decorations for the dance. Remember?"

"Oh yeah. The one your mom made you do."

"Uh-huh. It's part of my whole *high school experience*. Such crap. But I knew I had to. This way, she leaves me alone for everything else—which is what she's good at, anyway. Honestly, she pays attention to the strangest things. I think it kills her that I'm not the cheerleader type that she was. Not that there's anything wrong with being a cheerleader. If that's what you like, then cheer away. It's just not me."

"Okay, okay. I'm going in the shower."

Margaret glanced over at the monitor. "Hey, what's this you were reading? The fire again?"

"Yeah. I don't know. Something is really gnawing at me. I can't shake the feeling I'm missing something that's right in front of me. That night makes sense on the surface, but it's like a veil. There's something lurking underneath."

Alex zipped to the bathroom.

The hot water poured over his body in a pulsing stream, the nozzle setting that Wilby loved. Alex, not so much. But he left it alone for his little brother. He stood for a few moments, just soaking in the warmth and letting his mind clear. After a quick wash, he stepped out to the large steamy mirror in front of him. He turned to his right to grab the towel off the rack and caught a flicker of an image in the mirror.

He stood motionless. In the reflection looking back at him was a small child—maybe about ten or twelve. She was wearing a white nightgown with delicate pink flowers in the pattern. Her face was sullen, and her eyes drooped with sadness. Alex reached toward her, but she disappeared as quickly as she had materialized. He hustled to finish drying and threw on his clothes before dashing to his bedroom.

Margaret had left the door open. She had her backpack open and was stuffing it with clothes.

"Are you ready?" *Zip.* The backpack was ready. Alex hesitated and then sat down on the bed.

"I think I just saw Ester."

"What?" Margaret sat beside him.

"In the bathroom mirror. Unless there's the ghost of another little girl in this house, I'm almost positive it was her."

"Did she say anything?" Margaret's eyes widened.

"No. She just looked so sad. I think she might know what's going on. I've got to tell Mom and Wilby."

"Okay. I'll start the car and warm it up. Please hurry."

"I will." Alex grabbed some books and then scrambled down the stairs. As Margaret was heading out the door, she asked him to grab something for her to eat on the way.

He told his mom about the ghost child, and she said she would tell his brother. Wilby was still in his room, getting ready for school. She handed him two breakfast bars from a box on the counter. He grinned and bolted out of the house.

THE FIRST CLASS Alex had was Calculus. He hated math, but for some reason, he was good at it—which oddly made him hate it even more. Having arrived early, he decided to hang out on the bleachers until the bell rang. The varsity football team was training, and the cheerleaders were across the field, working on their routines.

The morning air was invigorating. The rich, brilliant blue ceiling to the globe was dressed with a single puff of cloud, perfectly hung in the center of it all. He loved this weather. Your senses could almost conjure up the smell of apples and cinnamon—the scents that ushered in Halloween and stayed until the New Year. A landscape for some of the most beautiful colors in nature, it made his soul come alive.

Alex reminisced about elementary school and the windy days he spent standing on the stoop, eyes closed and the imagination of his body lifting into the breeze. Seeing the neighborhood below glide by was magical. When he was younger, he hated the push to define who he was. Kids could be ruthless with their cruel remarks. Floating away gave him separation and peace. The coach's whistle brought him back to the present, and his gaze followed the students soaking in the routine. Life was normal for them, but his Fall magic had been shaded with darkness.

The loud clang of the bell brought him to his first class, and fifty-five minutes of boredom. There was more action going on around the school than in any classroom that morning. Students were speculating on Mrs. Nuncio's death, and Alex could swear he heard the reference to aliens at least twice. The administrator announced there would be a vigil for all the victims on Wednesday evening. It would be on the football field at seven o'clock, and please bring a candle.

Alex thought it seemed odd. They didn't know the true story surrounding the deaths. Their assumption was that a madman was running around town, randomly killing people. *Wouldn't it be better to stay home at night? Strange.*

The halls felt extra crowded that morning. Maybe it was because he had missed so many days last week. You get used to being in your house and your own space. Going to school was a little like lock-up. Not state prison, but maybe more like juvenile hall; something he hoped he would never experience first-hand. His cousin stole a car last year on a stupid dare, and they hauled his ass off. It was frightening to see him go.

The last class of the morning was English. He enjoyed this one. Mrs. Fisher had a way of grabbing your brain and reeling it in. She had traveled abundantly when she was in her twenties, and her classes received the full benefit of all the countries she had visited. Some days, she would bring in souvenirs she had collected, and on other occasions, a slideshow of brilliant destinations. How she managed to fit their required course in all that glory amazed him. But it worked. He had an A in that class.

Margaret had another meeting regarding the dance during lunch, so Alex was on his own—by choice. Seeing the dead had its disadvantages at times, and it was easier to keep his social circle down to one. The aroma of warm dough, garlic, and mozzarella tickled his memory senses, and he could have a reprieve from the prison gates for forty-five happy minutes.

The mild temperature and golden rays of sun peeking out from the clouds were the perfect recipe for a pleasant walk. Not to say he wouldn't be thrilled to have his license and a car, but he liked the serenity it brought him. A light wind scattered the fallen dried leaves through the street. The rustling reminded him of when he was younger, and his parents were still together. Wilby was just a baby, and his mom would put him in the stroller in the front yard while Alex and his dad would rake the leaves. The best part was making numerous piles and jumping in. Raking took twice as long, but the laughs made up for it. They were a happy family back then. Times had changed. Alex knew it was something he had no control over, but sometimes the loss consumed him.

Deep in thought, Alex never noticed his mistake in directions. Having taken a right at the corner instead of a left, he found himself standing in the front of the bagel shop. A tingle feathered its way up his spine, and the goosebumps stood at attention on his exposed forearms—bagels it was. Alex stood at the counter, surveying the menu before ordering. An onion bagel with ham and swiss, a side of chips, and a Pepsi. *Margaret is going to kill me; she loves onion bagels.* He chuckled to himself.

Opting for a window seat, he retrieved his cell phone from the front pocket of his jeans. He recouped the article on the Geranium fire and read it over several times before the clerk brought his sandwich to the table. He then glanced up and recognized the smiling face. Or at least he thought he did. The clerk bore a strong resemblance to the picture of Michael Kirkpatrick; could almost have been his twin. Alex's goosebumps stood at attention.

"Hey, dude, are you okay?" The guy set down a basket containing his food.

"Yeah. I'm good. Why?" Alex couldn't stop staring.

"You got like a surprised look on your face."

"I was wondering if we might know each other. You look super familiar." Alex grabbed the packet of mustard and lifted the top half of the bagel.

"Nope. Don't think so." The clerk was firm.

"I go to C.A.T. Academy, maybe I saw you there?" He smeared the mustard, letting it drip over the side.

"Uh, don't think so. I graduated from there two years ago." The clerk smiled.

"Oh, you're kidding. Well, I don't think much has changed since then. I'm still trying to break out."

The two guys laughed, then the clerk extended his hand. "I'm Tom. Tom Kirkpatrick."

Heart pounding and head buzzing, Alex focused on Tom. "I'm sorry. Did you say—Kirkpatrick?"

"Yeah. Why?"

"Any relation to Bobby Kirkpatrick?"

"He's my uncle. Well, my great uncle. Why, do you know him?"

"I do; my mom went to school with his granddaughter. So, you've lived here like forever."

"Actually, we lived out in Long Beach. We just moved here about five years ago. It's nice. Kind of small, but cool. My nana is from Floral Park. Her family has lived here since way back. After my parents divorced, my nana asked us to come and live with her. She's getting older and needed the help. Listen, I've got to get back behind the counter. It was nice to meet you . . ."

"Alex McKenna."

"Oh! You're *that* guy." Tom grinned.

"What guy is that?" Alex knitted his brows.

"Sorry, nothing. See you, Alex."

Alex knew exactly what he was referring to. *Some things seem to take forever to change.* He shrugged it off and gobbled down his sandwich. He couldn't wait to tell Margaret what he'd found out.

All the way back to school, his brain toiled with the possibilities. He knew in his bones he was right about his hunch. Like pieces in a puzzle, he needed to connect everything together. Then the picture would be clear.

As he crossed the grassy knoll in front of the administrative offices, the bell rang. Margaret would have to wait.

The afternoon classes were less boring than his morning sessions, but equally disrupting to his latest case. He caught a familiar face out of the corner of his eye—Kyle. The buffoon was sitting two rows over from his left, and a row back. They exchanged glances, but the teen kept his distance since their last encounter. Alex abruptly stiffened; the air grew thick and heavy with despair. He bobbed his head to survey the room.

Someone was giving off a strong trail of emotions. His chest heaved in a breath and held it when he realized the source—the bully himself. Alex glared at Kyle, who had turned and was facing forward, staring at the dry-erase board. His eyes were fixed and trance-like. Alex's palms were clammy, and the back of his neck dripped with sweat. Sadness choked him, tightening in his throat and seizing his ability to speak. Tears pooled in his eyes, letting droplets fall to his desk. *What the hell is going on?* Furiously, Alex fought to push back the boy's outreach of emotional overload.

Using a breathing technique similar to Lamaze, he slowed his body's response to the overwhelming sense of sadness and focused his mind. Bringing his thoughts back to the murders and the case yet to be solved, he slowly severed the tie between him and Kyle. Eventually, his mind wandered.

Searching for a scenario that would enable him to speak with Greta, it became clear, the only way to get to her was through Tom. He watched the minutes count down on the clock above the teacher's desk. It was the last class—thank the gods. He texted Margaret to meet him at the bleachers. He wanted to tell her about what happened and go back to the bagel shop. Hopefully, Tom was still working.

Ching-a-ling, the bell went off. Alex barely noticed any of the other students as he hastily made his way to the bleachers. Margaret was already there. He came up from behind and put his arms on top of her shoulders. Startled, she turned around and slapped his arm.

"Hey, what's that for?"

"You don't go sneaking up on a girl, especially after the last few weeks." She frowned.

"My apologies; you're right." Alex bowed his head.

"So, what's up? Why are we meeting here?"

Alex explained the chance encounter with Tom and the Kirkpatrick ancestry. She agreed it was underhanded to use Tom to get to Greta, but necessary.

When they got to the bagel shop, Tom had already left for the day. Disappointed, Alex thought about leaving a note for him, but changed his mind. As they walked back to the car, he got a chill. Daylight was fading.

On the way home, Alex got a call from his mom, asking if they'd stop and pick up Wilby from school because she was running a little late at work.

Margaret turned the car around and headed toward Our Lady of Victory Catholic School. Wilby was having a hard time with the constraints of structured religion. His mom wanted him in Catholic School for the smaller classes and better teacher/student ratio, but Wilby said he didn't see the point. He had enough spiritual interaction with his family, so why go and hear more junk in class? Besides, given his own mother's stance on the church, it never made any sense to him why she demanded he'd go. When they got there, the boy was waiting out in front of the school.

They pulled up to the curb and he hopped into the back seat. "Hey, buddy. How was your day?" Alex cracked the window.

"It was alright." Wilby sunk a little lower in his seat. "Alex, can I ask you something?"

"Sure. What's up?"

"Do you think I'm ever gonna be like you?" Alex exchanged glances with Margaret.

"I'm not sure. Why are you asking? Did something happen?"

"Nah. I was just thinking about it last night. I could have helped." Wilby laid his head against the window.

"Listen, whether it does or doesn't, you help. You're the one who pointed out the shadiness of Michael Kirkpatrick's story. Don't think for a second you're not a big part of all of this and the family."

Wilby curled half of his mouth in an attempt to smile, but Alex could see the anguish in his eyes. He knew his little brother wanted to be able to see and hear what he did—the lost spirits. The ones who really needed help.

"Hey, you up for hot chocolate before heading home?" Alex stretched his arm to the back seat and nudged Wilby's knee. "Because I know I could really use a hot caramel macchiato right about now."

Wilby had a full smile this time.

"Works every time," Alex whispered to Margaret. "Do you mind?"

Margaret knitted her brows in that *what are you, crazy?* look. She then turned on her left signal and they were are on their way.

They pulled up to the drive-through and placed their order. The cashier recognized Margaret from biology class, and they chit- chatted for a moment before she gave them their drinks. Alex reached back and handed his little brother the steamy cup of sugary goodness.

"Alex, can I ask you something else?" Wilby blew on the hot liquid.

"What's up?"

"Do you think the spirit in our house knows what it's doing?" He took a cautious sip.

"What do you mean?" Alex turned around to face the back seat.

"Well, you said that someone is sort of controlling it. Right?"

"Maybe not so much controlling but calling on it. The spirit is already full of rage. Someone is just using that anger for their own benefit. Keeping it here for what they need done."

"But how would they know the spirit was already angry?"

Alex paused. "That's a freaking good question. My guess is they knew the circumstances of the death and thought it would be angry enough to have some unfinished business here."

"Huh. That sucks."

Alex laughed. "Yeah, it does."

"Who do you think the spirit is?" Wilby took another sip.

"I'm pretty sure it's one of two women who were married to Jim Bishop. He's the guy who had our house built. Either Carol or Catherine, Ester's mom. I just need to figure out which one. And that should help us find out who the puppet master is."

"Okay." Wilby went back to enjoying his treat.

When they got home, the younger McKenna retreated to his room with a need to play his favorite video game.

Plopping down on the overstuffed tan couch, Alex grabbed his iPad off the charger. Finally, he remembered to plug it in. He Googled Greta Kirkpatrick. She lived only three blocks away from them. It didn't surprise him. Floral Park was not exactly a huge place. Cozy, yes. But definitely not big city.

Margaret was scrolling through Instagram on her phone. "You want to take a walk when you're done with your coffee?"

"A walk alone with you? Sounds dangerous." Margaret batted her eyes. "Where you wanna go?"

"Greta Kirkpatrick's house. She's three blocks away."

"Are you fucking kidding me?" Margaret stood up.

"Nope." Alex slipped his phone in his pocket.

"Forget waiting. I'll bring my coffee with me.'

Alex got up and shouted from the bottom of the staircase.

"Wilby, you want to go for a walk?"

"I'm playing my new game, so no."

"If you hear anything strange, you leave the house. I mean it. No investigating with this one. You get out and wait for us on the stoop. Besides, Mom will be home soon, and then it'll be homework."

"I get it, I get it."

"We won't be long."

"I don't know, Alex; maybe we shouldn't leave him alone. You know what your mom said." Margaret furrowed her brow.

"We're only gonna be gone a few minutes."

Alex grabbed his hoodie from the coat closet and clutched his coffee. The two set out like tourists gleaming with excitement; a benign act for an ominous mission.

The silence between them was comfortable. There was no need for words—they understood each other enough to be beyond that. Rounding the corner, Greta's 1928 red brick two-story caught Alex's eye. It was one of the few in Floral Park without a colonial facade. Puffy white smoke circled the rooftop, trailing into the atmosphere in slow curly Q's.

"It looks sort of picturesque," Alex commented.

"What are we looking for?" Margaret swigged her coffee.

"Honestly? Nothing in particular. Maybe a glance of Greta. I don't want to go up to the door; that just puts us in more danger if she has anything to do with this."

"Huh. More dangerous than being frozen to death in your house?"

"Again, with the smart-ass." Margaret rolled her eyes.

"Wait. There's an elderly woman stepping out of the front door. Looks like she's picking up the door mat. I can't make out her face."

"Let me see . . . If she would just turn a little—nope."

The woman rolled up the gray mat and brought it into the house.

"This was sort of a bust. The only thing we know is she has brown hair." Alex frowned. "Moving forward, the next step is to get to know Tom."

When they stopped at the corner to his house, Alex immediately shot his eyes toward the stoop. No Wilby. He let out a sigh of relief. As he put the key into the lock, he could hear his mom on the phone.

Margaret hugged him and got into her car to go home. She had been so scarce lately, she thought it was wise to make an appearance.

Walking in, he caught the tail end of a phone conversation.

"No, Gram. No. Really. Everything is fine. Alex and I have it handled over here. Lots of salt in the house. Yes—yes, I'll call if anything changes."

His mom tossed the phone on the couch.

"There you are. How come you left Wilby alone?"

"Ma, we were only gone a few minutes."

"It doesn't matter, Alex. That was reckless."

"You're right. Sorry. No more leaving him."

"That was Gram." His mom sat down.

"Is everything okay with her?"

"Oh, yeah. She was worried about us. She's having a little harder time with the spell than she thought, but she says it's almost done. How are you doing? Okay?"

"I'm good. I found out that Greta Kirkpatrick, Bobby's sister, is living only three blocks away."

"You're kidding me. How'd you find out?" Alex told her about his encounter with Tom.

"Greta is here. You know what that means, right?"

"She is at the top of the list," Alex surmised.

"The more interesting question is why did Bobby leave that important bit of information out?"

"Margaret and I were discussing that very same thing. Unless he knows more about this than he was telling us. We need to talk to him."

"I'd rather get this done sooner rather than later. Too much shit circling our family; we need to get to the bottom of this."

"I'm gonna call Margaret and see when she can get away. I know she just left, but I think if we do this without her, she'll kill me."

"Also, don't forget. Friday is your doctor's appointment. I'll pick you up after I get Wilby from school. It's at four o'clock, and we'll be cutting it close, so be ready. What about your birthday dinner?"

"Ma, this week is crucial. Can't we reschedule the doc appointment? At least until after Halloween."

"Nope. You know he needs to monitor your hormones.

He's got your latest bloodwork results, and I want to know what your levels are. Are you sure you're not having any nausea or other issues?"

"I'm good. I think I'd rather celebrate my birthday next week, though. I don't have the head for it right now."

"Okay. I get it. Call Margaret; we can pick her up if she's going. I'm not calling Bobby, I don't want to give him time to think."

"Margaret will drive over. I know her. This way, she can leave later when she wants to without bothering you. She hates being carted around."

Alex grabbed the phone from his back pocket and called Margaret.

"Alex, is everything okay?" Her tone was anxious.

"Everyone's fine. We're taking a drive to Bobby's, and I wanted to know . . ."

"I'll be over in ten minutes."

"What about your parents?"

"They're not even here. When I got home, there was a note on the fridge. They're off to some dinner party. Believe me, I won't be missed." Margaret sounded disgusted.

"I'd miss you," Alex spoke softly. Margaret had already hung up.

When Margaret got to Geranium, they all piled into Gina's SUV. Wilby sat up front, and Alex and Margaret were in the back seats. Alex brought his iPad with him so he could go over the article on the fire again. Maybe something would come to him before they got to Bobby's house. *Mr. Kirkpatrick said he saw flames and smoke coming from the Bishops' bedroom window. He immediately ran out of the house to go help. He could hear the sirens by the time he reached the house.*

"Whatcha doin?" Margaret laid her head back on the seat

and reached her hand out. Alex didn't notice; he was completely absorbed.

"This rendition of what happened the night of the fire by Michael Kirkpatrick bugs me."

Margaret leaned in. "Read it to me."

Alex read it over again for what seemed like the hundredth time.

"He said he saw smoke and flames from the parents' bedroom window?" Margaret's brows knitted.

"Yeah. Why?"

"He lied."

"How do you know?"

"Think about it, Alex. If Michael Kirkpatrick was in his house, he couldn't see the front of the Bishops'—your house. It would be impossible. His house is in direct line with the side and backyard of your house."

"Shit. You're right." Alex's eyes widened.

"And as for the sirens, didn't the article state they were late because of the weather?"

"Yup."

"Well, according to the fire chief, by the time they got there, Kirkpatrick had already gotten Mr. Bishop and Alister out and they were all on the front lawn." Margaret lifted her head up.

"Ahh. So he couldn't have heard the fire truck because he hadn't started his rescue attempt. No way could he have gone into the smoke-filled house, gotten Bishop and then Alister, and made it back out before the fire engine arrived."

"He never heard the sirens because they weren't there yet. He knew about the fire before it started." Margaret had a sheepish grin on her face.

"Damn, you're good."

"I know."

Alex played the scenario in his head. *Michael Kirkpatrick*

knew the fire was starting. He must have had someone do it for him. But why run over and rescue the family? Did he have a change of heart? Or was that planned, too? If so, then Jim Bishop was definitely in on it. Was it an oversight that Carol and Ester died? Alex still couldn't believe that as vicious as Jim must have been, he would murder his own daughter. It didn't add up to him. If Ester's death was an accident, maybe Carol's wasn't. Maybe she was the focus all along, like he thought. His theory about killing her for insurance money seemed to grow stronger. Now he had to see if he could find a copy of the policy.

"Ma, when we get there, we need to see if Bobby knows anything about a life insurance policy for Carol."

"You're thinking the murder theory again?"

"I am. But we need something more to prove any of this."

"Do you think the spirit is a pissed-off Carol?" His mom glanced at the rear-view mirror.

"I'm not too sure about that, either. I need to go and see Alister Bishop again."

"Okay. Let's concentrate on Bobby right now. You and Margaret can talk to Alister tomorrow after school. You know we still need to figure out how all these families are connected."

"I know. I'm hoping Bobby can shed some light on that." Alex shook his right leg.

When they pulled up to Bobby's, the outside was illuminated by a lone porch light. Alex got out and walked up to the front window and peered inside. He could see Bobby through the sheer drapes. He was sitting in a recliner with the television on and the sound down low, a beer in his hand. The rest of the first floor looked dark from what he could tell. Alex waved for them to come over as he walked up the four brick steps to the front door. He tried the bell first, but it was stuck. He pounded the door with a firm fist. Heavy footsteps creaking on a wood floor gave away Bobby's location before his gruff voice resonated from the other side of the door. Alex identified himself and heard the lock click.

"Alex. What are you . . .? What are all of you doing here?"

"Bobby, it's urgent. We really need to talk with you. Can we come in?"

Hesitantly, Bobby opened the door and moved aside so they could all enter. Wilby plopped down on the couch, and Gina sat next to him and whispered for him to keep quiet. He frowned but obeyed.

Alex was the first to speak.

"We're sorry for coming here without a call, but it's really important. I don't know if you saw the news, but Mrs. Nuncio was murdered yesterday in her home. You know, your old house?"

"Yeah. I'm familiar with what happened to Rose."

"We think her murder was connected to the others." Alex observed Bobby tapping his leg nervously, and although it was cold in the room, he had sweat beading up on his forehead.

"Listen, kid. I've told you, all of you, everything I know. I said things I shouldn't because I thought it might help. I even broke a promise to my father. What more do you want from me?"

"I want it all, Bobby," Alex replied firmly. Alex leaned forward and so did Gina.

"We know you're holding back. Your father's story about that night is full of lies. You know it and you know the truth. Tell us," Alex's mom demanded.

"Get the hell out of my house before I call the police. Get out now!" Bobby stood up. His fists clenched at his side, and his dark eyes glared with anger. Alex knew if they left right then, they'd never get a chance to talk to him again. He wasn't going to let them back into his home anytime soon. Trying to salvage the discussion, he softened his approach.

"Bobby, please. People we all know are dying. That's why we came to you to begin with. Let's just calm down and see if we can't get some answers together."

Bobby turned away, and Alex could see something caught his eye. He followed Bobby's stare to an old picture on the side table.

"Who's that, Bobby?" Alex asked calmly.

"That's me and my three sisters when we were kids." Bobby stood for a moment, seemingly locked in the memory, and then sat down. Alex took a breath and relaxed. He had him for a little while longer.

"Marilyn Monroe." Alex's mom smiled.

"Huh?" Alex was confused.

"Your mom noticed my sister Greta's beauty mark. Marilyn had the same kind of mark on her face. Our mother used to tease her about that. Calling Greta "Miss Hollywood.'"

"Your sisters were all so pretty," Gina said warmly.

"Thank you." Bobby gazed at the photo again.

"I met Tom at the bagel place. We started talking, and one thing led to another. I had no idea he worked there. I don't want to upset you, Bobby. But I'm worried about Tom." Alex used his words carefully.

"Worried? Why?"

"Well, it seems whatever this thing is that's killing everyone is targeting families who have a long history in Floral Park."

"Yea, but Tom wasn't born here. He just moved here a few years ago."

"Yes. That's true. But your family has been here for a long time. You and Greta were born in Floral Park. Right?"

"Yes."

"We've discovered that this dark spirit extends its deliverance of death to descendants. It doesn't have to be the person directly connected. Think about it. Almost everyone from the era when this started are gone by now. I think Rose Nuncio was the eldest. The rest of the victims were in their fifties or sixties. They wouldn't even have been born until after the fire. The fact that you're not born in Floral Park doesn't matter. What does matter is who you're related to."

"He's not in any danger. Can we just leave it at that?"

"No. We can't. Please, just tell us. Is Greta the one responsible for this?"

"Don't be silly. How could Greta do any of this? Why?" Bobby tapped his foot on the floor.

Alex glanced over at his mom and widened his eyes. She caught on. Her turn to ask questions.

"Bobby, it must have been hard for you to tell this to Alex and to us. I know how hard it is when a parent confides in you. When I was a little girl, my grandmother told me she knew the day she would pass on. I was horrified. She told me never to tell my father because he wouldn't be able to deal with it, but she knew I could. She said I was strong like her. So, for all these years, I've known the date, and have had to live with it. I've never told another a soul because I wanted to honor the promise I made. But I gotta tell you, it's damn hard." His mom's voice quaked.

Alex could see the pain painted on Bobby's face. He turned to his mom. She looked away.

Each one of them was forced to carry a burden. A pain that wasn't theirs to hold, but they did anyway.

Bobby took a deep breath and sat back in his chair before blurting out everything he knew.

ESTER SAT on her bed with the door to her room closed. She didn't want Carol accidentally hearing their conversation. Ester knew Carol wouldn't be able to see her mom—only she could do that. At least, that's how it used to be. Apparently now, so can Alister. She wasn't sure she was too happy about that latest development. He had Carol. She was his mom. He didn't need to be sharing hers.

Besides, Carol probably wouldn't care if Ester dropped dead right on the spot. It might even make her happy. Then she could have Daddy and her precious Alister, and they'd be the perfect little family. She did feel sorry for her little brother, though. He was good as brothers go, and he only irritated her occasionally. Having to go through life with Carol as his mom was going to be a rough road. She was nuttier than a fruitcake, or at least that's what her grandma—her *real* grandma— would say.

She sat on her bed, waiting patiently for her to show, but she didn't. This was their time together. They had been doing this every day for the past six years. Ester was not only upset, she was worried. Nothing would keep her from being with her daughter before. She glanced at the small antique clock on her nightstand. It was four o'clock. She loved that clock. When her mother died, her dad gave it to her. He knew she always adored it. The deep scallops along the edges of the sterling silver made her think of the nineteenth century—her mother's favorite era, and she passed that love down to her daughter.

Ester owned every trinket she could get her hands on that was forged in the eighteen hundreds, and her dad indulged her. She figured he must have felt sad for her—watching her mother get hit and then losing her. He didn't know the truth. She never really went away.

ALEX SAT ALONE in the dark room, cocooned in the familiarity of his own bed. Margaret had gone home, and Wilby and his mom were sleeping. Bobby's words were spinning around in his head like a tornado. He slid down between the sheets and pulled up the comforter. Staring up at the ceiling, he tried to envision the details of that night as told by Bobby Kirkpatrick.

Michael Kirkpatrick had confessed everything to his wife, who in turn told her son, Bobby, many years later. The guilt had eaten at Michael's soul, and he needed to tell someone. She had no idea her husband was about to take his own life.

By all accounts, Jim and Carol Bishop were the perfect couple. They seemed to have it all. They were deeply in love, had a beautiful family, and financially, they seemed to be on the mend. But all of that was a facade. In truth, their love spawned from a heartless murder, and their finances were drowning them. As for the family, Ester favored her mother in looks, and that infuriated Carol. She was horribly mean to the little girl and managed to keep that side of herself from Jim, reserving it for when he was at work.

Bishop would lose everything if he didn't do something fast. Included in that loss was the money that Michael Kirkpatrick had invested in his company. But it went beyond the two men. There were five other gentlemen who were indirectly involved. Bobby couldn't remember their names. Alex assumed they were all in some way related to the recent victims.

The men were part of a finance club. They would meet once a week and discuss investment opportunities and business partnerships that would be beneficial. When Bishop was at his lowest, he deceived the group to convince them to invest in his company. Michael gave them the largest amount, but each man had put some of their dwindling savings into their firm. What no one knew was that Jim Bishop had a very bad gambling problem—something he had acquired a taste for when he lived in the city with Catherine. That was the reason for killing her. He wanted the money because he was greedy, yes, but he also owed a large amount to some dangerous, underground poker bosses.

Kirkpatrick found out that all the money he and the other men had given Bishop went to feeding his gambling appetite. After several months of not seeing any returns on their investment, they pressured Bishop to reveal the financial books. He collapsed under the pressure and told them the truth. Kirkpatrick lost it. He had always had wealth, and now he was about to be as poor as a beggar on the street. He threatened Bishop physically, and that laid the groundwork for their plan.

Jim Bishop had been growing tired of Carol's insanity. It had gotten worse over the past year, and he was just waiting for the day she snapped. Besides, he didn't need her. Once the plan went through, he'd have enough money to hire a nanny for the kids. He could start a new company on his own. No more investors. He could get Kirkpatrick off his back permanently. They plotted the entire gruesome murder together, down to the last detail.

At first, Kirkpatrick didn't like the idea of doing away with Carol. Yeah, she was a loon, but this was cruel—until he found out the amount of the life insurance policy that Bishop had taken out on her. He would collect one million dollars if she died from an accident. An accident like a fire.

Bishop knew there would be damage to the home, but he had stayed friendly with Jake Warner—the foreman on the original build. He knew Jake was a good man. He'd probably feel sorry for him and do the rebuild for practically nothing. They'd keep the fire to the second story. The damage to the bedrooms would keep the ground floor livable for the time it took to repair. Bishop would call the fire department a few minutes before the fire was set. Kirkpatrick knew someone who could set the fire and make it look like an electrical issue. They left a small lamp on in the master bedroom at night.

Carol hated sleeping in complete darkness. He could go in after she was asleep, set the fire, and make it seem like the light had shorted out. Bishop would leave the door to the kitchen open. It was concealed by the hedges in the backyard, so nobody would be the wiser when the hired arsonist went inside.

They orchestrated the whole thing, leaving zero room for error. Or so they thought. Kirkpatrick watched the clock that night. He peered out the window to make sure he saw his acquaintance slip through the hedges to the back yard. He waited the allotted time, then yelled to his wife to call the fire department. The two men thought it would be more convincing if there was more than one call. Then he grabbed his coat, which he had conveniently left hanging on the doorknob of the entryway closet. He ran across the street and waited a few moments for Bishop to emerge with the children. But he didn't.

Panicked, he paced on the front lawn until he heard screams. He tried barreling into the front door, but it wouldn't budge. That's when he busted the glass on one of the French doors on the side of the house. Once he was in, he saw Bishop and Alister unconscious on the living room floor. The first floor was filled with smoke, and he could see the orange hue of flames peeking around the landing of the staircase that led to the bedrooms.

He picked up Alister first and brought him outside, using the front door this time. He then ran back in for Bishop. This was a much harder task, because he was a full-grown man. Kirkpatrick got a firm grip on his wrists and dragged him through the wall of smoke and onto the safety of the lawn. Alister had started coughing, and Kirkpatrick let out a sigh of relief. He then shook Bishop until he became conscious.

In a frenzy, Bishop started calling out to Ester. He told Kirkpatrick she was upstairs. Carol had locked the two of them in the attic. Kirkpatrick took his shirt off and wrapped it around his mouth and nose, trying to lay a barrier between his breath and the smoke before running back in. By then, the orange glow had progressed to an inferno. Flames engulfed the upper part of the staircase and created an impenetrable wall of heat. He ran back out.

Hearing the sirens of the fire engine in the distance, he ran to the right side of the house near the broken French door. There was a tall pine tree that ran alongside Alister's bedroom window. He climbed it to the second story. He stepped out onto the sloping roof and held onto the sweeping branches until he reached the window. He hoped Alister's bedroom was more accessible because it was down the hall and on the opposite side of the master, where the fire originated. Reaching the window, he crawled through. The heat smacked him in the face like a brick wall, and the smoke pumped into his lungs, stealing the air from his body. He tried frantically to get to the doorway and access the hall, but it was too much, and he collapsed.

He yelled out to Ester—nothing. Moments later, an ear-splitting scream that nearly stopped his heart directed his attention toward the doorway. Through the barrier of smoke, Kirkpatrick saw a disfigured woman floating toward him. At first, he thought it was his eyes playing tricks, but the closer it came, the more apparent that whatever this was, it wasn't Ester, and he needed to get the hell out of there.

Struggling to find balance, he clutched the windowsill. He pulled up his torso and swung his right leg over and onto the roof. He then slid his left leg out and steadied himself on the shingles by holding onto one of the extending branches of the pine tree. A glance back at the open window revealed the horrible thing hovering in the center of Alister's room. Slowly, he shimmied down the tree and wobbled to the front of the house, where he collapsed next to Bishop. By then, the fire department had arrived and praised Kirkpatrick for being a hero. He had saved Alister and Jim Bishop.

Bobby said his father never told Bishop about the thing in Alister's room. He thought it probably was a delusion from all the smoke he had inhaled. Kirkpatrick also said he never found out what exactly happened in that house that night. Why Ester was with Carol, or even how Carol had figured it out. His guy had lit the fire according to plan and gotten out. Bishop refused to talk about anything having to do with their deaths. The little girl's remains were found burned beyond recognition in the corner of the attic. Carol's fate was equally horrific. She had jumped out of the attic window, completely engulfed in flames, and landed on the cement walkway in front of the house. The fireman who witnessed it had to be put on leave. They had no idea how she was able to leap that far from the house.

Shortly after confessing to his wife, Michael Kirkpatrick took his own life.

For Bobby Kirkpatrick, the grief of losing his father and learning that the older man was responsible for the death of poor little Ester and Carol tortured him.

When he had finished his story, Alex asked Bobby if Greta knew. He issued a resounding no. He promised his mother he would never tell either of his sisters this horrid tale. It would reveal a side of their father they did not need to know.

Alex's mind focused on Catherine. She was the one there that night. He just felt it. He imagined her witnessing the death of her child, helpless to do anything to stop it. He needed to know more about that night—the parts that Jim Bishop refused to talk about. This is what would lead him to the identity of the spirit. He knew it. Up until now, he was leaning toward the insane Carol. But after hearing the events unfold and guessing the agony Catherine must have endured that night, it would be enough to make any mother lose their mind.

Alex shivered. He briskly rubbed his arms—goosebumps. Sitting straight up in bed, he scanned the room and saw a billowy shadow move across the floor. He wanted to yell out to his mom, but he couldn't. Something was constricting his voice. He leaped out of bed and reached for a small plastic jar containing holy water. He would occasionally go to the church and refill it. You never know when it would come in handy.

Mouthing a short protection prayer, he splashed the holy water on the shadow and then around his room. His heart was beating so fast, he swore he could feel it hit the walls of his chest. He reached for the door, but he was thrust backwards onto the bed. Again, he stood up and mustered all his strength.

He said the prayer again and again: *Evil spirit, I bind you in the Name of Jesus Christ, and command you to go to the foot of the cross.* He splashed the shadow repeatedly. Feeling his throat relax, the words became audible. With a loud voice, he reiterated the prayer once more, and it was gone.

TOM THE INNOCENT

Alex woke up with his iPad laying on his chest. He had dozed off while attempting to find information on the fifth man. He searched through names of residents in Floral Park at the time of the fire—none of them correlated to present day.

It was Tuesday, and they knew so much more than they did yesterday, but it was not enough. It still gnawed at him how this spirit was able to reside in the same house as him and his mom and they never knew it. Headaches, okay, but he should have known. That question was burning a hole in his stomach, and he abruptly jumped out of bed and ran to the bathroom to vomit. He had hoped his mom hadn't heard him; she would assume it was the shots. He didn't need to pile on more shit. He was already dealing with enough.

"Alex, is that you? You up?" his mom called out. The echo of her voice meant she was downstairs. "Gram's on the phone for you."

Huh. Why didn't she call my cell? "Okay. I'll be right down!"

He brushed his teeth and threw some cold water on his

face before grabbing his hoodie and some socks. The wood floors were really nice, but cold in the fall and winter. He didn't have a first period that day, so he could take a little more time in the morning. As he barreled down the stairs, he nearly slipped.

"Hey, there you are." His mom handed him a cup of coffee as he entered the kitchen. "Here. Talk to Gram." She handed him the land line. "But be quick, or you'll miss the bus."

"I don't have a first period today. I'll ride my bike. Why didn't Gram just call my cell?"

"Because I called her. Oh, and if you don't go in until a little later, I can drop you off on my way to work. I've got a conference call I need to take before going in."

His mom had turned a portion of her bedroom into a makeshift office with a desk in the corner. She used the land line strictly for work purposes. The real estate business was more than a full-time job.

"I'll be upstairs," she said.

Alex sat at the table. "Hi, Gram. What's up?"

"I was telling your mom when she called that I was just about to call you. Bonzetta, I found out why we can't sense this spirit."

Alex's heart quickened. Finally, an answer.

"I have a friend who I consult sometimes. She's from a small village in Naples. She tells me this is very rare, but it can happen. It's not the spirit. It's the person casting the spell. She —or he—creates a veil."

"That's just great, Gram. We're flying blind." Exasperation dripped from his words.

"No. There is good news. Once it has been revealed, the spell no longer works on us. I think, after the other day, when you and your mom had the first encounter, you broke its cloak of anonymity. Didn't you tell me the second time you saw the spirit that you had the goosebumps all over your arms?'

"Yes. I didn't put it together. But—yes! I could feel its presence, and so did Mom. Did Mom tell you what Bobby Kirkpatrick told us?" Alex switched to speaker.

"Yes, she filled me in on everything."

"Gram, do you have an opinion on who you think this spirit is?"

"I do. But without certainty, I'll wait. And so should you. Remember what your mother said. No doing anything stupid. Promise me, Bonzetta."

"I promise." Alex rolled his eyes.

"Good. Your banishing spell will be done tomorrow. In the meantime, do not stir up any unwanted house guests."

"Too late." Alex smirked. "You know what I mean."

"Yes."

Alex set the phone down on the table and gazed out into the backyard. He pictured the steps of the unknown fire starter, creeping through the hedges, and then to the porch, and finally in through the back door. Chills went up Alex's back, and he crossed his arms to seal in the heat. He knew the promises he had made to his mom and his gram, but there was no time for careful. He needed to do something drastic. And he needed to do it now.

After breakfast, he took a quick shower and was ready when his mom needed to leave. They briefly discussed his conversation with their gram before arriving at school. Standing in front of the gates to hell, Alex had an overwhelming sense that he should leave. His instincts told him to go back to the bagel shop and Tom Kirkpatrick. He knew he was risking his mom's wrath, but he had to follow his know. He texted Margaret so she wouldn't worry, but before he could make it halfway down the block, she pulled up beside him in her car.

"Go back to school. I'm not going to be the cause of you getting busted," he said, keeping a brisk pace.

"Alex McKenna! Get it in the goddamned car. You're not making me do anything. This is all me. I can't sit still through another class after all the crap yesterday."

Alex knew exactly how she felt. He hopped into the car.

"You know I can't wait to get my license and then a car. I'm gonna do all the driving then."

Margaret laughed. "Yeah, sure you are."

Driving was *her* thing. He saw stuff, encountered the other side, and felt when something was gonna happen. Margaret was the unofficial Joey Logano. He's the youngest NASCAR driver to win the Daytona 500 at the ripe old age of nineteen in 2015, and Margaret was a huge fan.

Alex pleaded silently to the universe when they pulled up to the bagel shop. He felt with no uncertainty that he needed to be here and hoped that fate was cooperating. Approaching the glass doors to the shop, he saw Tom behind the counter. *Thank you, gods!* he whispered to himself.

Tom flashed a wide grin and nodded his head toward the table by the window. They took a seat and eyed the menu behind the counter.

Alex leaned into Margaret. "What are you gonna order?"

"I'm having peanut butter and jelly on a raisin bagel." Margaret smiled.

"A woman after my own heart. Let's make that two. Coffee?" Alex took her hand.

"What the hell kind of question is that?"

"Yeah, I know. I heard the words but couldn't believe they were coming out of my mouth."

When Tom was finished with his customer, he greeted them.

"Hey, Alex. How's everything?" Tom said cheerily.

"Great. Tom, this is my friend, Margaret."

"Nice to meet you. So, what do you two want to order?"

"We'll have the P&J on a raisin bagel and two coffees, please."

"I'll be right back."

Tom returned a few minutes later with their food, and Alex offered him a seat.

"I'm not supposed to, but what the hell. No one's here." Tom shrugged his shoulders.

After a few minutes of unimportant chatter, Alex's patience was wearing thin. The words slipped from his lips.

"Tom, there was a reason we stopped by today. I needed to talk to you."

"Sure. What's up?"

"I don't have much time, so I'm going to get right to it."

Margaret shot him a wide-eyed, open-mouthed look. He knew what she was thinking, but they didn't have the luxury of tiptoeing into this. He decided the upfront approach, though risky, was the best way.

"I'm going to tell you a story. It'll probably sound unbelievable, maybe even ridiculous, and definitely crazy. But it's not. It's real. Tom, do you believe in ghosts?"

"Uh. I don't know. Maybe." Tom squirmed in his seat.

"There's something about me you don't know . . ."

Alex explained briefly about his *spidey sense,* using Margaret's terminology. After he knew he had Tom interested, he told him the real reason why he needed to speak to him. He gave as much information as he could without completely spilling everything. He felt too much might send his brain into overload.

When he was done with the story, he sat back and waited for a reaction. It was so quiet, it was unnerving.

Tom got up and went behind the counter and out of sight for a few moments. When he emerged, he was holding a large coffee.

"I'm not supposed to drink coffee unless I'm on break. I'm thinking it's break time."

Alex crossed his arms and rested them on the table. "You okay, Tom?"

"Yeah. Just a lot to take in."

"I know. I'm sorry." Alex sat back.

"I mean, when you came in the shop the other day and introduced yourself, I knew who you were right away. People talk, you know. But I had no idea how extreme you were. I mean, I thought maybe you were like one of those people who knew a plane was gonna crash before it did. But you're telling me you actually see people?"

"Wait, is that what you meant when you said I was *that guy* the other day?"

"Sure. What did you think I meant?"

"Nothing. Never mind." Alex grinned to himself.

"So, what are you asking me to do, Alex? You want me to spy on my nana? Or maybe just ask her if she's a heartless murderer? Because that's sort of what it sounds like. She couldn't do any of those things you're accusing her of. No way."

"I'm not saying it's her for sure. But if you're so sure, then help us eliminate her as a suspect."

"Forget it." Tom's face grew red.

"We could really use your help—please."

"We're done, Alex." Tom got up and went to the back room.

Margaret grabbed hold of Alex's hand. "Come on. I think we need to leave."

"I really saw that working out much better in my head." Alex shook his head.

"Not everyone's ready for Alex McKenna."

"I guess not."

Since the meeting with Tom was a bust, they decided to

switch their focus to the fifth and unknown family. This time, they were going to the library. Alex wasn't sure what to look for, but he wasn't finding anything online.

The lush topiary, leading up to the place where dreams were endless, was a testament to the original owner of the land that was now Floral Park. A lover of animals, the bushes were sculptured into the creatures that inhabited the neighborhood. Squirrels, birds, chipmunks, cats, and dogs. They all greeted you along the cobblestone pathway to the entrance.

Opening the door of the large brick building, Alex felt a shower of warmth melt over his body. They were stepping into the house of books. He took in the smell of paper, bindings, and endless possibilities. He loved the library. Maybe he was old fashioned, or maybe just an old soul for his seventeen years, but he felt at home here. Sure, having a computer, smart phone, and iPad were convenient, but there was nothing like holding a book in your hands. Touching the same pages of those countless hands who had held it before. Sometimes he would get pictures of people or events in his mind. Like a slideshow. Knowing what they felt made him love the place more. The experiences he could have through their imprinted emotions brought the pages to life—an added bonus, and sometimes sadness. The spirits also used the building as a connection to life that had passed them by.

Hazel would stand and greet everyone who came in, though of course they couldn't see her.

"Good afternoon, Mr. McKenna."

"Hello, Hazel."

The short, round, gray-haired woman had passed away while sitting at the information desk in the library over fifty years ago. She loved the place so much, she wouldn't leave.

"Can I help you and your friend find a book?"

"We're looking more for articles on the history of Floral Park and its residents."

"That would have to be on film." The woman pointed to a group of small rooms. "If it's here, that's where it will be."

"Thanks, Hazel."

"Yeah, thanks, Hazel." Margaret looked around at the empty space.

"What are you doing?" Alex looked puzzled.

"Just being polite." Margaret grinned.

Alex decided to start the search with the records of the town instead of focusing on Bishop. The twosome thought it would be better to split up and expand the search. They settled in after making several selections from various years from 1920 to 1935. Alex wanted to search a few years after the fire as well, hoping it might reveal a morsel of information to feed their hunger.

"I know we're looking for this fifth family, but it could be anybody." Margaret frowned.

"Yeah, but I'm getting this feeling that when we see him, we'll know."

"Huh. That's encouraging."

"Sarcasm?"

"No, really. That's encouraging. You know I trust your instincts."

"Never mind, just frustrated. Sorry to direct it toward you."

"Look how far we've come. Look what you've uncovered. Are you fucking kidding me?"

"Okay . . . okay. Let's just get back to the search." His skin singed from an irritated flush.

He rubbed his burning eyes; hours had passed with no more intel than when they started. He was exhausted and figured Margaret probably felt the same way. He suggested they break away for a while and grab a sandwich. She was up and, on the move, before he got the last word out.

Margaret sat with her hands on the wheel. "Where to? Any ideas?"

A picture of the local diner popped into his mind. "Let's go to the diner on Jericho Turnpike."

"Where did that come from? We never go there. You suddenly in the mood for greasy burgers?'

"Not sure, but I think that's where we need to be."

"Then the diner it is." Margaret threw the car into drive and hit the gas pedal.

The vintage eatery had been around for a long time. Judging by the articles framed on the wall, at least fifty years. The booths were in a turquoise blue with white tables that had a chrome base, typical of its day. The waitress was friendly and cheerful, and the menu was what you expected from a representation of the American greasy spoon. Alex ordered an egg on a roll with French fries, and Margaret opted for the grilled cheese and onion rings. They split a chocolate shake.

The framed black and white photos above their booth gave a visual depiction of the story of Floral Park. The diner was older than he'd thought. 1934 was the date on the first photo; two years after the fire. The town was just primarily homes, with a candy store, a local market, and the church. The diner was the main restaurant where, judging by the photos, everybody hung out. He loved the design of cars from that era. They had character.

"Cars today lack character."

"What did you say?"

Alex didn't answer. His thoughts were eighty years away. "Alex. Where are you?"

He peered over at Margaret. He knew he had heard something, but his mind was still off in another place.

"Hey. Come back." She brushed her foot against his leg.

He studied her face.

"Uh . . . I'm here. Sorry." He smiled.

"Where the hell did you go?"

"I was looking at the photos and then, well, my mind just wandered. Look at all of these. They're around the whole diner. It looks like they date back to the early thirties. So much town history is sitting right in front of us. Cool, right? And the cars . . . I mean, they were so much better back then."

"You know how much I love cars, but the old ones steal my heart." Margaret reached up, tracing the lines of the automobile with her fingers.

"We are definitely kindred spirits. I think we were both born in the wrong era."

"It's funny. When we met, you knew next to nothing about cars— didn't care. Now, you sound a little like me. I guess I'm a good influence." She laughed.

The waitress arrived with their food, and after she set down the hot plates, Alex stopped her. He glanced at her name tag—Bridget.

"Bridget, do you know how long the diner has been here in Floral Park?"

"Funny you should ask that. People usually don't believe me when I tell them this, but my grandmother actually worked here when it first opened in 1933. She was only sixteen and would serve soda and ice cream at the counter."

"Wow. That's so cool. So, your family is from Floral Park?"

"By way of Ireland." Bridget laughed. "My great grandparents came to New York and settled here when my grandmother was ten or eleven. We've been here ever since. I raised two kids here. And now, my grandchildren are here, too. I guess you could say we were meant to be here." She winked at the two of them, asked if they needed anything else, and went on to her other tables.

"Margaret, don't you find that strange?"

"What?"

"That we stop in for a quick bite and meet Bridget. I mean, we rarely ever come in here. For some reason, I've never noticed the photos on the walls before, but I was drawn into them today. Then, voila, Bridget emerges to tell us the story about her grandmother."

"I don't know. Could you be reaching? I know we're both frustrated. How's your spidey sense? Any goosebumps?

Alex pulled up his sleeves. His arms were covered in bumps. Margaret's eyes widened. "Well, I guess you're not reaching. What the hell now? The players in this little show just keep growing. I'm getting dizzy."

"Me too. But what if Bridget's family is the fifth investor in Bishop's failed company?"

Margaret shrugged her shoulders and offered her hands up.

They ate, immersed in their meal. A word here or there, but nothing to do with the case. When they both finished, Bridget came over to clear the table and drop off the check. Alex knew he had to be less than obvious, but also get as much information as he could. He figured he'd start with her grandmother's full name.

"That was such a cool story, Bridget. So much family history here in this town. It's got to be nice living somewhere surrounded by all your family."

"Oh, yeah. Growing up was the best. We never had to go far to run into one of our relatives."

"I'm doing some research on the town's history for some homework. Do you mind if I ask your grandmother's name?"

Bridget was more than eager to share her family's history and reveled in the notion that someone would be so interested.

"No. I wouldn't mind at all. It's nice to meet someone—especially two people as young as you—who are interested in this town's past. So much is forgotten these days. I do wish my grandmother was still around, though. She could tell you some stories. I know most of them, but she was so much better at really making you feel like you were there."

"What about your mom? She must have a few," Alex gently prodded.

"She did. But we lost her about five years ago. Actually, it was right around this time. Her anniversary is coming up." Bridget's eyes watered, and she wiped them with a napkin. "I'm sorry. I've been so busy lately with the grandkids. I didn't even realize the date."

Alex had figured Bridget had to be in her fifties, although her youthful appearance suggested otherwise.

"I'm so sorry. I didn't mean to bring up anything that would cause you pain."

"Oh, no. Please don't worry about it. I'm kind of glad you brought it up. She was just such a lively, strong soul, my mom. When my grandmother passed, we were all devastated, but she held us all together. I'm sorry, but I need to go. You can pay your check at the register."

She slipped away behind the counter and through the doors to the kitchen. Alex hadn't gotten the info he needed, but he didn't want to upset Bridget any further. He paid the check and they headed back to the library.

When they got there, he changed his search completely and focused on the diner and anything he could find on the opening. About an hour in, Margaret found something.

"Alex, check this out."

She had a snapshot on the screen of opening day at Floral Park Diner. It was from the local paper. The staff assembled out front, and from left to right under the photo were their names.

"Nice." Alex grinned.

He searched the group for the youngest looking female. She was easy to spot. She was the only one who appeared to be under the age of thirty—Maureen Quinlan. She looked so delicate with her petite frame and shoulder-length hair. It was hard to distinguish color, but you could tell her eyes were very light, and her hair was darker. A fresh face full of energy.

"Look. This has to be her. Maureen Quinlan. That's a start. We need to try and find her married name."

"She looks so young," Margaret said softly.

"Yeah, I know. She's like a year younger than us in this pic."

"Weird."

"What is?" Alex turned to her.

"We're looking at her, and so many years have passed. She's already been here and gone. But here in this picture, she had her whole life to live yet. We know more about her sitting here today than she did standing in front of the diner for her first job. So many possibilities. What were her dreams? What kind of life did she want? Did she get it? It kind of makes me sad."

Alex rubbed his stomach; it was as uneasy as his nerves. He was picking up on Margaret's emotions. She was the one he was the most connected to, and when she was sitting so close to him, it was a conduit for emotions.

He reached out and took her hand. With his thumb, he caressed the curves, gliding over each finger. She turned, eyes meeting his. He didn't need to speak; she knew he was feeling her pain.

"I'm sorry," she whispered.

"Why are you sorry?" he spoke gently.

"For giving you this sadness."

"I love that you can feel so much for someone you have never met. Sharing these emotions with you just makes us closer."

He wanted to kiss her, soak in the intimacy of the moment, but he didn't.

The librarian abruptly opened the door, and they quickly

pulled away from each other. Alex resumed his search for the married name of Maureen Quinlan.

Exploring the wedding announcements from the Floral Park newspaper circa 1937, he soon found what he was looking for. In 1938, the formal announcement of the nuptials joining Maureen Quinlan to Gregory S. Finley caught his eye.

"I think this is what we need." He pulled Margaret over.

"She married Gregory S. Finley. We just gotta see if this guy has any connection to Bishop and the others."

"He had such a formal name. Sounds like money. And look at little Maureen. She's just the cutest, but she doesn't look stuffy like he sounds." Margaret ran her fingers over the photo.

"You're right. If his family had money, maybe they lost it with Bishop. That would give us our connection and confirm our fifth family," Alex said eagerly.

"That's why you had goosebumps at the diner. Oh, jeez. Bridget could be the last victim."

"I know. We need to try and find out how her mother died." Alex furrowed his brow.

"Yeah. Bridget made it sound like it was unexpected." Margaret yawned.

Things are coming together. Maybe we still have a chance to stop this in time, he thought.

Alex rubbed his eyes, the burning signal that it was time to go. Margaret nodded in agreement; she had given up one too many yawns. As they returned each book to its rightful shelf, his mind wandered.

He knew what he must do to unveil the identity of the spirit. The plan would unfold tomorrow.

BRIDGET'S PAST

"I'm beat. I feel like we've been reading for days." Margaret checked her rear-view mirror.

"Close. More like hours." Alex grinned.

"Sarcasm? I don't have the energy." Margaret nodded her head. "Is that my phone?"

Alex reached down to the outer pocket of her purse. The light on the phone was blinking, and the Addams family theme song meant it was her mom.

"Can you put it on speaker for me?" Margaret glanced at him.

"Sure."

"Hello, Mom?" Margaret spoke up. "You're on speaker; I'm driving."

"If you're driving, why are you answering the phone?" Mrs. Kiley sounded curt.

"Alex is holding the phone. What's going on?" Margaret huffed.

"Your father and I want you home for dinner tonight. Just you."

Margaret rolled her eyes. "Okaaaay. Did something happen?"

"No. Just come home, please." The line went silent.

"What the hell? The last time they wanted me home for dinner, my grandpa had passed away."

"I remember."

"The good news is, I have no other close relatives. The bad thing is, I have no idea what they want. Normally, they're so aloof when it comes to me." Margaret turned on the left signal.

"Aloof? Where'd that come from?" He raised a brow.

"It's Cadence's new word. I guess it stuck with me."

She pulled up in front of Alex's house and promised to fill him in when she knew more.

Peering at the night sky before he went into the house, Alex shivered. His know was telling him they were close. And close meant danger.

He hung out in the kitchen, scouring his iPad for any information on Finley. Fully submerged, he never noticed the banging of pots while his mom put together a quick dinner.

"Hey, can you go get your brother? Dinner's ready." She set plates on the table.

"Huh?" Alex didn't look up.

"Alex McKenna, stop what you're doing and retrieve your little brother from his bedroom, so that we may eat this wonderful dinner I made for us."

Alex glanced over at the box of Hamburger Helper on the counter and then back at his mom.

"Don't even say a word. It's been a long day, and you have food. That's all you need to worry about." She glared.

Alex got up and ambled over to the staircase. Going halfway up, he shouted out Wilby's name.

"Alex, I could have done that myself. He has his door shut. Go up and get him, please."

"Okay, okay," he moaned.

Wilby's door was closed, and respecting privacy was a must in the house, so Alex knocked and waited for clear passage before opening it. Wilby was playing his favorite video game.

"Hey, come on, dinner's ready. You know Mom thinks you're up here doing homework."

"I was. But I finished."

"You know she's gonna check, right?"

"Yeah, I know. It's done. Really."

"Okay. Let's go."

The boom of Chuck Taylors hitting the oak stairs resonated through the house like a herd of wild animals. When they got to the kitchen, Gina was standing there with her arms crossed.

"Jeez. Did you two fall down the stairs?"

"Nah. We were just in a hurry to eat your delicious dinner." Alex flashed a wide grin.

"Always the smart ass. Sit. The both of you. I want to talk with you. I've made a decision on an issue that I've been wrestling with the past few days. Wilby, your dad's back home, and he's agreed to pick you up later tomorrow. I'm sending you there until this all blows over. It's getting more dangerous as time goes by—the little escapade from the other night really opened my eyes. I need to protect you, honey, and to do that, you need to leave the house."

"Mom, please. I want to stay. I want to help," Wilby pleaded.

"I know you do. And going to your dad's is how you can help us."

Alex wanted to interrupt, argue with his mother for his brother's sake, but he finally saw what she was trying to tell him a few days ago. Things were coming to an end; Halloween was almost there, and they were a bigger threat to whoever was doing this, now more than ever. Whether it was Greta or someone else, the more they meddled, the more danger they put themselves in.

Wilby wiped a tear away from his cheek, and Alex reached out and patted his back.

"Mom's right, little man. If we don't have to worry about you, then you're helping us more than if you stay. Do you understand?"

Wilby reluctantly nodded.

Alex tried to make his little brother feel better by changing the subject. He went over what he and Margaret uncovered at the diner.

"So, you're convinced that Bridget is the last victim?" his mom asked.

"I'm pretty sure. That's what my gut's telling me. But I need to back it up. I have to find out how her mother died. If I knew her last name, it would help."

"You found the grandmothers. Nothing on the mom?"

"Nope. We searched, believe me."

"Huh." His mom's mouth wrenched to the side.

"What?" Alex took a forkful of Stroganoff.

"Well, it's odd that you could find more information on something so long ago, and yet nothing on an event more recent."

"Maybe there were no announcements. Not everybody puts their engagement in the papers. I think we got lucky with the grandmother." Alex sipped his cola.

"Oh, honey, this is a small town. Everybody pretty much knows what's going on. I think there should have been something. Maybe you should just try talking to Bridget again."

"I don't know. She was pretty upset."

"The clock's ticking, Alex. How about I go with you? You in the mood for some pie after dinner?"

"That's a good idea. It might put Bridget at ease to have another mom there. Someone she could relate to."

"Wilby, finish dinner. We're going for pie." His mom grinned. Wilby clapped. His favorite dessert was chocolate cream pie.

THE DINER CLOSED at eleven o'clock; they had plenty of time. Bridget had been there late in the afternoon, so Alex crossed his fingers she had the closing shift. When they pulled up to the parking lot, Alex spotted her serving coffee to a booth filled with customers.

"She's here." Alex grabbed the door handle.

"Great." His mom unlatched her seatbelt.

The counter was fairly crowded, but luckily, just as they were entering the diner, a booth opened in her area.

The waitress smiled when she recognized Alex. "Hey, back for some more?"

"Yeah, this time it's dessert."

"All of our desserts are on the back of the menu. Why don't I give you a few minutes to look it over?"

"Nah. We're good. We all want pie." Alex grinned.

"Decisive. I like it." Bridget winked.

After they went through the verbal rendition of homemade pies, Bridget retreated to the kitchen. Minutes later, she arrived with two empty cups, a coffee carafe, and a large chocolate milk for Wilby.

"Your pies will be out in a moment." Bridget poured the coffee.

"Thank you. My son tells me he had an interesting

conversation with you earlier. Your family has quite the history here." Gina stirred in a drop of creamer.

"Yes, we do. It was so nice to share with someone who actually seemed interested."

"I'm sorry I upset you, though," Alex interjected.

"Oh, no worries. I'm fine. Just miss her; that's all." Bridget patted his forearm.

His mom knocked his foot under the table. That was Alex's clue to let her handle it.

"Wow. I mean, to think you're working in the same place as your grandmother did when she was just a girl. Amazing. How long have you been working here?" Gina asked.

"Man. It'll be ten years this November."

"That's a long time."

"Yeah. I started right after my mom passed away. Me and my kids were living with her, and I was working in the city. The commute was long. After she was gone, it was clear I needed something close to home. You know, with the kids and all. The manager knew me from high school. And it didn't hurt that my grandmother's picture is up on the wall."

"I wonder if I knew your mom. She would have been about my grandmother's age. Maybe a little younger, but Gram had so many friends. What was your mom's name?" Gina smiled.

"Evelyn Fitzgerald. She married a real Irishman. Had the wedding in Dublin."

"No. Not ringing a bell. Well, it was worth a shot. You never know in this little town of ours."

"I know, right? I meet people all the time that I had no idea they knew my family. In fact, I ran into a woman just the other day. Oh! I better go get your pie."

"That was great, Ma. I didn't know your grandmother lived here," Alex blurted.

"She didn't."

"Huh. You got skills you've been hiding."

"Oh, you have no idea, son."

Bridget pushed through the swinging door from the kitchen with three plates of chocolate cream pie. Setting them down on the table, she resumed her story.

"Where was I? Oh, yes. I was telling you I had met this woman the other day. She came into the diner for a quick coffee, and it seems she knew my grandmother. Apparently, when they were little, they went to school together. She was a bit odd, though."

"Odd how?" Alex's interest was aroused.

"Um, I don't know. She asked a lot of questions about me and my kids. Things that seem personal to me. It was just eerie."

"That is weird. Did she tell you her name?" He was crossing his fingers.

"No, I'm sorry."

"Anything else you can remember? Was she young? Older?"

"Oh, this woman was definitely elderly—maybe late eighties."

Bridget wrinkled her nose.

"What kind of questions did she ask that made you feel uneasy?"

"Like what my shifts were? Who lives at the house with me? Do I feel lonely when they're gone? Just weird stuff like that." Bridget glanced at the counter.

"That is more than strange. I'd stay away from her next time." Alex shook his head.

"I don't think I have to worry. She didn't like the coffee. Complained to the manager." Bridget chuckled.

When they had finished their dessert, his mom got up and paid the bill while Alex and Wilby went to the car. Alex sat in the passenger seat, gazing out at the town. It was below freezing, and the cool air cut through his skin like a knife. He put his hand on the window. *Why ice?* he thought. *If it was Carol, she died by fire. Catherine, by the hand of a hired driver. It doesn't make sense.* He had asked himself these questions before, and still could not come up with a logical answer.

He sat in awe of the stars. There were so many out, they blanketed the sky. He hadn't seen a view like that in a long time. He caught a glimpse of his mom out of the corner of his eye. He turned to see her walking toward the car. Then he glanced back at Wilby, who had dozed off. Rubbing his hands together to ward off the freezing temperature, he turned toward her again, but this time, the window had fogged up. He cupped the sleeve of his jacket and smeared away a clear line of sight. She was standing in the middle of the parking lot. He scanned the lot and pivoted around in his seat toward the back of the car. There was a figure standing on the other side of the car, about thirty feet from his mom.

Alex threw the door open and leaped out.

"Alex, get back in the car!" his mom ordered.

He turned around and squinted to get a better look, but it was nearly impossible to get a clear picture of what—or who —it was. Shrouded in a long black veil, the figure blended into the darkness, blurring the lines of reality. It clutched a small statue to its chest, and a deep, melodic chant filled the air around them.

"Ma, come over here to the car," Alex pleaded.

"I can't." Her voice fractured.

"What do mean?"

"I mean I literally can't move." His mom struggled to take a step. Alex took a step toward the dark figure.

"Alex, no!" his mom shouted. "Stay where you are. Protect Wilby."

He checked on his little brother—still sleeping. He felt helpless. Not sure if he should ignore his mom and rush the unknown or wait like she told him to. The silhouette took a few steps toward the diner. It was then he realized it wasn't his mom she was focused on; it was Bridget.

"What the hell do you want?" Alex yelled.

The shadow slowly turned its attention to Alex. He stood tall, not showing the fear that was ravaging his body.

"Alex, be careful," warned his mom.

"It's okay." Alex stood firm.

The dark figure let out an ear-piercing screech, and Alex buried his head in his jacket. Again, it changed its focus and twisted toward the back seat of the car—Wilby. It held the statue down toward the earth, and the car started to rock back and forth.

"Wilby!" his mom screamed as she struggled to break free.

Alex's heart pounded; the death freeze of the dark spirit was coming, and it was very close.

"Ma, that thing is summoning the beast!" Alex's voice dripped with fear.

"Alex, I don't know what to do. I can't move. Is Wilby still sleeping?"

"Yes."

"Good." She wiped her upper lip with her sleeve.

"What if he wakes up?"

The vibration in his front pocket distracted him. Alex slipped out his phone; his gram's picture lit up like a beacon.

"Gram, we're in trouble," Alex whispered.

"I know. Listen carefully, Bonzetta. Tell your mother we are going to use the prayer of light. I will do what I need from here."

"What do I do?" Alex's palms dripped with sweat from anxiety, and he nearly dropped the phone.

"Just repeat what we say, okay?"

"Okay."

He didn't want to shout their plan, so he texted it to his mom. "Ma, look at your phone."

She slipped it out of her purse and read the message. Then, nodding in agreement, she waited.

ALEX'S GRAM instructed him to have his mom start the prayer, and he was to repeat it after each sentence. This would give her time until she could get all the ingredients together. Swiftly, she gathered the ingredients she kept in the kitchen.

4 tbsp frankincense or myrrh 4 tbsp black powdered iron 4 tbsp sea salt

4 tbsp orris-root powder (or oak moss) 1 white candle

1 bottle with a cork or lid mortar and pestle parchment paper

black ink or black ballpoint pen black thread

She mixed the sea salt, orris-root powder, and the iron in a bowl, then cut a piece of parchment to fit inside the bottle.

ALEX HAD the phone to his ear, listening for further instructions. He breathed a sigh of relief when he heard his gram's voice.

"Bonzetta, don't be afraid."

"But Wilby."

"Everything will be fine," his gram said in a soothing voice.

ALEX'S GRAM wrote the words "shadow demon" on the parchment paper in black ink, along with the spell. Then, she rolled up the parchment, tied it with a black thread, and placed it in a bottle. She then filled it with all the dry ingredients, then took a white candle and, while turning them counterclockwise, dripped the wax over the cork to seal it. She put the phone down and went to her garden in the backyard to bury it. When she got back to the kitchen, she called out to Alex.

***

"Hello, Alex? Alex?!"

"Gram, I think it's working. The air is changing. It's like I'm almost floating."

"Good. Tell your mom to try and move."

"Ma, see if you can . . ."

His mom made a dash for the car and jumped in the driver seat before Alex could finish his sentence. Alex quickly shut the door and hit the automatic locks.

"I think we need to get out of here. Now. That thing is pissed." Alex's attention was fixed on the silhouette—its fists damned them as they pulled away.

His mom shifted the car in gear and floored the gas pedal. The tires screeched as they left the parking lot with the shadow growing smaller in the rear-view mirror.

"Holy shit. It's a good thing Gram called when she did. I've never been restrained like that. I mean, I could not move one muscle in my legs." His mom tried to catch her breath.

"Hey, why are your guys shouting?" Wilby yawned as he rubbed his eyes.

"Nothing, honey. Go back to sleep. We'll be home soon."

"Ma, what about Bridget? We left her there all alone."

"She's fine for now. Whoever that was has five more days before she can commit another sacrificial murder. She probably went to the diner to watch Bridget. She's consumed with whatever it is that's causing her to commit the murders.

She tried to kill us for convenience. I doubt she had a clue we'd be there."

"Great. So glad we could accommodate," Alex said sarcastically.

"We need to be extra careful these next few days." His mom gripped the steering wheel.

***

FLORAL PARK, New York 1932

CAROL BISHOP HAD GONE to bed early. She had been nursing an extremely bad headache and listening to Jim's gibberish just made the pounding worse. As she lay under the warmth of her fluffy bedspread, she reflected on her life. How could she have married such a weasel of a man? He couldn't do anything right. He even screwed up his wife's murder by losing all the money he'd inherited. Now they were in deep. So deep, she feared, they'd lose their house. What would the neighbors say to that? And her poor, little, precious Alister. To be humiliated in class and knowing his father was a failure. Not to mention the extra money they spent on feeding that cow of a girl, Ester.

Honestly, she really is an idiot. Always talking to herself when she thinks no one is watching. Jim should have let her go with her mother. At least they'd have less of an expense, and they need to save every penny they could.

It was her turn to host the ladies' luncheon on Thursday, and she needed to pull out all the stops. It would be scandalous if they were to find out how bad things were before she had put a recovery plan in place.

Having their pity would probably work best. She could still uphold her status if it got out that Jim was beating her or cheating or something. Anything to make her appear that all of this had been done to her and poor Alister. That's it! If they think Jim had a dark side and favored Ester, he could take his anger over Catherine's death out on his new family. This could work.

As her eyes grew heavy with the relief that she had solved her problem, she thought she had gotten a whiff of smoke. Thinking it was probably Jim lighting up another one of his smelly cigars, she let sleep carry her away.

THE VISION

By the time they got home, and Gina had put Wilby to bed, it was nearly eleven. Alex hunkered down on the couch and called his gram. It was a quick conversation, just to recap what had happened and to tell her about Wilby. She confirmed the spell would be ready in the morning, as there was one last ingredient she was waiting for. It was being personally delivered. Alex hung up and traipsed up to bed. He was exhausted.

The alarm on his cell went off right at five-thirty a.m. He wanted to be sure he went through all the motions of a normal day before enacting his plan. The house had to be empty, and Margaret couldn't know anything. He'd go to school, and since he didn't have any classes with her until the afternoon, he'd slip out after first bell. She'd be none the wiser. He could still text her to keep up his charade. Wilby was running late, and his mom was a little on the frenzied side. She had a meeting at work, and the traffic in the morning was always congested.

"Alex, I need you to come home right after school. Your dad is going to pick up Wilby and bring him home to pack a bag and get some of his things. Wilby is complaining of a stomachache, but honestly, I think he's probably just a little tired from being up so late. If I didn't have this meeting, I'd stay home with him."

Alex panicked. He definitely needed the house empty, and the last person he wanted home was his little brother.

"No, Ma. I think you're right. He seemed okay earlier. When I got up to get breakfast, he was playing a video game. I think he's probably feeling a little lazy."

"Yeah, well, no time for that. Especially in this house."

Alex grabbed his pseudo lunch, shouted a goodbye to his brother, and ran to catch the bus. He met Margaret in their usual place on the bleachers. Talking with her, he felt his secret pushing up into his throat and almost passing his lips. He wanted to tell her. He never hid things from her in the past, but this time, he wanted to protect her. He clenched his fist that was nestled in the pocket of his hoodie. He had never been so happy to hear the bell ring for first period. He walked Margaret to class and told her he'd see her later at lunch. *He hoped.*

He had to walk home, but it gave him a little more time to solidify his plan. He pulled a folded piece of paper from his back pocket. Most of the family's spell books were at his grandmother's house, and the books his mom kept were in her closet. He didn't have the time to flip through all of them looking for the right spell. Alex had scoured everything on the internet he could find on a holding spell. He needed to keep the spirit paralyzed long enough to get what he wanted. Fingers crossed the powers that be who shared this spell on their site knew their crap.

The neighborhood was pretty sedate during the week. Most of the residents were at work. There were a few old timers that you'd see raking leaves from time to time, but for the most part, he could get home undetected.

Normally, he would have enjoyed this stroll. But given what he was walking toward, all the joy had been squashed. As he rounded the corner of his block, he saw a car in front of Mrs. Rice's house. It was probably her son, Howard. He would visit every two weeks like clockwork. You could time your watch by him. His mom said it was because he was waiting for her to keel over so he could sell the house. She had lived there for over sixty years. Jewel Rice and her husband, Timothy, had bought the house shortly after they were married. She was now eighty-six, and he had been dead for nearly ten years. Alex would rake her leaves for her sometimes. They'd have conversations on the stoop. He genuinely liked her.

He was fairly certain Howard wouldn't care what he was up to, as long as he stayed off the front lawn.

Locking the front door behind him, Alex went straight to the kitchen. His mom had a bottle of wine on the counter. In the LaBoccetta family, you practically grew up with wine in your formula bottle. Okay, that was a huge exaggeration, but you were allowed to take a sip here and there. Alex, being nearly seventeen, was allowed half a glass on holidays, some Sunday dinners, and special occasions. He opted to have his half glass now. Yes, it was the morning, but he wasn't sure if he was going to see the end of this day, and he really didn't want his last drink to be something as mundane as soda or as benign as water.

He grabbed the bottle and a wine glass from the cupboard. Sitting at the table, he poured a smooth, full-bodied Merlot into the fragile, shapely glass from Naples. He took a few sips and envisioned how his plan would play out. He would stand in the center, surrounded by the circle of salt. He was going to call out the spirit and hope it would respond. It was pretty pissed on their last encounter, so he was betting that, given the opportunity to get him home alone, it would take it. A long shot, yes, but the whole scheme was a long shot. When they had their face-to-face, he would start with the holding spell. This *should* keep it there with him.

He took his last sip of wine, washed out the glass, and placed it back in the cupboard. He then grabbed the large box of salt and made a complete circle before stepping into the center. He spoke in an authoritative voice, commanding the spirit to come. He repeated this three times. With the holding spell in his hand, he waited.

The sudden cloud of frost in the air burnt his lungs. It was working.

Poised, he waited.

Boom! Boom! Boom!

He swiftly pivoted in a clockwise motion, scanning the room. Nothing. Above his head, heavy footsteps sounded. Someone, or something, was walking around the second story.

He hesitated for a moment. "This could be a trick the spirit is playing to get me to leave the circle," Alex murmured to himself.

Once again, he heard the rustling of steps from above, but this time, it was followed by the flush of the toilet. Because it was an old house, when someone used the water upstairs, you could hear the swoosh in the pipes downstairs.

Damn. His worst fear was materializing. He leaped out of the circle and raced up the stairs. Standing in the hallway was his little brother.

"What the hell are you doing home?" Alex was light-headed with anxiety.

"Why are you yelling at me?" Wilby whimpered.

"I'm not. I'm sorry. But you are supposed to be at school."

"Yeah. Well, so are you," Wilby replied in a snarky tone.

Well, the kid has a point, thought Alex.

"I needed to pick up some things I forgot. And you?" Alex peered down the stairs.

"I threw up in the car on the way to school. Mom's gonna come back after her meeting. She tried to text you, but you didn't answer. She tried Margaret, too."

"Mom texted Margaret?"

"Yeah."

Alex panicked. "Damn! Shit!" Alex panicked.

"Alex, what's wrong?" Wilby widened his eyes.

"I need to get you out of here."

Alex heard pounding on the front door.

"Hello? Alex! Wilby! Open the door," Margaret shouted.

Alex grabbed Wilby's hand and flew down the stairs with his little brother in tow. He reached for the knob of the front door and felt a cold chill raise the hairs on the back of his neck. He glanced down at his arms—goosebumps.

"Crap," he muttered.

As he opened the front door, Margaret pushed through.

"What the hell is going on? Your mom texted me and said you weren't answering. What are you doing home?" She was irritated.

"I need you to leave now. Take Wilby and go, wherever. But get the hell out of the house," Alex commanded.

"What have you done?" Margaret crossed her arms.

"Just go. I'll explain later."

"No. I'm not leaving you. Wilby, go wait in my car." Margaret handed the keys to the boy.

"Listen to me, the both of you. You're gonna put all of us in danger. I'm not sure I can protect you. Hell, I'm not sure I can protect me."

Alex reached for the knob to open the front door, but it slipped through his fingers as the door slammed shut.

"Oh no." Alex grabbed his little brother and Margaret and ran for the salt circle. "Remember, whatever you do, do not look at it. You hear me? Just keep your attention on me."

When they got to the kitchen, Alex was horrified. The

circle had been demolished. There was salt all over the floor, and the room was like an icebox. Furiously, he scanned the space—nothing. His goosebumps told him otherwise. Then it hit him. Slowly, he tilted his head up and, hovering with its back to the ceiling, was the malevolent spirit.

Alex yanked them both toward the back door, but when he tried to open it, the door wouldn't budge. He swung around, leading them into the den. He strained in an attempt to open the window. It was sealed as if it had been nailed shut. They ran through the living room and up the stairs, the cold chasing at their heels.

The first bedroom they tried was Wilby's. On the street side of his window stood the large pine tree. They could easily climb down from there. But like the window in the den, it was sealed shut. Room to room, they tried everyone until they ran out of windows. Margaret tugged Alex, yanking him toward the door to the attic. There was a small window they could probably fit through, but before Alex could reach for the knob, the door opened.

He quickly realized the attic was exactly where it wanted him to be. No attic.

They fled downstairs, slipping on the icy residue left behind by their enemy. Clutching the banister, Alex stopped himself from knocking Margaret right over the railing. He desperately ran to the kitchen, wracking his brain for a plan to get them to safety. The basement was not the ideal place to go, but they had run out of options, and it was the complete opposite of where the thing wanted him.

Alex crossed his fingers and reached for the knob—the door opened. Moving aside to let Margaret and Wilby through, he gasped. Wilby was gone. The spirit was no more than ten feet away, watching them with an evil grin of enjoyment on its distorted face. Lime green eyes glowed, illuminating the dark circles under the beast's lower lids, creeping like a fungus over its cheek bones. Pasty gray flesh, riddled with red sores, infected the rest of the killer's identity —leaving no resemblance to human form.

At least Alex knew it didn't have Wilby.

He shoved Margaret through the door frame and followed on her heels. When they reached the basement, Margaret shouted out Wilby's name. Alex put his index finger to his lips. She nodded. He pointed toward the boiler room, and they slipped past the unfinished pine door to the dark room.

They huddled together behind the furnace in the basement, and Alex hoped the heat coming from the unit would be enough to throw the beast off their trail. Alex held Margaret close with a firm hand pressing her head onto his shoulder. He couldn't understand why, but for whatever reason, the rules didn't apply to him. He had stared into its malevolent black eyes and nothing. The only lasting effect on him (other than a moment of paralyzing fear) was complete exhaustion. But Margaret wasn't like him, or others in his family. The tighter he held Margaret, the more worried he was about Wilby. His little brother was somewhere else in the house. He knew he was smart, but this thing was stronger than anything else they had encountered in the past. Systematically, his mind envisioned every room in the house, searching for a way out.

Peering his head out from behind the hot metal tank, Alex was careful not to touch it. He made the mistake a few years back of carelessly brushing up against it while moving some boxes for his mom. The scar on his right arm left a reminder never to do that again.

The damp, musty smell and the pipes hanging below the ceiling gave the room an ominous air. It was dark in every corner except for a sliver of light emanating from the single, ground-level window. He hated the basement—especially the furnace room. It was the part of the basement that wasn't finished, and he felt like he stepped into a glimmer of hell every time he was in it. He could sense the thing was still lurking in the shadows, but he had no real fix on it—just the goosebumps that were standing at attention, coating his arms. He eased back behind the tank again. His plan seemed to have worked for the moment, but it also limited their options. It was only a temporary reprieve from the chase, and now he needed to come up with a solid way to find Wilby and escape.

"I think I know how we can get out of the house." Alex kept his voice low. "But you're gonna have to trust me."

Margaret nodded her head, and a quick shiver shook her body. She was not one to frighten easily, but this one had them both off- balance.

"I know you're really scared right now. So am I. I also know you can do this. I'm going to lead it toward the attic."

"Alex . . . no." Margaret grabbed his t-shirt and gripped tightly.

"It will follow me. Then you get the hell out of here and find Wilby. Senses tell me he's in my mom's room. After I get its attention, I'll run for the stairs. You give it a minute or two before following. Get my brother and then head back down here and out that window." Alex pointed to the ground window. It was big enough for Wilby and Margaret to fit through. "See the large wrench on the bench?" She nodded. "Use it to break the window. My mom has rags over there, too. Line the ledge so you don't get cut."

"Why don't we just break one of the windows in the den? They're larger." Margaret's voice trembled.

"No. It would be harder to break through the double panes, and it would attract a lot more attention. I need you to do this for Wilby." Alex rested his forehead on hers. "Text me when the both of you are out."

"Okay. But what about you? How are you going to get the hell out of the house?"

"Don't worry. I have a plan." He gave her a reassuring smile. He knew he had no plan, but he had to tell her something so she would agree. Margaret was as strong as they come when it came to protecting the important people in her life . . . especially him.

He pulled away and eased out from behind the furnace. A chill ran up his spine, and the goosebumps running along his arms stung to the touch. It was close. Alex squinted, trying to distinguish the differences in the shadows. He took a step forward and hit a cloud of cold air. He was headed straight toward it. A deep, gravelly sound flowed like a wave in the ocean to his ears. He wasn't sure if Margaret could hear it too, but he was not about to take the chance and give up her location by calling to her. He shifted his eyes toward the right —toward the door. He was waiting for the perfect moment.

The beast lunged forward and reached for Alex with its icy arms. Alex ducked and swerved. He spun around and ran straight for the door. Leaping onto the staircase, he turned back to make sure it was right behind him; it was. Halfway up, his feet betrayed him, and he fell body-flat with his legs stretched out on the stairs below. A frigid grip on his leg triggered his reflexes, and kicking furiously, he broke free. Quickly, he scrambled back to his feet and up to the first level. He ran through the kitchen and dining room before reaching the steps to the second story. The entrance to the attic was in the hallway between all three rooms. Once he got the creature there, he could buy Margaret the time to find Wilby and get out.

The burning in his lungs gave a small distraction to the fate that lay before him.

Hesitating to take the next step, the creature set out a welcome mat. The attic door flew open and slammed into the wall. Shards of plaster catapulted outward, grazing the corner of Alex's eyelid.

He pressed his palm on the wound to stop the bleeding and used the sleeve of his hoodie to smear the blood out of his eyes before running up the staircase. The musty odor soured his stomach, and his gag reflex rendered him motionless.

He bent over and placed his hands on his knees, taking several short breaths before his body would allow the passage of a deep breath. He searched for a place to hide, but every corner of the space was cluttered with remnants of generations before him. The only clearing left him completely exposed in the center of the room. He might as well hang a sign around his neck that said, *come and get me.*

A sudden boom startled him, but it was a familiar sound. The door had been slammed shut. His plan had worked. He was alone with the darkness and nowhere to go.

Alex backed up until he felt the cold air hitting his back. He was leaning against the only window in the room. In front of him, about fifteen feet away, hovered the grotesque entity of something that once had a life. Droplets of sweat descended from his brow, leaving a salty taste on his pursed lips.

He clasped his head, a piercing pain forcing him to close his eyes in agony. It stopped. Slowly opening them, the attic blurred, spilling images into one another before settling into a different landscape in the same space. An old bed lay up against the wall to his right. To his left, boxes of children's toys were stacked on each other, some spilling out onto the floor. In the center of the room, more boxes, neatly sealed and labeled. A ray of sunlight caressed the room, highlighting an old desk near the staircase.

Startled by a sudden gush of air, Alex jumped away from the window. A man—about forty years old—wriggled through the open window. He clutched a glass bottle containing a clear liquid in one hand, and several large rags in the other. Alex stood, unable to move. The movie was playing out, and he had to see how it ended.

The perpetrator drenched the rags with the mysterious liquid before scattering them around the attic. In getaway mode on the staircase, he pulled a box of matches out of his pocket, struck them, and released the flaming sticks into the air. In moments, the rags ignited, building a wall of flames that engulfed everything in its path. Shielding his face from the intense heat, Alex collapsed on the floor, struggling to breathe through the thick smoke.

And then, quiet.

Still crouching, he lowered his arms. The fire was gone, and he no longer found himself in the confines of the attic. A mahogany dresser with an overly ornate mirror masked the familiarity of the room. It was his mother's bedroom, but not. A woman lay sleeping in the bed, the covers drawn to her shoulders and shrouding her face. The arsonist took out two more rags from his pocket, and once again, drenched them with the clear liquid. He staged a semblance to his actions moments ago, and the room ignited. The arsonist quickly opened the window and hopped out to the roof, jumping to the safety of the grass below.

The woman grunted and then coughed before groggily sitting up in bed. Alex immediately recognized her. It was Carol Bishop. Her eyes widened with astonishment when she realized there was a blazing fire at her feet. Leaping from the bed, she called out for Alister.

She fled to the hallway and ran into a man waiting for her —James Bishop. He punched her in the face, and she went down with a large *thud*. Bishop ran into the bedroom that was now Wilby's. He emerged with a small boy and rushed into the second bedroom. A young girl of about ten or twelve followed him out. "Damn, that must be Alister and Ester," Alex murmured.

Jim ran down the stairs with Ester close behind. He didn't hear Carol call out to his daughter. The child turned and ran back to her stepmother. When she reached the hallway, the woman was waiting for her. Consumed with anger, she latched onto the child's arm and squeezed tightly. The little girl screamed and tried to fight back, but Carol was too strong.

Alex turned away, distracted by Jim Bishop's yells and the pounding of shoes as he came running back up the staircase. Carol, blinded by hate, yanked Ester up the attic stairs, dragging the child as she screamed and latching the door behind them. Reaching the inferno, Carol gasped. She hadn't any idea the fire had originated in the very room she had boxed them into. The smoke swallowed the attic in moments, rendering her incapable of finding her way.

Alex squinted to distinguish them through the smoke. It was impossible to navigate; he could barely get a fix on them. Carol gasped, struggling for air. Crawling to get to the window, she collapsed unconscious on the floor. Jim pounded furiously on the door, trying to break it down. "Ester!" He screamed for his child, but only silence returned his call.

Crying, the child couldn't speak. She clutched her throat, gurgling, and huddled further into the corner. Finally, she surrendered, and her lungs succumbed to the suffocating smoke.

Alex inhaled clean, cool air. He was sitting on the snowy front lawn. Two men and a boy lay next to him. The boy—Alister—was unconscious, and Kirkpatrick was attempting to revive him. Jim Bishop was catatonic with grief.

The sirens of the fire trucks blared in the distance, and when he turned to look for them, he found himself back in the attic. The malevolent spirit hovered no more than ten feet away as it glared at him.

Alex felt a connection. It was showing him the events of the fire back in 1932. It wanted him to know. *But why?* The hate from the creature was matched by his own confusion. *Why bother to let him see this?*

Again, Carol appeared. She crawled on the floor; the smoke had nearly taken her, but the fire reached out, consuming her flesh. The woman screamed in agony before shattering through the glass and plummeting to the ground below. Alex quickly looked away.

The spirit moved closer. Alex stepped backward and pinned himself to the wall. Swooping toward the ceiling, it circled the room and let out a high-pitched screech. A stack of unpacked boxes lifted off the ground and thrusted toward him. Alex managed to dodge most of them, but a corner clipped his right shoulder and knocked him off his feet and onto his ass.

Struggling to recover, he limped toward the staircase, only to be thrown across the room and against the wall. The spirit opened the window with a glance. Alex groggily crawled a few feet and held onto an old nightstand to leverage himself. But halfway through his struggle, he found himself levitating off the floor and hovering midway between the ground and the ceiling, his body floating toward the open window.

For the first time in his life, Alex McKenna felt his death nearing. The only thing he could think about was Margaret. He saw her face. So beautiful. The life he had hoped they would have together seemed so clear a few hours ago.

"Why show me?" he whispered to the darkness. "You're just going to kill me anyway."

The creature pointed toward the window.

Alex turned his head. Straining, he could see part of the driveway. The shadowy figure from last night's encounter in the parking lot stood facing the attic window. Slowly, it pulled the black veil from its face. An elderly woman stood glaring at him; her eyes filled with hate.

"Marilyn Monroe," Alex murmured. "Did she want you to show me?" He pointed outside the window.

The spirit grew impatient and flung him against the wall

by the window. He reached out and grabbed the framework. He was able to wrap his fingers around the molding. The spirit grew furious and, with a nod, Alex went sailing outward and through the open window. He clasped the other side of the frame with his left hand and held on, suspending his body in the opening.

"You fucking son of bitch! I'm not letting go!"

Alex heard a loud crash from across the room. He tried to maneuver to see who it was, but all he could do was hold on to prevent plummeting to his death.

"Nel Santo Nome di Gesù, sigillo me, i miei parenti, questa casa, e tutte le fonti di approvvigionamento del Preziosissimo Sangue di Gesù Cristo."

"Leave us, spirit! Go back to your keeper!" the voice commanded. *"Nel Santo Nome di Gesù, sigillo me, i miei parenti, questa casa, e tutte le fonti di approvvigionamento del Preziosissimo Sangue di Gesù Cristo."*

Alex smelled incense of basil fill the room. "What the hell?"

"Alex, hold on. This thing is dissipating."

"Ma?"

"Yeah. I'm here."

"Wilby and Margaret?"

"They're safe outside."

He blinked his eyes, trying to flutter away the tears. He thought he had been alone. He knew now he wasn't going to die today.

His mom ran to the window, placed her right arm around Alex's waist, and pulled him in. The two stood in an embrace for a few seconds before, overcome with exhaustion, Alex slid to the floor. His mom sat down beside him until he was ready to talk.

"How did you know to come here?"

"Alex, you called me."

"What?"

"Maybe not consciously, but you did. I got your screams in my head. I knew you were in danger. I came straight home."

Alex sighed. "I'm really glad you listened."

"Me too. Now, do you mind telling me what the hell you were trying to do?"

"I thought if I summoned it, I could figure out who it was. Carol or Catherine."

"And did you?"

"I'm convinced it's Carol. She showed me her death. In fact, she showed me everything that happened that night."

"Damn it, Alex. I can't believe you did this after I told you not to do anything dangerous. You endangered your brother and Margaret, without any thought of the consequences. "

"But it worked! Please, listen to me. I said I saw everything. Bishop had the fire set. But he had intended to kill only Carol in the fire. He took out a huge life insurance on her. Ester was not supposed to die. Carol did that. When she realized it was Bishop who was trying to kill her, she grabbed the little girl, too. They both died in the attic."

"This doesn't make it better."

"I know. It was stupid. But they weren't supposed to be home."

"No. Alex, skipping a class is stupid. This is—there are no words for this. Your impatience is going to really backfire one day. And I may not be there to help you. You need to think more clearly. Act with your heart, yes. But do not forget to use your brain, too."

"Ma." Alex spoke softly. "I saw who it was."

"Who?"

"Greta. She had a beauty mark just like the picture at Bobby's house. I think Greta Kirkpatrick blames everyone involved with Bishop's financial failings for her father's suicide. You should've seen the pure hate in her eyes."

His mom stopped talking. Alex had hoped it was because she was thinking about what he had told her, and not all the ways she could torture him for the rest of his adolescent life. She helped him up and held onto his arm as they walked down the stairs. Assuring her he was alright, she let him go and opened the front door before going into the kitchen.

Margaret immediately went to Alex. She didn't say anything; instead, she threw her arms around his neck and kissed his unsuspecting lips.

"W-w-what was that for?" Alex's eyes widened.

"You almost died. We almost died. Look, I know you like me, McKenna. More than just best friends. Although, you'll always be my best friend. Never mind that. You like me, and I'm saying it's alright, because I like you too."

Alex pulled back and studied the truth in her eyes. Darting his gaze to soak in every curve of the beauty that made up Margaret Elizabeth Kiley, he wrapped his arms around her waist and tugged, pulling her body into his. Slowly, with the tilt of his head, he moved in, tasting the strawberry cream he had yearned for all these months.

"Yuck," Wilby remarked before going straight to the kitchen. A few minutes later, he emerged with a large salami sandwich.

When Alex and Margaret saw him, they laughed.

"Only you, little brother, would be thinking about your stomach after nearly being killed."

"Nah . . . I knew you'd get us out."

Alex cringed. He wasn't the one who rescued them. Their mother was. He would have failed his little brother.

"It wasn't me, buddy. It was Mom." Alex put his head down.

"No. Margaret told me you sent her to find me by getting that thing to follow you. We went out the basement window just like you said."

"Margaret, would you mind taking Wilby in the kitchen to finish his sandwich, and let me know when the coffee's ready, please?" Gina was standing in the archway to the living room.

"Come on, little man."

After Margaret and Wilby had gone, Gina sat down beside Alex. "Listen, I didn't mean to sound so harsh. I was worried about all of you. But the truth is, you did get them out. You saved them. But it would have been better if you had never done this. Understand?"

"Yeah. I get it. Really, I do. It won't happen again." Alex looked away.

"Oh, sure it will. You are who you are. Just make sure that when it does, you remember you're not alone. We are stronger together."

Alex nodded.

"Ma, something is really bugging me." Alex sat up. "Why did she bother showing me everything? I mean, it made no sense. And why freezing?"

"What do you mean?"

"Carol died by fire. Why not burn your victims? You'd want them to feel your pain, right?"

"I would think so."

"See? It's so screwed up," Alex said exasperatedly.

"Well, we have the rest of the week. We'll figure it out." Gina kissed the top of Alex's head.

Sometimes, Alex still felt like a kid, and other times, much older than his years, but having the added strength of his mom near him definitely fed the child inside. He always tried to be the leader and take on the responsibilities that the universe had bestowed on him, but it was good to have someone else take the lead sometimes.

Margaret shouted from the kitchen. "Coffee's done. You want it in there?"

They both got up and went into the kitchen. Sitting

around the table, Alex was reminded of something he'd forgotten to mention.

"Ma, I think I just bumped up to the top of the list."

"What do you mean?"

"I think Greta definitely wants me out of the picture."

"You're sure this dark spirit is Carol?"

"Well, that's whose death I saw. Why show me if it isn't? I think it was Greta being evil right before she killed me. Sort of, 'I told you, but now you die and can't help anyone with your knowledge.'"

"And why are you so sure? This spirit could have tricked you. It could have let you see whatever it wanted to."

Alex hadn't thought about that, but the feeling he was getting was that he saw it happen exactly the way it went down. He was going to trust his own instincts on this.

Margaret went back to school, and Wilby up to bed. Alex was on lockdown—no leaving the house for the day.

Alex felt like a prisoner in his own home. He decided to try and distract his thoughts, so he plopped down on the couch to play a video game. He really wasn't into them, not like his little brother. Alex swore that if they left him alone, Wilby would probably play all day, every day.

The game worked for a little while, but then his mind wandered to faces. The one that kept coming into view was Alister Bishop. Since Alex had seen the events that lead to Carol and Ester's deaths, he wasn't sure what else Alister could offer them. He was only a young child when it happened and, from what Alex saw, he was unconscious for quite a while. Yet, there he was, like a framed piece of art just hanging in his mind's eye.

He needed to get back to the Assisted Living facility.

Floral Park, New York 1932

Jim Bishop sat in the church with Alister beside him. In front of the pulpit were two closed coffins. The church was packed. It looked like the entire town had come out to show respect to Carol and poor little Ester. Across the aisle sat Michael Kirkpatrick and his family.

Behind them and filling the pew were the remaining five families involved in the financial cover-up. Jim looked at them, all crying and comforting each other. Everyone had remorse, but no one was innocent. They all had blood on their hands, and his were the most stained. He glanced back at the tiny coffin that contained his once beautiful, vibrant little girl. She lay there because of him and his greed. He then glared at the coffin containing Carol. Near the end, he'd grown to hate her. She was maniacal, manipulative, and horrible to Ester. He must admit her death didn't bother him in the least. She thought he didn't know how badly she had mistreated his innocent little daughter, but it was her own son, Alister, that told him her secret. Knowing made it easier to plan her death.

The priest said mass and then gave a brief eulogy for both victims. Afterward, he asked if anyone would like to come up and say a few words. Michael Kirkpatrick was the only one to rise. As he walked to the pulpit, he stumbled and caught himself with the back of one of the pews. His face was drenched with tears and puffy from all the crying. He had a handkerchief wadded up in his right hand, and he could barely keep his composure. His left hand shook as he removed a folded piece of paper from the inner pocket of his suit jacket. Unfolding it, he placed it on the pulpit and smoothed it out several times before reading the heartfelt words.

Jim listened, choking on every syllable. He knew the truth —the pressure that Kirkpatrick put on him to recover the lost money. He was the one to enlist and deceive the five families. Making his life miserable. They had threatened to go to the police and tell them everything. The gambling, embezzling, and fraudulent companies. Kirkpatrick was the real reason Ester lay in the coffin, and he knew it. That's what all the tears were for. His guilt.

After the services, everyone followed the procession to the gravesite. A few more words from the priest and tears from the phonies, and it was over. Jim just stood there with his hand on his daughter's coffin and Alister by his side.

"Your sister's in heaven now. No more pain or tears."

"I know, Daddy. The lady told me."

"The lady? What lady?"

"The lady in our house."

ALISTER'S CONFESSION

Alex waited until his mom had fallen asleep. She was exhausted from work and all the recent crap that was happening. She decided to take a nap. Not a normal practice, but Alex figured she needed it.

He texted Margaret at around three o'clock.

"My brain keeps focusing on Alister. I need to go over there again and see if there's something else he might remember."

"Okay, give me a few minutes to finish this homework, and then I'll be over. I don't want to leave in the middle of this English crap. Honestly, why do they give us this shit?"

He grabbed his keys and decided to wait outside. He gently closed the front door and, twisting the key, he winced. He didn't want to make any noise that would disturb his mom. His little brother was already gone. After the incident in the attic, Gina called their dad and asked him to pick up Wilby early. His dad came about a half hour later, and his reluctant little brother was whisked off to safety.

Alex stood on the stoop while he waited. There was a light breeze. He raised his arms, reaching toward the sky. He closed his eyes, and the air lifted him up, higher and higher. He elevated to the top of the trees, floating through the neighborhood. He twirled and then swooped past the elementary school and to the park. He flew straight up and then down again, barely missing a rooftop. This was his dream. To fly. How freeing to be a bird—to have wings. Able to go anywhere you want on the sheer highway of air. It was so clear to him. His mind took him away from everything when he flew.

A hand caressed his cheek, and he abruptly opened his eyes. Margaret was smiling at him. "Flying again?"

Alex blushed a little and then nodded.

"I didn't want to beep my horn and risk waking your mom.

"Where'd you go?"

"Everywhere."

Alex stood up and shakily took Margaret's hand in his; he tried to recapture the kiss they had shared after his fortunate rescue. But he hit her nose instead of her waiting lips.

"Ouch." Margaret laughed.

"I think I'm going to need to work on that." Alex nervously placed his hands in his pockets.

"We'll work on it," Margaret whispered in his ear.

They walked to the car holding hands, only parting to get in.

Alex cringed as they pulled away from the house; he knew if his mom woke up and he was gone, the shit was not only hitting the fan—it would obliterate it. It was a risk he had to take.

"I'm not trying to sound like a bummer, but what are you gonna tell your mom if she finds out? You promised her this morning that you wouldn't do anything else crazy."

"I know. I was just thinking about that. You getting psychic, too?"

"Nah. I just know how the mind of Alex McKenna works." She pursed her lips.

"She said I was on lockdown for today and yes, I'm breaking that rule. But I don't think going to visit an elderly man at a care facility is dangerous."

"Maybe. She'll still be pissed, though."

"Yeah, I know." Alex checked the time. "Maybe we'll get back before she wakes up."

"One can hope," Margaret said sincerely.

When they arrived at the assisted living, they used the same plan to get in as they did the last time. Why mess with perfection? Thankfully, this trip, they knew what room Alister was in. The door was closed, and Alex knocked loudly.

A gruff voice called out, "Come in."

Alex pushed open the door and then closed it behind them.

"Oh. It's you again. What do you want from me this time, boy? I told you everything I had to say. There isn't anything else to the story," Alister said sternly.

"Alister, we found out much more about that night of the fire. We know what really happened to Carol and Ester."

Alister looked up at Alex with venom in his eyes.

"Boy, you have no idea what you are talking about. How could you? You weren't there."

"But I was. Alister, you said the last time I was here that you could tell I saw the monster. I did. But there's more to it. I have a gift. I can see the dead and experience things not everybody can. I saw the whole thing. How that man set the fire that killed them. But Ester, she was a mistake. Just your mother was supposed to die. Did your father tell you that? Or that he was the one who set it up?"

"He doesn't understand what you're talking about." Margaret stepped in front of him. "The man is in distress. Can't you see that?"

"I understand that, and I don't mean to upset him. But we're running out of time."

"Alister, Alex is not trying to upset you. But his vision is proof your dad and Michael Kirkpatrick planned everything. He's just trying to stop more people from dying, and we need your help."

"You're insane. Get out of here, both of you! My father would never put me and my sister in such danger. And kill my mother? You know nothing. He loved her." Alister shook with anger.

"There was a conspiracy to recoup their lost funds by committing murder and collecting on the fire insurance and the life insurance policy your father had taken out on your mother. You don't have to believe me. You can check for yourself. Life insurance is a public record. He was a murderer and a thief. People have been dying all these years, and one more is coming in four days. If we don't stop this, it will just happen again next year and the year after that until Greta Kirkpatrick dies."

"Greta? What does she have to do with any of this?" Alister's eyes widened.

"She's the one that controls the spirit of your mother."

"My mother?"

"Yes. I think Greta is enacting revenge on all the families who were involved in the fire—the event that caused her father to commit suicide. He couldn't live with the guilt. She's been killing one member of each family every year since his death."

"Why would you think it was my mother?"

"This spirit is full of resentment. Your mother found out in her last minutes alive that your father was trying to kill her. She purposely took Ester with her to get back at him. She knew you were safe. She hated Ester. You already know that. Your mother was so full of rage and hate, she got the two of them trapped in the attic where they both died. Who else do you think it could be?"

Alister covered his face with his hands and slumped in the chair.

"Not my mother." Alister sobbed.

"Alister, I just told you . . ."

"Catherine," he whispered.

"What do you mean?" Alex raised his voice.

"Catherine. Ester's mother. It could be Catherine."

"Why would you think that?"

"Because she was there that night. She woke me up and told me to get out of bed." Alister wiped his tears.

"Are you sure it was Catherine?"

"Yes. She would visit with Ester all the time. And once, I saw her. She scared me, so I think she stayed out of sight when I was around."

"Was she angry?"

"No. Not at all. Ester loved spending time with her mother. She was a kind spirit."

"Then why do you think it could be her? If she was not full of hate, then . . . Ester's death. If she was there, she would have witnessed her child die tragically." Alex ran his hand over his mouth.

Alister nodded his head in agreement.

"Fuck. Now we're back to where we started from. It could be either one of them." Alex huffed.

"Watch your language, young man," Alister snapped.

"Sorry. But I have no way of knowing which one it could be. And in order for the spell to work, I need to know the spirit by name."

"Spell? What are you kids up to?" Alister leaned forward from his chair.

"We're trying to end this for good. Remember I told you a little bit about me and my family?"

"Yes. But how are you going to do this? How can a spell help?"

"It will banish the evil spirit back to where it belongs. No more summoning it up next year. Greta will be done. Did your mother have anything happen to her related to the cold? You know, freezing, like maybe a childhood accident or something?"

"No. Not that I'm aware of. In fact, she loved the winter. Hated the summer." Alister grinned slightly.

"Maybe that's it. Maybe she's freezing them because she likes it." Alex stared out the window.

"Okay. Alex, do you hear how lame that sounds?" Margaret frowned.

"I know. Grasping here." Alex rolled his eyes.

Alister narrowed his eyes. "What are you two kids talking about? Freezing who?"

Alex let out a sigh of frustration. He had told this to Alister the last time they were there.

"I told you, the spirit is freezing its victims' heads."

"Well, Catherine lost hers," Alister said promptly.

"I thought you said she was not an angry spirit." Alex raised his eyebrows.

"No. Literally. In the accident that killed her, she was decapitated."

"What? There was no reference to that in anything we read!" Alex exclaimed.

"No, there wouldn't be. My father told me about the accident when I was older. She was hit by the car and decapitated. He said she was bending down and looked up just as the car smacked into her. Anyway, her family didn't want anyone to know the gory details. They paid the papers to leave it out. It was a closed casket. Sad part was, it took so long to bury her." Alister dropped his chin to his chest.

"Why?" Alex inquired.

"There was only one coroner in town back then. He was away on vacation, visiting relatives in Germany. Catherine's body and head had to be kept in a large, stand-up freezer, covered in ice to preserve her until he arrived home. After the coroner was done with her, my father told me the mortician sewed her head back on. It looked awful, and that's why they closed the casket."

Alex crumpled to the floor.

"Are you alright?" Margaret knelt next to him.

"I'm better than alright. That's got to be it. The reason I was supposed to come here. It's Catherine. Why else would they be freezing? She wants them to feel her pain. The horror of seeing her dismembered body on ice like a slab of meat for all that time. Then she sees her daughter die by the hands of the same man that killed her, and in a gruesome, torturous way. All she could do was watch the whole thing unfold. It's her. It has to be."

Alister eyed Alex, and then Margaret. "The both of you, please leave now. And don't ever come back here. I don't want to see you ever again. You have caused me so much pain, making me relive the past. Do whatever it is you have to but leave me out of it." Alister turned away.

Alex spoke gently. "We're sorry. I don't know if it helps, but you might have just saved a lot of lives. I promise you won't see us anymore."

Alex got up and grabbed hold of Margaret's hand. As he was walking out the door, he glanced back for one last look at the old man. Alister was staring off into the distance, a single tear running down his cheek.

When they got home, his mom was waiting on the couch in the living room. Alex swore he could see the steam shooting out of her ears. She was not happy.

"I cannot believe you did this again. You promised me! You better have a damn good explanation. By good, I mean life or death, because you are not going to see the light of day after Sunday if this isn't a great story."

With Margaret's help, he explained the whole thing. The details of Catherine's horrible death that were kept secret, and the connection between freezing and her severed body on ice for all that time.

His mom softened her tone. "So, it is Catherine we're dealing with."

Alex nodded his head in agreement.

"It all makes sense, Ma. The only thing I can't wrap my head around is why she showed me their deaths."

"Tesoro, she wasn't showing you their deaths. She was showing you Ester's death. Her whole reason for her rage. You said Ester used to get visits from her before all that happened, right?"

"Yeah. Alister said he even saw her once. She scared him, though."

"She scared him because she was a spirit. Not because she looked like this thing now."

"Ohhhh. I see what you're getting at. When she saw her daughter die, the rage inside grew to this insatiable need for vengeance. Greta must have known about Catherine. How else would she know who to summon?"

"Maybe. Maybe not. She might have cast the spell, and Catherine was close when it happened. It sort of locked her in. By that time, she was probably so fueled by hate that it was easy to grab her. Once Greta got her, there was no escape. Each year, she became more and more of what she is now. An evil, malevolent bitch."

"So she showed me Ester's death, but only to kill me afterward? That seems off."

"Maybe she wasn't going to kill you." Gina crooked her mouth.

"Uh. Sort of felt like it," Alex replied.

"You said Greta was outside. Maybe that's what she wanted you to see. She's struggling with both sides of her being—the one that Greta controls and the real Catherine buried deep inside."

"Oh, so she's not a malevolent pain in the ass?" Alex smirked.

"No, she's definitely one of those. But maybe there's a piece of her that's holding on and needs help to break free. If something like that happened to either you or your brother, you might as well pick up what's left of me and toss it in the sea. I can't—don't want to know the anguish she felt."

"Are we good now?" Alex nervously waited for an answer.

"Oh, we are so far from good. We're on opposite ends of the world. But I get why you had to go. You should have told me, though. I know you're getting older, Alex, but we're still a family, and we still look out for each other. You can't think everything is just up to you."

"Got it."

"I'm not so sure you do." His mom put her hands on her hips.

"No, I do. I get what you're saying. I'm sorry; I put lives in jeopardy. I do want to find the killer, but not at the cost of innocent bystanders. I promise, next time, I'll discuss it with you first."

"Yup." His mom folded her arms.

"We have four days left until Halloween. We're getting the spell from Gram later today, and we know who the murderer really is—Greta. We know Catherine is the means, and that Bridget is more than likely the last victim this year. What we need is a way to bring everyone together. When I spoke to Gram last night, she told me all elements need to be joined for this to work."

Margaret interjected, "All elements?"

"Bridget, Greta, and Catherine. We need them all present

when the spell is cast. The spell will release Bridget from Catherine's rage, send Catherine back permanently, and leave Greta drained from doing this again. It's a one-stop shop kind of thing." Alex smiled to reassure her.

"Oh. Okay. That makes sense. But getting them all together with no murder—death—kill as the end result is going to be hard." Margaret bit the inside of her cheek.

"I know. And there's more. Gram says it would be best cast on Halloween. This means fending off any other Greta encounters for the next few days." Alex took a deep breath to stop his voice from shaking.

Gina got up and started pacing. "Margaret, honey, please don't take this personally, but I think you should spend more time at home until we're done. It's one less person for us to worry about and for Greta to go after."

"Gina, no. I want to help and be here with all of you," Margaret demanded.

"I know you do. But you would be helping by thinning out the targets." Gina rubbed Margaret's arm affectionately.

Alex stood up. He didn't want Margaret alone, and he knew she was a fighter. Yes, he wanted her safe, but he felt like being with the family was safer. If Greta decided to go after her to get back at them, she'd be far worse off on her own.

"Ma, you said I should have trusted you earlier. Please trust me now. Margaret is much safer with us. If Greta were to go after her, at least if she's here with us, we can protect her."

His mom sat down. She looked up at her son; dark circles under her eyes were the reward for the worry she'd endured the past few days. Nodding in agreement, she smiled.

"What about your parents? Won't they object?" Gina asked Margaret.

"Well, my dad is away on business in California—again. And Mom is happier in the city. If she knows I'll be here for a couple of days, she'll probably stay at my aunt's. She has a loft in Manhattan. I'll call her now." Margaret pulled her cell from her pocket.

After Margaret left the room, Gina sat down next to Alex.

"I don't know, kid. I love Margaret, but her family is really bizarre."

Alex laughed.

"Why are you laughing?" his mom asked.

"We're standing here, discussing banishing an evil spirit, and Margaret's family is bizarre?"

"Well, when you say it like that."

His mom smirked. "No. What I meant was, how lax they are with her. They never spend any real time with her. What would she be doing if you two weren't together?"

"Thankfully for me, we don't have to answer that question." Alex beamed.

"Ahem. I can see that things have changed." She grinned.

Margaret flung the front door open. "All set. I'll run home and grab clothes and be back in a few."

"I'll go with you." Alex grabbed his hoodie from the closet. "I want to stop by the bagel place and see if Tom is there. I hated how badly it went the other day. Maybe I can smooth things over. I really feel sorry for him. Greta is still his grandmother. What she's done is despicable, but he doesn't know that side of her. To him, she's just Nana."

"It's kind of sad. He has no clue what's really going on. I mean, hearing it from you is one thing, but accepting it— that's an entirely different set of emotions."

———

THE STREETS WERE LITTERED with leaves. The season had arrived, not only for brilliant color, but for the changing of life. Winter would come soon, bringing sleep with it. Alex didn't mind having trees with bare branches. It was comforting knowing that, with each season, there was beauty. Soon, the bare branches would hold up layers of white powder. Spring brought new life. Summer, with everything in full bloom, endless possibilities. Fall was a time to prepare. Getting back to school, the bursts of golds, oranges, and reds surrounding the town invigorated him. It was the segue to the holidays, the first snowfall, and peaceful chilly nights, spent snuggled in blankets with a cup of hot chocolate cupped in his hands and a good movie.

He loved this town. Being in the city was electrifying but living there wouldn't be for him. He needed a slightly more laid-back pace. Besides, if he stood on the steps of a brownstone in the city, he couldn't fly. Not like here. So many trees to glide by in Floral Park made his flight feel like he was a small and yet significant part of the universe. They'd probably think he was crazy.

Here in this neighborhood, no one cared. Well, mostly no one. His thoughts traveled back to some of the crueler kids in school, but they were just a minuscule blip compared to all the good people he knew. Those days had pretty much melted away, and life had gotten sort of good. Except for the occasional encounter with Kyle, he was getting a handle on things, and that made it easier. Although, if there was still more to come, at least he had a great cheering section.

However, that didn't mean the harsh words wouldn't occasionally creep their way back into his memory, dinging his shiny armor and roiling the acids in the pit of his stomach.

It was the first week of ninth grade. New school, new neighborhood—new bully. Alex was having issues with his medication, and his doctor was trying to regulate them. Alex knew who he was, but sometimes other people were the ones with the clarity issue. Hidden under baggy clothes and a hoodie, occasionally the right sway could reveal the curves that he was desperately trying to prevent. Cal Parks was one particularly clouded individual who would go out of his way to relentlessly fling insults regarding Alex's blossoming shape. Tranny, he-she, thing, and it, were all part of Cal's daily vocabulary. For almost a year, Cal tortured him. Slowly, Alex retreated. No interaction with other students became the easier way to deal with the anguish. That is, until Margaret came into his life.

Cal tried a few more new, creative uses of the English language, but she shut him down one day with a swift kick to the place no boy wants with the heel of a combat boot. Cal retreated after the embarrassment of having his ass kicked by someone who was half his size.

When they reached Margaret's house, he stayed in the car. Although her mom was lenient about her schedule, she wasn't crazy about their friendship.

It was about six months after they became friends; Margaret invited him over for a birthday celebration that her family was having for her dad. The teens were paralyzed with astonishment when her mother introduced him as Margaret's little transvestite friend. The both of them immediately got up and left. Alex hadn't been back inside her house since.

He rolled down the window—Margaret's car didn't have power windows. Alex liked it. You didn't need a key for everything. He rested his arm in the window frame and brought his mind back to the case. He felt now with no uncertainty that the evil spirit was born out of the horror of watching her daughter perish by the hands of her own father. Accident or not, he was responsible. Catherine's rage was formed that night. Never mess with a mother's child—words he often heard pass through his mom's lips.

Margaret came out with two stuffed backpack-style bags. Alex chuckled to himself. The girl could pack. They once had a weekend getaway to his cousin's house in Manhasset, further out on Long Island. They were only going to be gone for three nights and two days. She had brought enough clothes for the next ten days. A minimalist at heart, prepared for anything. A perfect contradiction.

Margaret threw them into the back seat, and they headed over to the bagel shop. He didn't know what he was going to accomplish by trying to talk to Tom again, but he felt he needed to try. Hearing your grandmother might be a maniacal killer isn't exactly easy to swallow. Alex felt responsible for causing the pain that had been inflicted on Tom. The bagel shop was only a few minutes away, and yet, the closer they got, the further away it seemed. He was going into anxiety mode— a side-effect of his other heightened senses. He felt things with more intensity than most, and this little outing had him in high-gear. He wanted to do it, and yet, on the other hand, he wanted to run screaming in the opposite direction.

Margaret pulled up to the shop and found a parking spot right in front. Alex hesitated a moment before getting out. He could see Tom in the window. *No going back now,* he thought. Margaret reached for something out of one of her bags. She drew out a hoodie. Alex felt the cold for the first time. He had been so preoccupied with talking to Tom that he didn't notice it. Zipping up his own, he reached his arm out and they clasped hands. Alex had waited too long to be able show his affection for Margaret, and he wasn't about to let one chance slip by. Besides, he needed some of her strength right now.

As they passed through the threshold of the bagel shop, his stomach churned.

They walked to the counter and waited. Tom had his back toward them, but when he turned around, his smile quickly faded into a scowl.

"What do you want, Alex?"

"Just a few minutes to talk and explain."

"I don't have time for this. If you're not going to get anything, then just leave."

"Okay. I'll have a large coffee and an everything bagel. Ciucciamia?" Alex turned to Margaret.

Margaret was scanning the shelves for something that caught her eye. She decided on an old favorite—a cinnamon raisin bagel with peanut butter and jelly; toasted, of course.

Alex gave Tom his debit card, and when the transaction was complete, Tom swiftly turned away and proceeded to fill their order.

Sitting in the familiar window seat, Alex gazed out at the streetlights, getting lost in their glow.

Margaret reached out and grabbed his wrist. "You got this."

He half smiled. *How the hell am I going to explain all of this to Tom? What the fuck do I think I'm going to accomplish by this, anyway?* His mind raced; nothing made sense. He only knew he had to try.

Tom brought their food and coffee and set it down on the table. "Tom, please let me explain what's going on. I'm sorry for hitting you with it the other day like I did. Could you just give us a chance?" Alex pleaded.

"You know what, Alex? I talked to my Nana. She said you're crazy and so is your whole family. She told me not to listen to a word you say. All of you just like to stir up trouble in the neighborhood. She also said that your so-called powers are a lie. Just a way to get attention, or maybe a distraction from other things."

The hairs on the back of Alex's neck rose. The heat swelled in his body and filled it up like the hot coffee in the cup he was drinking. He felt Margaret's hand once again. Glancing over, he knew by the look in her eyes what she was conveying. *Cool down.*

"Tom, I get that you're pissed. I don't blame you. But at least hear us out. Get both sides of the story. I promise you I'm not making this shit up."

"You two are customers, so eat and let me get back to work. When you're done, don't come in here when I'm working again."

Alex dropped his gaze to the floor. He knew this was it. He wasn't going to get the chance to redeem what was done. When you do something just to make you feel better, sometimes it's better to walk away. Margaret agreed with him —it was time to leave. Grabbing their coffee and food, they headed back to his house.

Midnight blue was a perfect backdrop for the scattered, charcoal gray puffs in the starless night. Static electricity thickened the air with impending rain and ignited the senses to the lurking storm. Alex had a quivering in his chest—a hint that things were about to go from bad to worse. Greta would put up a ferocious a fight; he knew it.

<hr>

ALEX SLIPPED his key into the deadbolt and opened the door to an intense conversation. His mom was on the phone, and she put her index finger up to signal he needed to wait. When she was done, his mom threw the phone on the couch, as if the very act would make her anguish go away.

"Your grandmother has written the spell out, and there is one for each of us. At twelve o'clock Sunday morning, we will start preparing the house. After that is done, we will wait until dawn and start summoning the spirit of Catherine. I cannot wait for this crap to be over."

"But what about Bridget and Greta? They both need to be here, too. How the hell are we gonna get either one of them over at six a.m.?" Alex questioned.

"As stupid as it sounds, we're going to invite her. We're hoping her hate and need for vengeance will guide her right to us. Bridget is a different problem. I think that one might be up to you and Margaret. You were the ones who first responded to her family stories. I think the truth might be on your side. Especially with the peculiar death of her mother."

"You find something out on the death of Bridget's mom?"

"Evelyn Fitzgerald died from overexposure to the cold—in her bathroom," his mom responded.

"What? That's it. Right?" Alex shook his head.

"I would say so. It seems Bridget was the one to find her. She was in a bathtub that was filled with hot water. Her body was frozen solid, and her neck broken. This is why I'm hoping, if you tell Bridget the truth, she'll come on her own."

"And if she doesn't?"

"One problem at a time, bella mia. Let's just hope she does," his mom sighed.

"Margaret and I will go to the diner tomorrow. If Bridget's not there, we'll find out her address."

"48 Pansy Ave," his mom responded.

"What?"

"That's Bridget's address."

"Okay, Ma. That's the mechanics. What about the spell itself? If we're all taking part, shouldn't we go over it?"

"No."

"What? Why?" Alex was astonished.

"Because we don't want to show our hand. Read it to yourself. Become familiar with it, but do not say one word out loud. Understood?"

"We get it, don't worry."

"Oh, it is much too late for that, mio figlio. Worry is now my middle name."

A cold blade of shivers ripped up Alex's spine, and goosebumps skittered down both arms. He surveyed the room. In the far-left corner was a shadow of a little girl—Ester. Soon, he thought.

THE PLAN

Thursday morning, Alex woke up with Margaret safe in his arms—a very different arrangement from the night before.

He was thankful to have a mother like Gina. He knew no one else would let his girlfriend stay the night in his bed. His girlfriend . . . it sounded so cool.

He pulled up his comforter and draped it over the both of them. Getting out of bed could wait a little longer. This felt so good, which was something that was not in their daily adventures the past few weeks. He caught a scent of pumpkin spice—Margaret's fall shampoo. He nestled his nose into her soft, shiny locks. He loved that smell. She stirred a little, and he lay still for a moment as not to wake her. She had been beat last night, and a few extra minutes were his gift to her.

As he gazed up at the ceiling, a shadow emerged amid the nubby popcorn finish that was left over from an eighties remodel. He hated that look. The longer he stared, the clearer the shadow became. Alex wasn't afraid. He glanced at his arms —minimal goosebumps. It was Ester. The little girl hovered just a few feet above them. Her eyes drooped and the corners of her mouth turned down. Sadness dripped from her small spirit. Alex slowly slid his free arm from the warmth of the comforter and waved slightly to Ester. The ghostly child descended until she was inches away from the two of them.

Alex lifted his head and turned it away from Margaret. Then he whispered to Ester words he hoped would comfort the little girl. "I know who you are, Ester. I will set things right. Your mother is not in full control of what is happening. I will do my best to save her spirit and send her back to you."

Alex heard the words slipping from his lips, but he wasn't quite sure why he said them. He had no idea how to save Catherine. Up until now, the plan was to banish her to where she had come from; but seeing the anguish and lost, lonely expression on the young girl's face—his instinct to help kicked in.

Ester reached to Alex, and her hand caressed his cheek. Her eyes softened with what one might assume was hope. She glided toward the window and was gone as quickly as she had appeared.

Crap, he thought. *What the hell did I just do?*

Margaret stirred and then rolled over with her back to him. He wanted to get up but decided to wait just a little longer before disturbing her. Hoping to find an ally, he was going to talk with Gina. He may be able to appeal to her maternal side.

Margaret turned again; this time, she was facing him.

"Hey. Good morning." Margaret bunched the comforter up to her neck. "What's going on? I heard you talking to yourself."

"I saw Ester," Alex whispered.

"Catherine's daughter?" Margaret propped her head with her hand.

"Yup."

"Where?"

"Here, a few minutes ago."

Margaret sat up. "What? Did she say anything?"

"No. She just looked so sad. Tesoro, you should have seen her. It was killing me."

"What are you gonna do? Or can you do anything?" Margaret ran her fingers through his hair.

"I think so. But I don't think it's going to go over very well with everyone else."

"Okay. Tell me."

Margaret wiggled and pulled the comforter up to her neck as she listened. When Alex was done, she took a deep breath and sighed.

"I'm not gonna lie; you've got your work cut out for you. Everybody in the house has nothing but venom for Catherine."

"See, I think that's not exactly true. I think they all have venom, but I think it's mostly for Greta. Remember what my mom said earlier? She thought that maybe Catherine was reaching out with some small part of the human side that might remain."

"Yeah. I do remember her saying that."

"Maybe if she believes it's true, then she'll think we might have a chance to save Catherine's spirit. I'm not saying murder is excusable, but Catherine is the puppet. It's Greta who is orchestrating all of this. She just used Catherine's anger over the death of her daughter to benefit her maniacal plan."

"I'm on your side. I get it. Now you just need to win over your mom like you did me." Margaret kissed his cheek.

"That's not fair."

"What? Why?" Margaret snuggled closer.

"I'm your partner in crime; you need me for your cookie cravings." Alex winked.

"Oh, McKenna. You couldn't be more mistaken. I'm the one with the car."

"Ouch."

"Come on. Let's go and talk to your mom."

They threw off the covers and quickly dressed. The wood floors were pretty, but not so much on the cooler days. Alex put on a pair of heavy white socks, and Margaret slipped into her Uggs. Zipping their hoodies, they traipsed downstairs.

His mom was in the kitchen, fixing a bowl of oatmeal. "Good morning." Alex kissed his mom's cheek.

"I'm sorry about the house. I know it's really cold, but the heater is slow this morning. It's old. I just need it to hold on through this winter, and then in the spring, I'll look into a loan and getting a new one." His mom pursed her lips.

"It's okay. We have winter armor." Alex tugged at his hoodie. "Listen, Ma. I need to talk to you. Could we go in the other room?"

His mom knitted her brows.

"I'm okay. I just need to run something by you," Alex said reassuringly.

He figured he'd have a better shot at persuading her if they were alone with no outside opinions.

He led his mom into the sunroom. It wasn't a very large space, but it was his favorite in the entire house. It was surrounded by French doors on three of the walls, and the fourth housed an antique upright piano. The only one who played was his grandpa, but his mom kept it because she loved hearing her dad play, even if was only occasionally. Alex enjoyed the solace of the room. It's where he would sit and think. During the day, the room soaked in the light and heat of the sun. It was always bright. It gave him hope and cradled his soul even on the lowest days.

"Uh-oh. We're in the sunroom. What's going on, Alex?" his mom probed.

"I got a visit this morning." Alex sat on the piano bench.

"Oh?" Her eyes widened.

"It was Ester."

"Catherine's daughter?"

"Yes. She was so sad. You could see how lost she was. I really want to try and help her."

"Um. Okay. I understand where you are coming from, and when this is over, we will help her cross over; I promise. But right now, honey, we have bigger and more dangerous issues. She's waited this long. A few more days won't be too awful." His mom sat next to him.

"No. That's not what I mean."

"You don't want to help her cross over? Then what? Ohhhh . . . no. You can't be serious."

"Ma, just listen," Alex pleaded.

"Alex, you want to unite Catherine and Ester. Am I right?"

"Yes." He nodded his head.

"Have you lost your mind? We have enough on our plate with crazy Greta. How the hell do you propose to get mother and daughter together when mom is a raging serial killer?"

"Come on. You said it yourself. Catherine must have a piece of her true self in there somewhere."

"No. What I said was, there's a *chance* there's some of her humanity left in her. Big, huge difference."

"And if it were Wilby?" Alex played the mom card.

"What do you mean?"

"If Wilby were stranded between worlds and looking for you, wouldn't you want everything possible done to get you together again?"

"That depends."

"On what?"

"Am I a sinister, hateful, malevolent spirit? Or am I me?"

"That's not the point." Alex furrowed his brow.

"That's exactly the point." His mom's tone was sharp.

This was not going the way Alex had seen it in his head.

She was being infinitely more stubborn than he had anticipated.

"I promised her." Alex glanced past his mother.

"You promised her what?" His mom narrowed her eyes.

"That I'd help her get to her mom again."

"Damn it, Alex. You had no right. You have just put everyone's life in greater jeopardy than they were before," she said angrily.

Alex understood the scope of what he had done. If they tried, they were all at great risk. If they didn't, he lied to the spirit of a lost little girl. Getting her to trust him—or anyone again—so they could help her cross over might prove near impossible.

"You didn't see her face or feel her overwhelming sadness. She needs us."

His mom's choice of silence left Alex with uneasiness. He nearly expected her to explode. Turned out not to be the case at all.

"I'll talk to Gram. Maybe there is something we can do. Once we've trapped her and have all three of them here, we might be able to pull her away and reason with her. I'm not making any promises," his mom said sternly.

"Thank you." Alex paused. He couldn't let it go. "Ma?"

"Yeah?"

"How come you changed your mind?"

"Because you're my child, and I could see the sadness in your face."

Alex stayed in the sunroom after his mom left. He contemplated her words. As a child, you never really understand why your parents do the things they do. They all seem crucial to you. But what Gina said struck him. To save her own child anguish, she would try. Maybe that's how they get through to Catherine. It wouldn't be enough to have Greta, Catherine, and Bridget there. They needed Ester, too.

New Hyde Park, New York- 2002

Jim Bishop sat alone in his living room. The television was on some comedy show. He didn't really care. He wasn't paying attention. The gun he had bought ten days ago from the Arms Show at Madison Square Garden lay loaded in his lap. The melted ice and residue of bourbon in a short bar glass stuck to the tabletop next to his chair. The nearly empty bottle was beside it. He had done so many wrong things in his life, yet his only real regret was Ester.

There was a loud knock at the door. He could hear the postman identifying himself. He apparently had a package to be delivered. Jim ignored him. It didn't matter. Whatever it was, he would have no use for it any longer. He was ninety-five, for Christ's sake. How many more years would he have to endure? He was too tired for all of this. He hated to leave Alister alone, but let's face it—he was getting on in age himself. With no children of his own and the move into the retirement community, he plotted his own course. He no longer needed Jim, and he certainly didn't need the responsibility of taking care of him. No. He had spent enough time on this dreadful planet. Enough time dealing with *her*.

If he had known then that she would never leave him, then killing her would not have been an option. Maybe just had her committed.

Crazy was easy to prove back then. But her death had brought about a life of misery for him. Now, he would finally be free. Why he chose to hide it from his son all this time was never clear to him. They had a conversation once after he spotted her the very last time he set foot in 55 Geranium. Nothing was mentioned after that.

He pulled up the afghan that was covering his legs. The temperature had plummeted suddenly, and he knew damn well what that meant. She was coming. The horrible, disfigured thing that was once his wife.

He lifted the gun from his lap and clicked off the safety. Then, reaching over and grabbing his glass, took the last sip of watered- down bourbon before placing the nozzle under his chin and pulling the trigger.

THE FINAL VICTIM

The entire afternoon was spent preparing for Sunday. Alex's mom took every precaution to make sure all the ingredients they needed were readily available and the house was as safe as possible. Anything breakable was packed and placed in the garage. The larger, heavier, pieces of furniture were moved to the basement. Once that was done, she installed a bolt on the door just in case anyone decided it was a good idea to run down there in a frenzy. It wasn't.

Alex agreed he should be the one to talk to Bridget. Margaret was going to stay home for this one. He didn't want it to appear as if they were ganging up on her. He did bring some of the articles regarding the murders and the fire, along with the death of Catherine in the obituaries.

Margaret had offered to drive him to the diner, but he wanted to walk. He needed to walk. His head was clouded. A few weeks ago, his largest concern was passing his driver's test and getting a car. Gina had rescheduled it for mid-November.

Most of the trees had completed their change and had started to lose their leaves. He walked through the rustling splashes of brown that laid on the sidewalk. He used to like raking them with his dad.

He knew his friends thought he was crazy, because it was a hassle, but for Alex, it was like this walk. Time to clear his head with the added bonus of spending time with his father.

He gazed up at the vast emptiness and welcomed the open door of change in the air. The longer, darker days were almost here, and would be submerging them under the cloak of winter for the next several months. He had hoped this walk would reveal some epiphany to him. A clue he had missed, or perhaps a significant word or sentence in the dialogue of the people he had spoken with this past week. His stomach churned from the burning acid cooking inside his belly. He felt inept with this case. It was nothing like the ghosts of past experiences. This time, the living depended on him. He needed to perform with the utmost caution and precise execution.

First, however, he needed to get Bridget on board.

The diner was crowded, every window filled with faces of conversation and chewing. After he was inside, he spotted a seat open at the counter. Luck was on his side; Bridget was serving a customer who sat beside the empty barstool. Hastily, he claimed it before anyone else noticed. Bridget saw him and waved. She put up a one with her index finger, signaling she'd be over in a minute. Alex opened the menu and searched for a dish that would take longer to prepare. Since the diner was so busy, he didn't know how much of her time he'd be able to steal. If the food took longer, then there would be more chances for him to catch her in between customers.

Chicken pot pie. That was one of his faves, and a recipe he never got homemade. His mom was a great Italian cook, but American comfort food was not on her list of accomplishments. Although, she never really tried . . . so who knows, maybe. Anyway, they made it fresh here, so it would take some time. A disclaimer was included on the menu. *Made fresh just for you! Patience please when ordering this item.* He laughed to himself. *Perfect.*

"Back again? You're becoming one of my regulars." Bridget flipped open her pad.

"I'm on my own for dinner tonight, so I thought I'd spend it with a friendly face." Alex smiled.

"Are you sure you're only seventeen?"

"Old soul. Or at least, that's what I'm told."

"I'll say. Where's that pretty little girlfriend of yours?"

"She had to hang with her parents tonight." Alex frowned.

"Well, what would you like?" Bridget had a pen in hand.

"I'll take the chicken pot pie and a root beer." Alex handed her the menu.

"Good choice, if you don't mind hanging around for a bit. Cook makes it fresh."

"So I hear. I got nowhere else to be, so I don't mind. Besides, maybe you can tell me some more stories." Alex made a pleading gesture.

"You got it! Let me go put your order in. I'll be back in a few minutes."

Bridget disappeared through the double door to the kitchen. Alex rubbed over his heart. A familiar pain squeezed his chest. There were so many people, an eclectic ensemble of emotions consumed the room. It could be hard to control. Protecting himself was something he learned at a young age. His gram had showed him how to create the white light in his thoughts. It radiated around him, acting as a shield. He was doing the same for Wilby.

However, on rare occasions, an event could be strong enough to penetrate his shield. With no warning, Alex found himself grappling to breathe. He swiveled around in the chair and panned the room, attempting to connect with someone.

At the far end of the diner, in a booth against the window, a small boy sat with his parents. The adults were engaged in conversation, and he was coloring. He had dropped his crayon on the floor and lay down on the seat, hanging over the edge to pick it up. The little boy sat up, his face red, and grabbed his throat.

Alex labored to take in air, his mind struggling to focus. He tried to yell out, but he couldn't. A phantom obstruction blocked his airway. He got up, struggling to make his way to the child. Thankfully, the mother noticed what was happening and screamed. The dad responded quickly and grabbed his son, immediately turning him around and slapping his back. A piece of hamburger flew out of the boy's mouth, landing on the restaurant floor. The boy lay cradled in his mother's arms for the remainder of their meal.

Exhausted, Alex collapsed on the floor directly in the aisle of exiting diners. Bridget came running over and helped him back to his seat. She brought him a glass of water and a cold rag.

"Hey, you okay, honey?" She blotted the rag on his forehead.

"Yeah, thanks. I saw that boy choking and went to help. I must have tripped over my own damn feet," Alex lied.

It sounded lame, but doable. He took a sip of water—the coolness soothed his throat, but not his nerves. He hated those intense encounters. He plugged in his earbuds and allowed himself to be lulled to a calmer place while keeping one eye on Bridget. He didn't want to miss his opening to speak with her.

"Alex, your order should be up in about fifteen minutes." Bridget gently touched his forearm. "Can I get you another soda while you're waiting?"

He glanced over at his empty glass and nodded his head in agreement.

"Thank you." He removed his earbuds.

"No problem. What are you listening to?" Bridget leaned on the counter.

"The soundtrack from The Nightmare Before Christmas."

"Oh, brother. You're just like my sister's kids. They love everything and anything related to Halloween. Me, I'm more of a Christmas girl myself."

"Christmas is great. But Halloween is when it all happens. Ghosts, goblins, vampires, witches—they all come out on Halloween. Bwahahaha!" Alex laughed.

"That, they do." Bridget grinned.

"Listen, Bridget. I was wondering if you had a few minutes to talk after your shift?"

"Actually, you are my last customer. Let me go see if your food is ready, and then I'll check out and grab a cup of coffee."

"Great. Thanks."

Bridget came back with the piping hot pot pie and a soda refill. Alex waited for it to cool down before cracking the top crust. He loved that part. By the time he'd had a few bites, Bridget came over with her purse and a cup of black coffee. She sat down on the open stool next to his and took a sip.

"Ah. That is so good after a long day on my feet. Honestly, I'm getting too old for this kind of work."

"My mom always soaks her feet in a hot foot thingy." Alex took another bite.

"Is that the technical term?"

"Ha, ha. You know what I mean."

"I do. I have one of those. Sometimes it helps. So, kid. What did you need to talk about?"

Alex finished chewing. He figured that would be his last good bite; the rest would probably go down like lumps after he told Bridget why he was really there.

"You remember my mom?"

"Sure. I said I was too old for this work. I'm not feeble." She smirked.

"Well, I need to tell you something about her and me. In fact, about all of us. Please don't judge. Hear me out, and then if you want to leave, then go. I won't bother you." Alex knew that was a lie. They needed her there on Sunday morning and, whether she came on her own or they intervened, she would be there.

He started the story with Jim Bishop and Catherine. He showed her the obituary of Catherine's death in the newspaper. She fidgeted when he mentioned her own family's involvement, but she didn't leave, so that was promising. When he got to the present day and the current victims, he could see the light bulb go off by the widening of her eyes. Then he laid out the details of the death of her own mother and the gruesome similarities. He paused, waiting for her to either hit him, walk out, or call the police to have him arrested.

But she didn't.

"Bridget? Are you okay? Do you understand what I'm saying?" Alex spoke softly.

"I do. And yes. I'm fine. You're telling me that you think I am the next victim."

"I do—we do. Greta was here the other night when you were working. She summoned Catherine. We think she was watching you. She tried to kill us. But thankfully, I have a brilliant grandmother. I'm so sorry about this. Believe me, I know how ridiculous it all sounds. And I wouldn't have told you if I wasn't one hundred percent sure you are in grave danger."

"I know. I believe you." Bridget patted his hand.

"Okay. That was a little too easy."

"Ever since I found my mother, I've been looking for answers. You just gave them all to me."

"Well, it's not over yet. Halloween is Sunday, and that's the last day for her to complete her murder spree for this year. We want to end this permanently. My family thinks we can do it. But we need all the elements involved in the same place. Back where it started, 55 Geranium Ave. It means . . .”

“I know what it means. I have to be there with this thing and Greta. And Ester? Is the little girl there, too?”

“She is. Listen, I will explain everything to you. What needs to be done and how. But for now, I need to know you will be there. I also should tell you that it doesn’t matter where you are—she’ll find you. I’m not trying to scare you, but we are your best chance to survive this.” Alex waited.

“Okay. When should I be there?”

“Saturday night before midnight.”

“I’ll be there. 55 Geranium Ave, right?”

“Yup.” He shook his head.

Bridget reached out and squeezed his forearm once more, her gaze soft. He knew she would be there. He stayed to finish his pot pie before calling Margaret for a ride home. He was drained, and the walk back didn’t sound as appealing as the journey up.

He waited by the door, opting not to tempt fate in the darkness. When Margaret pulled up, he vigorously slid in, belted, and sighed in the security of the steel carriage. She had the heater on, and he held his hands to the vent to warm them. He didn’t say much; he was too tired. It had been a long day. His doctor’s appointment was in the morning, which was an unwanted distraction. Normally, he didn’t mind going. It was a chance to get one step closer to his goals. But not this week. There was too much going on, and it was more of an inconvenience than a solace. Missing it was not an option, though. His mom insisted. And since he didn’t want to rock the hormonal boat and crash into the thousand-foot wave that sometimes fueled his mom, he kept his thoughts to himself.

His mom was still up when he and Margaret got home, and just as he had figured, she reminded him about his appointment in the morning. He nodded and focused on his prize—sleep.

THE DOCTOR

eep, beep, beep. Alex swiped to turn off the alarm on his phone. He rolled over and expected Margaret's warm body, but instead, an empty pillow lay waiting. Groggily, he sat up and threw the comforter to the bottom of the bed. He shivered. No worries about Catherine killing me; the broken furnace could do that.

Wrapping himself in the security of his comforter, Alex ambled toward the bathroom. Unfortunately, when he turned the knob, it was locked. He pressed his ear to the door—the shower pulsed in a stream resembling heavy rainfall.

He knocked with a heavy hand and was greeted with the lovely melody of Margaret's reply.

"Who is it?"

"Ciucciamia, it's me. When you get a chance, can you let me in?" He leaned into the door.

"Sure. Just give me a sec. I'm rinsing my hair."

Alex slid down to the floor and propped his back against the wall until the click of the lock summoned him. Margaret was standing in the steam-filled room with wet hair, wrapped in a towel.

"Get in here. It's freezing out there." She tugged at his arm.

"Tell me about it." He swiftly gravitated to the heat of the steam. "A little privacy, please?"

Margaret sheepishly grinned and turned around.

"Why do you still keep calling me your friend?" Margaret briskly ran a towel over her hair.

"What do you mean?" Alex hesitated at the shower curtain.

"You called me ciuccia-something again."

"Oh." He laughed. "Well, I have a confession. It doesn't really mean 'my friend.'"

"Well, what does it mean, then?" She turned around to face him.

"It means . . . my baby." Alex lowered his head.

"Really?" Margaret wrapped her arms around his neck and softly pressed her lips against his, sharing the smooth balm of strawberries and cream. "Okay, you're free to shower now."

Alex twirled his index finger, and she abruptly turned around again. He unwrapped himself from the plush warmth, slipped off his boxers, and stepped into the shower. The hot water hammered his back, prickling his skin. It felt good. When Margaret had finished drying her hair, she told him she'd meet him downstairs. He stood in the sauna-like stream a few minutes longer before soaping up and rinsing.

Venturing out wasn't quite as easy. He hesitated, dreading the cold gush that awaited him. He pulled the towel off a nearby rack and stepped onto a small but welcoming bath rug. Clearing the mirror with his hand, he half-expected and fully hoped to see Ester again. Leaning in toward his reflection, a hint of disappointment filled the void of the empty-looking glass.

After he was dressed, he joined everyone in the kitchen. Silence pervaded the air, which was another rare occasion in a gathering at the McKenna household. Too busy with their consumption of early morning fuel, no one looked up except for Margaret.

"Hey, Alex, what are you gonna have for breakfast?" She took a bite from a cream cheese-smothered onion bagel.

"I think I'll stick with a bowl of Cheerios." His stomach fought off the flutters of his impending doctor's visit.

"Are you worried about your doc appointment?" His mom frowned. "Is there something you aren't telling me?'

"No. I'm fine, Ma. You know I always get anxious before a visit." Alex rolled his eyes.

He didn't know why; it didn't make any sense. He wasn't afraid— in fact, it was the exact opposite. He liked finding out about his progress. But nonetheless, here were the butterflies, floating around in his stomach and causing just the slightest bit of nausea.

Maybe it was because, for the first time, Margaret would accompany them to the doctor. She had talked about taking a more active role in his transition in the past. Even when they were just friends, Margaret wanted to understand everything about the process he would endure. But Gina had held her at bay in the past. Whatever changed her mind made them both very happy.

Doctor Freeman was a kind man. He was also the leading pediatric endocrinologist in New York. Alex just knew he liked him. The doc explained things in terms that were simple and clear.

The waiting room was packed—the downfall to seeing a great doctor. They were there about forty-five minutes before the medical assistant called his name. She was new and petite, with short blonde hair that was shaved on one side, and several piercings in each ear. A tiny blue stone on the left side of her nose completed her fashion sense.

The three of them herded to the waiting girl

"Alex McKenna?" She directed her question to Alex.

"Yes." Alex smiled.

"Hi, my name is Ryan."

"Nice to meet you. Where's Mickey?" Alex inquired.

"She has the day off. But she'll be back tomorrow." Ryan grinned.

"You're new here?"

"Yes. I started last week."

"Cool."

Ryan led Alex to a large, electronic scale and asked him to step up—one hundred and forty pounds.

"Great. If you follow me, I'll get you to your room."

The room was uncharacteristically warm that day. Usually, Alex would be crossing his arms to hold in the heat, but today, he was relaxed. The decor was meant to appeal to younger kids: the light blue walls had two murals of giraffes, elephants and zebras in the midst of green trees, and a brilliant blue body of water. In the corner was a small table with two chairs and a plethora of coloring books and crayons. Two chrome and black adult-sized chairs butted up against the wall, and a physician's stool floated in the middle of the room. The most cumbersome and attention-grabbing piece of furniture needed no announcement—the examining table.

Both women took a seat while Alex had hopped on the table. Ryan took his blood pressure, then pulse and temperature. There were the usual questions about his overall health and history since his last visit. When she was done, she told them the doctor would be in shortly.

Alex wriggled on the table; it wasn't the most comfortable position.

"I hope he's not late today." Alex lay back on the table and then sat up again.

"Why? Is he normally late?" Margaret got up and took his hand.

"Sometimes," he grumbled.

Thankfully, a short, light knock at the door was followed by Dr. Gerald Freeman. He sat down on the stool and glided over to Alex. "Alex, how are doing today?"

"Good, Doc."

"I see we have a visitor." Doctor Freeman glanced at Margaret.

"Oh, yeah. This is my girlfriend, Margaret." The words fumbled from his mouth.

"Nice to meet you." Margaret smiled.

"You too." Doctor Freeman resumed. "So, let's get down to it. Your blood test results were excellent. You're right where we want you to be. You know my concerns are comfortably maintaining the levels we need you at so you don't experience any female puberty. No signs of a menstrual cycle, right?"

"Nope. None." Alex shook his head.

"Any problems with the shots? Nausea? Joint pain?" Dr. Freeman opened his notebook and started typing.

"I feel good." He lied—the nausea was with him as they spoke.

"How about any concerns? I think your voice has deepened since your last visit. Are you happy with the progress?"

"I am. Well, I wish it would get just a little deeper, but hopefully with time." Alex raised a brow.

"I won't lie to you, Alex. It might, but it might not. There is the option of training your voice, which we can discuss, but I don't think we're there yet. What about your hair growth? I see a little stubble on that chin." The doc lifted Alex's chin with his index finger.

"I'm stoked. I haven't tried shaving it yet, but I'm going to," Alex said gleefully.

"Great. You might see that increase as well. It's all a waiting game. But you're right on the mark, and I don't think

I'd advise any increase of hormones at this time. How do you feel about that?"

"I mean, if you think we shouldn't, then that's okay. I would just like to have more hair growth and the voice thing like I said. But I do see the changes; I just wish they were faster. I don't want to risk feeling bad, so I guess we leave it for now."

The doctor turned to Alex's mom. "He's right where we want him to be. Do you have any questions for me, Gina?"

"Actually, I do." She crossed her legs and leaned forward. Alex felt the flutters in his stomach take a nosedive.

"I've been reading about the surgery. Doc, it seems very risky."

"It can be." Dr. Freeman turned to Alex. "But is this something you've been thinking about lately? Because on your last visit, you had decided to wait."

"No. I haven't thought about it. Not yet. I do know eventually I want the top surgery. The sooner the better, but for anything else, no. I need time to think."

"Well, you know we can do the breast surgery whenever you're ready." Doc patted Alex's shoulder.

Alex nodded. He knew the insurance wouldn't cover it, and his mom didn't have ten thousand dollars just sitting in the bank. He would have to save up his own money for this one. First a car, then surgery.

"Thanks, Doc."

"How about we discuss this some more the next time you come in?"

"Sounds good." Alex hopped off the table.

"Gina, are we good?" Dr. Freeman stood up.

"For now, I guess we are," she agreed.

Doctor Freeman sent an electronic prescription renewal for Alex's hormone shots to his pharmacy and left the room.

Alex could feel his mom's confusion over the conversation. She really didn't get any answers. Or, at least, not the ones that she wanted. The truth was, this was his body, and he would discuss topics like surgery when he was able to. Not now.

He opted to ride in the back seat with Margaret on the way home. They held hands, soaking in the silence. They didn't need to speak. All Margaret wanted was to be included and be there for him in whatever decisions he made. He never had to explain to her why, just how.

The aroma of fresh garlic browning in olive oil immediately awakened Alex's taste buds as he entered the house. His nostrils flared with delight from the fragrant scent. The robust melody of Come Back to Sorrento vibrating throughout the house meant only one thing: his gram was in the kitchen cooking.

"Gram! What are you doing here? I thought you were staying home?" Alex hugged her.

"Your mom and I thought it would be a good idea to have extra forces. They've told me what you intend to do with Catherine's spirit and Ester."

"I feel it in my bones. It's what I have to do." He sighed.

"I agree. And that's why I'm here." His gram took a sip of wine.

"But Gram, this might be too hard on you."

"Let me worry about what I can and can't do. Now, everyone sit down, dinner is ready."

His gram kept it simple. Spaghetti and garlic bread with a little vino, and insalata with balsamic vinegar and olive oil. As long as it was his gram's homemade dressing, Alex didn't care if she decided to drench it over cardboard—he'd eat it.

"Now, what exactly are your plans?" His gram set her fork down on the plate.

"Our biggest problem will be getting Greta here," Alex replied.

His gram sat back and took another sip of wine. "Use me.

Let her know I will be here, too. I should think she couldn't resist having the matriarch of the LaBoccetta clan wiped out."

"Uh. Okay. Not sure if I like your word usage, Gram. Wiped out?"

"How about the boy? Tom. This is her grandson, right?" his gram inquired.

"Yes."

"Maybe pay him another visit and tell him exactly what's happening."

"I don't know. He made it pretty clear never to go to the shop again when he was working. I may get in, but that doesn't mean he'll listen."

"I'll go," Margaret cut in. "He might be a little more lenient with me."

"I don't think it's safe for you to be there alone," Alex opposed.

"Alex, for Christ's sake. I'll go tomorrow in the daylight. There's a good chance there will be other customers. You can wait outside in the car and watch the whole thing. As long as he doesn't see you, I think we'll be fine," Margaret said firmly.

"I don't think . . ."

"I'm going. You can either wait here or in the car. That part is up to you. The part where I go and see Tom and tell him everything, we need for him to know—that's all mine," Margaret said.

Alex held his words. He knew he was getting nowhere with this.

He also knew she was more than capable, but it still worried him.

After dinner was over and the dishes were washed and put away, his gram went up to Wilby's room to rest. Alex's mom was at the kitchen table going over bills, and Margaret had turned on the TV.

Alex, however, couldn't relax. His head was spinning with

thoughts that were about to become a reality, and he worried for his family and Bridget. A walk might help him clear his mind. Margaret offered to go with him, but he needed some alone time. She got it. He knew she would. He grabbed his heavy pea coat from the hall closet and a beanie for his head. He didn't bother with gloves—that's what pockets were for. There was no plan for his destination: the night sky and cement walkways would be the guide to where his soul wanted to be.

As he stepped onto the stoop, he had the urge to close his eyes and take flight. The air was exhilarating, and the trees against the moonlight painted an inviting landscape. But not tonight; there was too much clutter. Skipping steps, he jumped onto the pavement below.

To some, darkness brought terror of the unknown, but for Alex, it was peace. Untouched by the perils of daylight. All the hustle of people rushing to places they had to be—or worse, didn't want to go. The endless anxiety spent on just getting through the day. In the evening, and in the shadows, it slowed down. The night was his time for sanctuary.

In the cloak of the midnight blue sky, he strolled down Geranium Ave, first passing Mrs. Rice's house. It was all locked up for the evening, and he could see the light of her television shining through the half-closed blinds. He pictured her sitting in her usual recliner, asleep with a cup of tea on her side table.

A pang of sadness pierced his heart. Her son only visited out of obligation. A few houses past were the Bensons. Sam Benson was an attorney and worked in the city. His wife was a stay-at-home mom, who Alex only knew as Mrs. Benson. Their hedges were always exceptionally neat and tailored. Alex figured it was because Sam Benson was probably a real type-A personality. Coming to the end of the block, his feet took him in a straight line instead of turning. Shivers rippled down his spine; the uneasiness, an unwanted passenger.

For every good spirit that just needed a little nudge to find its way, there were dark souls content in being lost. Looming in the corners of despair, they'd wait to get Alex alone. Separated from his family, he was more vulnerable. They were not victims like Catherine, but rather people who in life embraced the evil in this world, drinking it up like a smooth scotch. They enjoyed the darkness as it slithered down their throats, warming the fires of hate and igniting their thirst for more. Floral Park was no stranger to one or more of these cursed souls.

You'd better pick up your pace, my young friend.

Victor, who's out there?

No one you want to meet, Alex.

Alex quickly turned back and around the corner. The cold air crept into the open collar of his jacket, and he shuddered. Luckily, he was only a few minutes away from uptown and a group of shops and convenience stores that were across the street from the church. Like a magnet, his know pulled at him and led him to the coffee shop.

As soon as he entered the place, he was hit with a wave of regret. Standing in front of him was Tom. He quickly turned to leave, but he was stopped by a tight grip squeezing his arm.

"Alex, why can't you just leave my family alone? My nana hasn't been the same since you started harassing us. I don't get you, dude."

"I'm sorry, Tom. I wish I could change things. I really do."

"She says really weird things now. I don't know . . . She's scaring me."

"Tom, leave. Get out of Floral Park and go someplace safe."

"See? What does that even mean? Someplace safe? I can't go anywhere. I'd never leave my nana alone."

"Greta has done some really terrible things, and I don't think she's gonna stop on her own. But there's no reason for you to get involved."

"Sure, there is—she's my family. I gotta go."

Tom pushed through the door, and Alex just watched. There wasn't anything he could say to change the guy's mind. But he was right—he and Greta were family. And Alex understood the full weight of those words. Family was everything, but unfortunately, Tom's family had to be stopped. *Please, universe. Keep him safe.*

Clutching the warm cup between his hands, Alex crossed the street. The church had been a place he always enjoyed spending time in. He loved the art of the stained-glass windows, the statues that dressed the altar, and the mystery of the confessional boxes. He wasn't sure exactly where he stood in the whole catholic belief system. It was definitely flawed, but the rituals of robes, incense, and holy water intrigued him. So he wasn't surprised when his journey ended at Our Lady of Victory.

He hoped it was unlocked. There were a couple of break-ins the year before, and Father Martin had started locking the doors after dark.

Alex stood in front of the structure of brick, mortar, and celestial windows and held his breath. He reached for the heavy oak door and pulled. It was a struggle, but it opened. He walked about halfway down the center aisle and took a seat at the end of the pew. It was serene. No one else was there. At first, he soaked in the variety of prismatic tints in the glass and the harvest decorations that adorned the altar. All Saints Day was the day after Halloween, and the church was ready to receive its people with orange and yellow floral arrangements—the gateway to the winter holidays. Leaning back, he closed his eyes and let his mind wander. The best way for him to clear it was to unleash it.

He found himself relaxing while his anxieties slowly melted away.

Clarity filled the crevices of his brain, overflowing them with pure, white light. It consoled him, but more importantly, brought empowerment. He followed the light in his mind as it unveiled the plan for Sunday morning. All the players were there, and they each had their part. The frames of film unfolded, working out the possible errors that he then corrected. His confidence rose the further he went; he knew this was possible without jeopardizing his family. This was one of his gifts—the ability to live the experience without harm, making the necessary corrections before it happened.

He opened his eyes and sat for a moment—this gift cost him a good amount of energy. Soaking in the spiritual aura of the altar, he pondered the question of whether this religion, or any other, had complete truth in it. Whatever portion was based on reality, at times it had its comforts. That alone was enough for him. He didn't need confirmation. He already knew that life existed after death. He needed hope for the living.

As he pulled again on the cumbersome wooden doors, they felt lighter this time. Since his mind had worked out the issues he was having, the walk home was just for him. He could soak up the darkness and the contrasting sliver of illumination from the waxing crescent moon. He melted into shadows. For someone who saw the essence of those who had passed, the shadows were filled with possibilities, not fear. Nearing the corner to Geranium, his trip home had passed much quicker than the one to the church. He felt a little disappointment cradle itself in the pit of his stomach. He took the first step on his stoop and turned back to take one more look at the enchanting night. Then, leaping two steps at once, he opened the front door to a glowing low light and voices from the television.

HE AND MARGARET woke at the same time and cuddled in bed before going downstairs. It was going to be a busy day.

Alex's gram and mom were in the usual family hangout. Three coffee cups, crullers, and crumb buns were in the center of the table. Alex filled two cups of black liquid and handed one to Margaret. They both took a seat at the table.

His mom leaned into Alex. "You got home late last night."

"Yeah. I needed to clear my head. You know, prepare for tomorrow."

"Did you do that thing?"

"Yup."

"Did it work?" His mom sipped her coffee.

"It did. I also saw Tom Kirkpatrick." Alex reached for a napkin.

"You didn't tell me that last night." Margaret took a bite of her cruller.

"I know. I was too beat when I got home."

His mom furrowed her brows. "Did something happen?"

"No. Just tired from the night air." Alex knew mentioning his encounter with Tom would only fuel a fire that didn't need to be ignited. Tom really had nothing to do with any of this other than being Greta's grandson. Sometimes, his quest for answers lead him down the wrong road. He lost sight of the players. Tom was swooped up into the main characters, when truthfully, he was only a bystander.

After they finished their coffee, Alex and Margaret went upstairs to shower and dress. It was about eleven in the morning when they finally made it to the bagel shop. Alex had a clear view through the front window of the shop. Tom was there, and so was one of his friends.

"You sure you're good?" Alex held Margaret's hand tightly. "I swear, if you ask me one more time . . . I'm fine."

"Okay. I get the picture." He let go, and Margaret's hand slid away.

"I'm gonna keep it short and simple. I'll tell him that we're taking care of Catherine tomorrow, your gram is here, Bridget is under our protection, and there isn't anything Greta can do about it."

"I think that should be enough to get Greta there. She knows it will end for good without Catherine." He kissed her forehead.

"Can't she just summon another dark spirit?" Margaret wondered.

"No. Not according to Gram. Once this spell is cast, it will bind Greta from casting any spells in the future."

"Okay. Well, that's good."

"Yup. It's the little things."

"Smart ass."

"Well, it's better than being a—"

"Don't you even go there. Okay, I'm going in." Margaret blew him a kiss.

"I'll be right here."

"Yes. And right here is where you shall stay." Margaret smirked. Standing at the window, Alex tapped his thigh with his fingers.

Margaret talked for a couple of seconds, then Tom started waving his arms like he was showing her the exit. She didn't move. She just kept talking. At one point, his friend stood up and started to come near her, but she just re-positioned herself. When it appeared their conversation was over, she walked up to the counter and ordered two bagels and two cups of coffee. Before grabbing the items, she dropped a dollar in the tip jar and then walked toward the door. Alex quickly opened it and grabbed the two cups of coffee.

"What the hell are we gonna do with these bagels?" he questioned.

"Alex, he really is struggling with this. I don't know, I felt obligated to buy something."

"I know. Last night, when I saw him, it killed me inside to see his anguish. Do you think he got the message?"

"Did you see him wave his arms for me to leave? He got the message."

"Let's go home; we did what needed to be done. I just wish we could've left Tom out of it." Alex sighed.

"You're one of the good ones, Mr. McKenna." Margaret ran her fingers through his hair.

Alex set the coffee down on the hood of the car and grabbed her. Pulling her close, the scent of cherries and vanilla captivated him before he immersed himself in her lips.

THE BATTLE OF DARKNESS AND LIGHT

It was about eleven forty-five in the evening when the doorbell announced the arrival of Bridget. Alex invited her into the living room, and, within a few minutes, the entire family had joined in welcoming their guest.

Bridget anxiously intertwined her fingers while Alex explained their strategy step-by-step. He tried to ease her fears by explaining his gift of vision, but her nerves clearly were not cooperating.

"I understand you're confident about this plan, but I'll be honest— I'm frightened out of my mind." Bridget's voice cracked.

"As soon as we have confirmation that Greta is on the property, I'll summon Catherine and then call out to Ester. I believe when Catherine sees her daughter, we'll be able to bring her around. I know you're scared, but we will all be with you the entire time." Alex smiled gently.

His gram explained that she had two spells. The first would hold Catherine, and the second would banish her. If the plan went the way Alex had hoped, they wouldn't need the second spell. If they could get back Catherine's humanity by bringing Ester to her, they could help them both cross over together. Greta would be powerless.

Literally. His gram was going to cast a binding spell, preventing her from doing anything to anyone else.

Since Gina was more experienced than her son, she would be the one to execute the holding spell along with his gram. For a spirit as powerful as Catherine, it would take two of them.

Alex worried about his grandmother. This was going to be exhausting emotionally, and she hadn't had to do anything this dangerous in a very long time. His mom assured him she was up for it, but it didn't ease his fear.

The preparation for the spells were complete, and salt garnished every exit to the outside world; they had created a containment center.

Alex stood up in the center of the room.

"Gram, when I call out Catherine, please be cautious. No one here can look directly at her except me. I'm not sure if you can or can't."

"I will be fine. You just worry about bringing Ester to her mother. I believe the child will be able to bring her back."

"Okay, I guess that's all. We should all get some sleep; we're going to need it."

Alex turned and caught his mom smiling at him. "What?"

"Nothing. Just that you're not a little kid anymore."

"Now you get it." He realized then that he sounded a bit snarky.

"Sorry. I meant you finally see who I am."

"I know. Goodnight, my baby. I love you."

"I love you, too."

His mom ambled upstairs to bed. Alex had given Bridget his room, while he and Margaret camped out in sleeping bags on the living room floor.

"Hey. You worried about tomorrow?" Margaret yawned.

"Sure. My insides are churning. I want it to work out for Catherine and Ester. And then Bridget . . . We're putting her right in the middle of the chaotic dead. I also feel something heavy weighing on me when I think of Greta—and Tom."

"Tom? You think he'll come, too?" Margaret was surprised.

"I don't know. But I'd be lying if I didn't say there's a possibility."

"Man. That could really screw things up."

"I know."

Alex rolled over and grabbed Margaret, pulled her close, and melted into her body. He gently kissed the top of her head, resting it under his chin. They both were out in minutes.

Alex had several dreams that night, and none of them ended well.

New Hyde Park, New York 2002

Alister stared at the corpse of his father lying in the coffin. He had never missed his mother or sister as much as he did now. He was completely alone.

Reaching into the glossed wooden box, he straightened his father's tie. Jim was a perfectionist about his wardrobe. He never would have worn his tie crooked. Alister had picked out a dark blue suit with a white shirt. Blue was Jim's favorite color. The mortician did an exceptional job covering the bullet wound. Otherwise, this would have been a closed casket.

Fighting to hold back the tears, Alister wiped his eyes with the sleeve of his blazer. His father would have been mortified. No gentlemen should be without a hanky at all times.

Confusion clouded his mind as he thought about the last few days. When he got the call from his aunt informing him of his father's passing, he never would have thought it had been by his own hand. *How could he commit suicide? For the love of God, he was ninety-five years old. How bad could it be that he couldn't wait?* The questions burned through his brain like battery acid eating its way through an engine. He clutched the envelope left behind. It was addressed to him. His aunt found it the day she discovered the body. He hadn't been able to bring himself to open it.

The last words his father thought were forever imprinted on that piece of paper. It almost seemed sacrilegious to break the seal. He stepped out of the viewing room and into the chapel. Taking a seat in one of the pews, he gently ripped open the envelope with a pocketknife he carried. It was a gift from his mother as a small boy. Not expensive, but to him—priceless.

With his index finger and thumb, he lifted the page out as if it were a newly discovered excerpt from the Bible. He unfolded it with equal delicacy. It was his father's handwriting, and the contents filled both sides of the page. It was a confession.

ALISTER,

Over the years, there were many secrets. Some, I've shared with you, but others were kept close to my heart. One of them was about your mother. I know you have nothing but fond memories of her, and I wish that was all I could say on the matter. But the truth is, she aided me in the demise of my first wife, Catherine. Carol was a greedy woman with nothing in her heart for anyone except herself. I do believe she truly loved you, son. We both did. As for Ester, my poor little girl. I feel Carol hated her most of all. Maybe because she favored her mother in looks, or maybe because she kept the bond to my past alive. I am not sure. What I can tell you is she killed your sister that night. She didn't start the fire or directly take the air from her lungs, but her willingness to hate would not allow her to let your sister run to safety. For this, I fear she will burn in hell. We both will. As much as I do not want to find out if this is truly my fate, I cannot go on any longer. I have been haunted every day of my life since the first time you found me paralyzed with fear. Catherine has become in death the complete opposite of who she was as a person. It is my Ester that holds all of my regret, and the pain has become too much to bear. If Catherine wants her revenge, then it is up to me to give it to her.

In the beginning, I thought it was Carol who was haunting me. This creature that I would see could not be Catherine. But I was wrong. With the deaths throughout the last sixty plus years, I have come to suspect otherwise. Then just last week, my suspicions were confirmed. For the first time since the fire, I saw my little Ester. She came to me in a dream. She told me it was her mother who was lost and needed help. I didn't know how I could help other than to give her the one soul I thought she had wanted the most—me. I pray this will end the torment I caused my beautiful girl, Ester. That she might find her mother and live out eternity in her arms. My regrets are meaningless now. I chose the path I walked, the people I hurt, and the life I threw away. I'm sorry, my boy, for all that I've done to cause you pain. Please know this last and final act has nothing to do with you. It is my way of fixing a wrong that should have never happened. Use this letter as my confession to free Catherine's soul and bring her to your sister. Tell the world that Jim Bishop was a faulted man with no regard for anything but the dollar. I pray you carry this out as I requested and be the man I could not.

Your Father,
James Bishop

IT WAS ABOUT five o'clock in the morning and the aroma of coffee spread throughout the first floor. Alex's mom and gram were in the kitchen, and Bridget was already in the shower.

Alex was awakened by his shaking body.

"Hey, you okay? You scared me. You were shaking so violently; it woke me up." Margaret stroked the back of his neck.

"Yeah, I'm sorry. Just had a vivid dream. I think Jim Bishop told everything to Alister. He wrote a note right before he committed suicide."

"Weird. I guess Alister thought he was protecting his father somehow," Margaret whispered.

"Yeah. He's a broken man. His mother, father, and sister all lost because of greed. What are you doing?"

"Practicing the banishing spell. You know I don't know how to speak Italian. I wanted to get it right."

"Cenere alla cenere, polvere alla polvere, che il vento si soffia, vagando fantasma e cancellare il mondo dei vivi, si gira a cui si appartiene, e che tu possa scomparire senza lasciare traccia." Margaret let out a deep sigh. "Does that sound right?"

"Actually, it sounds great. You sure you're not from the old country?" Alex grinned.

"Are you humoring me or telling me the truth?"

"No. I'm serious. You were dead on. You know you can say this in English."

"No. All of you will be using Italian. I want to do the same. Now tell me what the hell I'm saying."

"Ashes to ashes, dust to dust, may the wind blow you, wandering ghost, and clear the world of the living, turn you to where you belong, and may you disappear without a trace."

"Harsh. I thought you were trying to save Catherine's spirit?"

"I am. I will. This is what we will do if it doesn't work. It has to work, though. Ester is all alone. She won't cross over without her mother. I can't fail her." Alex buried his head in the pillow.

"Whoa. Wait. This isn't all on you. It's your idea, but we are in this together. All of us."

"I get it. I do. But I feel responsible because she came to me," he confessed.

"I get where you're coming from, but it still doesn't change the fact that it's not just you. Okay?"

He let it go. Margaret couldn't change how he felt any more than he could do it for himself. No words were better right now.

The house was quiet for the next several hours. Their timeline had changed. His gram insisted they summmon Catherine closer to noon. She *felt* that would be the time that Greta would show up. Like Alex, she feared for her.

Antsy, Alex decided to go outside and try to clear his mind; bring everything into focus. Sitting on the top step of the stoop, he checked his phone: it was ten minutes before noon.

A small voice resonated behind him. "I'm scared."

"Of what, buddy?"

"There's a bad ghost here, Alex. I think it wants to hurt you."

"It's okay, Jacob. We're already for her. But I want you to stay away."

"Why?"

"Because I'm not sure what she's capable of, and I don't want you to get hurt."

The little boy laughed. "Alex, I'm dead."

"Yes, there are things that dark spirits can do to hurt other spirits. You told me a minute ago you were scared. Listen to your instincts; stay away."

"Alright, Alex, I will."

The little boy vanished. Alex checked his phone again—two minutes until D-day.

He was only inside a minute before his mom came rapidly out of the kitchen.

"Everyone, Greta is here!"

Alex ran to the back of the house and peered out the sliding glass doors that led from the kitchen to the backyard. Greta Kirkpatrick stood on the paved walkway.

They had placed a table in the center of the room, containing three white candles, a statue of the Virgin Mary, Jesus, and a silver bowl filled with holy water from the Our Lady of Victory. In the center of the table, two larger bowls of incense scented the air. The first contained Dragon's Blood—used for ridding negative influences. In this case, Greta. Beside it, white sage. This was used for cleansing and purification.

Alex grabbed a box of wooden matches from the table. He struck one, lighting the candles and silently praying to himself. It was a religious ritual that he often questioned, but today, he wasn't leaving anything out. Gram burned the incense, while the family stood around the table and held hands. Alex had Margaret on his right side and Bridget on his left. The temperature in the room plummeted to an uncomfortable glacial chill.

"Do you guys smell that? It's putrid." Alex scrunched his nose.

"It's vile. This odor was not present before." His mom winced.

"Gram, does this mean something?" Alex coughed.

She nodded. "Someone else is here. It's not just Catherine. I can feel her."

"I feel something, too. It's bad. Are you sure it's female?"

Alex was confused. The only other spirit that had been in the house was Ester, and the little girl came with no odor.

"Yes. This spirit is a woman. She's bringing death with her."

"Great. Another fucking insane spirit."

Bam! Bam! Bam! It was coming from upstairs. "It's one of the bedroom doors!" Alex bellowed.

"Footsteps!" his mom exclaimed. "They're coming down the staircase."

"Everyone, get ready," Alex commanded.

Alex squeezed Margaret's hand. She gave him a half smile, but he couldn't acknowledge her. His attention was diverted from the threat coming down the stairs to the one that was hovering in the dining room.

"Catherine's here. Bridget, Margaret, whatever you do, remember, eyes shut. I don't care if you can feel her icy breath on your face—do not look at her. Stay in the circle and don't let go of each other. Ma . . ."

His mom whispered, "Don't worry about me. I'll be fine."

Margaret leaned into Alex. "What about Gram?"

"She's okay."

Catherine drifted toward the family, an icy halo adorning her.

Alex swiped his left hand across the side of his thigh. Bridget was dripping with fear. Cupping her hand to reaffirm his grip, he held it tighter.

"I'm not gonna let her harm you," he whispered in her ear. She squeezed his hand.

The spirit positioned itself directly behind Bridget. Alex hunched his neck and shoulders; his spine tingled. He tossed his head back, and a piece of frost-laden hair had brushed against his brow. A whistle of wind swept the center of the room, bringing with it the pungent scent of burnt lilac. The thud of heel-to-step resumed, until the final boom settled in the living room. A dark, shadowy figure stood at the bottom of the staircase, facing the front door.

Catherine shifted her gaze toward the levitating silhouette. But when the darkness gazed back, her jaw dropped, exhaling a painful wail.

"Gram, I'm going to call out Ester," Alex asserted. His gram nodded in agreement.

The howling of the wind penetrated Alex, his body swaying with the circle.

"Ester, it's Alex. Can you show yourself? I have someone here. Someone I promised I'd bring to you."

He waited a few seconds, but nothing happened.

"Ester, please. Show yourself. Let me help you," Alex pleaded.

A blur of color streamed through the den, and Ester shimmered in. The trilogy was complete: Catherine, Greta, and Ester. The moment was now. He let go of Margaret and Bridget and joined their hands together. Standing beside Ester, he faced Catherine, the pain of death staring back at him.

"This is who you've been missing all these years. Catherine, I know you're in there somewhere. Your daughter is right here. She's been looking for you."

The malevolent spirit would not look at the child. "You can be together again."

Ester reached out for her mother, but Catherine did not respond. "Alex. Alex . . ." His mom's voice quivered.

"Ma, I'm a little busy."

"Alex, the shadow."

He peered over at the shadow that was once by the bottom of the stairs, but it was now standing beside him. The little girl's sad face abruptly changed to horror, and she disappeared. The wind was steadily increasing, and Catherine once again moved closer toward Bridget.

His thoughts flew, and he had to focus. *Who the hell could this be? Why would Ester be so frightened? Oh god . . . It can't be.*

Alex tried to get the words out, but he didn't have time. An instant, sharp splash, followed by a crackling crunch interrupted him. Standing in the den was Greta and—Tom.

"Shit. Tom, get out of here!"

"Alex, I can't leave her. She's my grandmother!" Tom's eyes widened with fear when he spotted Catherine.

"Tom! No. Don't look at her!" Alex shouted.

Greta's face contorted with dread. Her grandson had locked eyes with her instrument of death, and she couldn't stop it. Catherine swooped through the room, turning the air to ice. Chunks of the hardened O2 rained down, pummeling their heads. Tom remained motionless. Greta stepped in front of him, but it was too late. Catherine had found a new victim. Since Tom's great grandfather was Michael Kirkpatrick, he was fair game. Catherine threw Greta across the room with one glance from her hate-stained eyes. The spirit may not be able to kill Greta, but apparently, she could restrain her.

"Tom!" Alex tried to go to him, but he felt a grip on his left forearm. His mother was holding him back.

"You can't. There's nothing you can do for him now." His mom's grip firmed.

"Ma, I have to try!" Alex pleaded.

"No. You don't. She will kill you."

"She can't freeze me. I'm immune."

"Are you immune from broken bones? You saw how that thing just sailed Greta through the air with just a look. What do you think she will do to you if you were to interfere? No. I'm sorry, but I won't let go." His mom averted her eyes.

Alex struggled, but he wasn't going anywhere. He could only watch as Catherine enveloped Tom, encasing him in a tomb of ice. When he stopped wiggling, she reached out with a long, skinny finger and cackled—his head lay beside his body on the floor. Greta shrieked, which got the shadow's attention. As it swooped its willowy figure around the room, the wind responded with a vengeance. The family was in a war zone. Dropping to the floor, they tightly rejoined hands, resuming the strength of the circle. Alex called out to Ester several more times, but the child remained hidden.

Alex shouted to be heard over the wind. "Gram! I need to find out who the shadow is. I have an idea, but I don't know how I can get her to identify herself. If we do, can you banish her?"

"I can. But it's going to get worse in here, and I don't know how long we can hold on while the spirits are locked in their pissing contest. We might have to banish both of them."

"No. Please, Gram. Give me a little more time," Alex begged. "This is what you do. Address the shadow directly. See if you can appeal to its ego, and then it might identify itself. Once you get it to say its name, I'll do the rest."

"Okay."

Alex pushed against the wind toward the two spirits, who were waiting to rip each other apart. He could see out of the corner of his eye that Greta was slowly getting back on her feet. He knew she would try to resume her attack on Bridget, but he needed to get rid of one problem at a time. He knew his family would watch out for the final victim. Struggling, each step pushed the barrier further back. By the time he was close enough to engage with the shadow, it was well-aware he was there. The darkness spun around, leaving Catherine to finish the murder she had intended to commit that day.

"Ma! Watch Bridget!" Alex raised his forearm to his eyes.

"Just worry about what you're doing, Alex. I'll get this."

"I've got her, Gina."

Margaret tightened her grip on Bridget. "We'll do this together. You stay steady; I'm not leaving your side."

"Ladies, allow me." Gina swiftly moved in front of Bridget

and Margaret, breaking free from the circle and using her body as a shield. Catherine tried to maneuver herself around her, but Gina didn't budge. Alex had seen her do this before. He knew she was envisioning a white light surrounding all of them, encasing them in its warmth and protection.

"Remember, keep your eyes shut tight," Gina whispered.

"I will," Bridget said weakly.

"Don't worry about me; that piece of shit is not breaking us," Margaret roared.

Alex inched closer to the silhouette of destruction and whispered, "Carol." The shadow retreated. Alex moved forward. "Carol, no more hiding in the shadows. Show us who you are. Or can you?"

The creature remained motionless.

"I know why. It's because Catherine is so much stronger and smarter than you, right? You have been reduced to just a shadow when you're in the presence of her greatness." Alex smirked.

Alex gripped the archway of the dining room, his fingers struggling to hold on. The dishes that decorated the shelves of the buffet hutch plummeted to the floor and splattered shards of glass across the wooden planks.

"You were in her shadow when you were alive, and now, even in death, you are still sloppy seconds. Your little boy, Alister—he knows the whole truth. Jim told him in a letter just before he committed suicide. He hates you." Alex sneered.

His remark cut through the cloak that had been hiding the woman underneath. Shedding her skin of anonymity, Carol had taken the bait.

"Gram! She's here. It's Carol!" Alex sensed the essence of a small hand clasping his; Ester stood beside him. Carol's face hardened with rage at the sight of the young girl.

His gram stepped out from the circle, and, falling into a trance- like state, began reciting the spell to banish Carol.

"Carol Bishop . . . *Cenere alla cenere, polvere alla polvere, che il vento si soffia, vagando fantasma e cancellare il mondo dei vivi, si gira a cui si appartiene, e che tu possa scomparire senza lasciare traccia.*"

Carol thrashed around the room, unleashing an energy that tore at the walls, sending bits of plaster flying aimlessly into anyone in its way. Alex watched the wind as it began to funnel into the center of his family's circle. A small, spinning cone twisted violently, growing with every passing moment. She would have her revenge.

"Gram! I think we're running out of time! Hurry!" Alex gasped.

His grandmother's hands cut through the smoke of the incense and blew it in the direction of Carol's maniacal spirit. She grabbed the bowl of holy water, splashed it over the deadly apparition, and called to the strength of her past ancestors to aid them.

She repeated the incantation again.

Alex rubbed the bumps that had infested his forearm. He shuddered. The tremors in his chest vibrated with an intensity of the power of a hundred souls. He raised his head toward the ceiling—hovering above, filling every inch of space, was the family his gram had summoned. They were nothing like Carol and Catherine. Basking in the glow of white illumination, they were warm. Rays emanating from their celestial bodies engulfed Carol. She couldn't move.

The wind calmed, leaving only a light so bright they had to partially shield their eyes. The bitter cold of Catherine's ice melted. The souls descended and overwhelmed Alex with love and strength from the generations of family he had never met. He had never felt so aware of the life around him. The *know* of being a part of something that had no end. They had come before him, and one day, he would join them and pave the way for future generations of their bloodline.

Catherine cowered in the corner of the adjacent dining room. Several of the spirits surrounded Alex and his family, keeping them safe. Black muck churned beneath their feet, erupting violently and splattering against the wall and dripping to the floor. A deep rumbling under the oak planks lifted the boards up one by one and threw them across the room until they came to rest in a pile by the door. Smoke puffed from the large crater that had been forged, opening a gateway to the underworld.

A groaning beast, surely representing Hell itself, rose up head- first. It stood hunched over, and large tumors ravished most of its body. Its twisted face oozed with droplets of puss, while misshapen eyes glowed a fiery red as it searched for its prey.

It surveyed the room, passing everyone, until its glare locked onto Carol. With a guttural roar, it reached up, and the white souls released their grip. Screaming, Carol plummeted right into its waiting arms. She struggled helplessly, but there was no escape. The beast unhinged its enormous jaw and dropped her squirming body in head-first, devouring each morsel as if it were a rare delicacy prepared especially for him. When the last bit of Carol disappeared, the vile creature licked its cracked lips, wiped its mouth, and descended back to the depths of terror. The crater closed with a howling wind and snapped the floorboards back into place, leaving no evidence of the underworld.

Alex collapsed. His chest heaved with each breath he struggled to pass air through his lungs. The gentle stroke of a small hand on his head calmed him, allowing his lungs to welcome the oxygen they needed. He looked up to a smiling Ester. He gripped the door frame and pulled himself up on struggling legs.

"Gram, I have to try with Catherine one more time."

"You're not going to try anything. You are all going to die now!" A voice cackled.

Alex whipped his head around and saw Greta by the front door. She lunged for him but was paralyzed in mid-air. Surrounded by the spirits, they pulled her into their circle, completely covering her body with the warmth of the white light. In moments, she was gone.

The souls gathered by Alex. They reached out and touched him; he felt the goosebumps again, but this time, instead of a chill, he felt warm. They peered back to Catherine, and then to Alex again. He nodded. He understood what they meant. This was his one shot, or they would have to take her.

Slowly, he moved toward the dark spirit with Ester by his side. Her master was gone, and she had no one controlling her. Alex hoped this would be enough to get through to the person he knew was buried inside. When he was about a foot away from her, he stopped.

"Catherine, I know you're there. You don't have to be afraid or angry anymore. Look. See who is with me."

The child reached out her hand to her mother. Catherine backed up.

"Mommy, don't."

Catherine halted and Ester reached out again. This time she clasped her hand. Alex smiled; the air was changing. The heaviness lifted, and the scent of flowers in spring replaced the consuming odor of burnt lilac left behind by Carol. The layers of ice melted, dripping in a puddle onto the floor and uncovering the person that had been buried inside for so long. Standing in a soft green dress was a lovely brunette with blue eyes—Catherine. She grabbed her daughter and lifted her into her arms.

When Catherine saw the family and Bridget, she bowed her head and turned away. Alex placed his hand on her shoulder, and she turned to him.

"It's not your fault. This was Greta and Carol, too. Their hate just fed on your sadness and turned it into something you couldn't control. You have Ester again. You are not being held here any longer. You can both cross over now."

Catherine looked beyond the family to the light of the souls who were waiting.

"They won't hurt you. They're only here to show you the way."

A few of the souls reached out to Catherine and surrounded her with their essence. Mother and daughter ascended with the glow of the circle, and in moments, the room was bare.

There was a calm in the silence.

Gina surveyed the mess of broken glass and disarray that the dueling darkness had left behind. Sighing, she poured a glass of wine and sat at the dining table with gram. Exhaustion had gotten the better of them, but no one nearly as much as Alex. He struggled up the stairs to the bathroom. Sitting on the edge of the tub, he looked at his reflection in the mirror.

Alex felt no guilt or sorrow over the loss of Greta. As far as he was concerned, both she and Carol got what they deserved. But losing Tom really cut him at the core. Fate had dealt him an unfair hand.

He rose, took a few steps to the sink, and turned on the cold water. He splashed his face and swallowed, trying to push down the bile that had forged its way up. He couldn't get the expression on Tom's face out of his head; the fear that he knew he was dying.

Alex had been seeing the dead since as long as he could remember. But watching someone's life slowly be pulled from them was something entirely different. If he hadn't talked to Tom, he would have never been there. But he did. He did it to get Greta and to save Bridget, Catherine, and Ester. That didn't ease his guilt.

He dried his face and stared into his reflection before heading downstairs. When he was halfway down, he glanced into the living room. Tom's body was covered in a sheet. His stomach convulsed, sending vomit to the back of his throat. He grabbed the railing and clutched it firmly. He could hear his family in the kitchen, and he followed their voices to solace.

He ambled in and noticed Bridget was not there.

"Did Bridget go home?" Alex sat down and turned away from the Italian bread in the center of the table.

Margaret reached out and touched his arm. "She left a few minutes ago."

Alex rested his elbows on the table and put his head in hands. "What are we going to do with Tom? Did anyone call the police?"

Alex muttered.

His gram gently stroked the back of his hair. "I've called some friends. They will take care of him. We can't call the police—not without sounding suspicious."

"But what will they do with him?" Alex glanced at her, tears flooding his eyes.

"They'll do what's right. Don't worry." Gram got up and kissed the top of Alex's head.

There was rapid knocking at the door, and Alex's mom went to answer it. Alex could hear the deep voices of at least two other men. He assumed they were the *friends* his grandmother had spoken of.

He heard the crunching of heavy plastic, and a few minutes later, the front door closing. He imagined Tom was gone. He stood up and walked to the glass doors. Gazing out he felt himself wanting to fly— the need to soar far away and bring his soul to a place of peace.

Alex's gram gave him a hug. "Bonzetta, are you alright?"

He didn't want to talk about it. This was something he had to work out for himself.

"I'm fine, Gram. Just tired." She didn't press him.

"Get some more rest."

"I will."

Legs trembling from the weight of grief mixed with terror, Alex fumbled upstairs. As he passed by the empty spot Tom's body had occupied, he could only recognize sadness. He needed the coziness of his comforter and soft bed. He was drifting into the abyss when he heard the door squeak open. He knew who it was.

Margaret slipped off her shoes and then slid under the covers. She never uttered a word; she just held him. As he allowed the in- between to carry him off, his last thought was, seventy years would never be enough time with her.

If you enjoyed this story set in the Alex McKenna universe, there's plenty more paranormal mystery waiting for you. Dive deeper into the series to uncover more secrets, suspense, and the unknown lurking just beneath the surface.

And if you have a moment, please consider leaving a review—it truly helps others discover the books and keeps the stories coming.

Alex McKenna and the Academy of Souls
Alex McKenna and a Winter's Night
Alex McKenna Death is Not the Beginning

ACKNOWLEDGMENTS

To Holly and A.J., the community...the world, needs so many more of you. Thank you for giving Alex a proper introduction.

Samantha, for every literary meltdown you got me through and every time you brought reason into my world of chaos, thank you.

Mom & Dad, you gave me everything...thank you.

Quote

"Grow old along with me. The best is yet to be."
——— Robert Browning

Visit us online:
creativejamesmedia.com

creativejamesmedia

@creativejamesm1

@creativejamesmedia

@creativejamesmedia